THE MORE VIOLENT THE STORM
THE DARKER THE NIGHT

FORGED

-BOOK THREE OF THE GLITCHED SERIES-

EISLEY ROSE

Majestic Pen
PUBLISHING

❀ Formatted with Vellum

If you feel triggered while reading this book, then I've done my job.

CONTENT WARNING

There is a list of content warnings available near the back of this book.

- Forged Inspirational Playlist -
    (Found on Apple Music & Spotify)

Chapter 1:
    "A Little Bit Off" by Five Finger Death Punch

Chapter 2:
    "Wolves" by Sam Tinnesz & Silverberg

Chapter 3:
    "Come Around" by Papa Roach

Chapter 4:
    "You Were Mine" by Forest Blakk

Chapter 5:
    "Until the End" by Breaking Benjamin

Chapter 6:
    "The Red" by Chevelle
    "I'm Not Okay" by Citizen Soldier

Chapter 7:
    "A Symptom of Being Human" by Shinedown

Chapter 8:
    "Toxic" by 2WEI

Chapter 9:
    "Burden" by Citizen Soldier
    "Beat Up Guitar (Acoustic)" by Darling Brando

Chapter 11:
    "Zombie" by Yungblud

Chapter 12:
    "I Believe in a Thing Called Love" by The Darkness
    "You're the One That I Want (feat. George Madrid & Clejan)" by Manuel the Band & Crosev
    "Say You Won't Let Go" by Boyce Avenue
    "Zombie" by Bad Wolves

Chapter 13:
    "Bodies" by Drowning Pool
    "Wish I Could Cry" by Citizen Soldier & Halocene

Chapter 14:
    "All Eyes On You" by Smash Into Pieces

Chapter 15:
    "Heavy" by Citizen Soldier & SkyDxddy

Chapter 17:
    "Dark Thoughts" by The Funeral Portrait

Chapter 19:
    "ICU" by Citizen Soldier
    "Reason to Live" by Citizen Soldier

Chapter 20:
    "You Are Enough" by Citizen Soldier
    "Lovely" by Lauren Babic & Seraphim

"Ashes of Eden" by Breaking Benjamin
"Pass Slowly" by Seether

Chapter 36:
"Better Than Me" by Hinder
"Half hearted" by We Three

Chapter 37:
"Before You Go" by No Resolve & Katey x Krista
"Wish You The Best" by Lewis Capaldi
"Only When It's You" by Bleeding Verse

Chapter 38:
"Euclid" by Sleep Token

Chapter 39:
"Issues" by Julia Michaels

Chapter 41:
"Easy On Me (Duet Version)" by No Resolve, Halocene, & Noise Machine

Chapter 43:
"Cold" by Crossfade
"Rain" by Sleep Token

Chapter 44:
"Forever Again" by Matt Hansen
"Look What You Made Me Do" by Our Last Night

Chapter 47:

"Flow" by Smash Into Pieces
"Real One" by Smash Into Pieces

Chapter 48:
    "Shadow" by Livingston

AN ANCIENT PROPHECY

"Fear not the one soul split in two, for they are destined to save this realm. Both bathed in blood and consumed by fire, absolution must be at the helm.

"One of the two souls forgotten, the other believed to be dead. Their lives painfully intertwined yet distanced by fated bloodshed.

"Violence and rage shall threaten the world in the guise of a humanlike creature while a deception most keen must be severed unseen to secure the twin flames' future."

—The Oracle at Delphi (371 BCE)

CHAPTER ONE

Five months later...

The wild birds' boisterous chirps echoed off the tall trees amongst the thick forest, awakening Damon from his unhinged dreams.

He inhaled sharply, and his eyes opened wide as he sat upright in a pile of dirt. Damon's eyebrows furrowed in confusion. "What? Where am I?" he asked while looking down at his dirt-covered, naked body.

At some point during the night, he had unknowingly dug a place to rest in the forest floor.

While rubbing the sleep from his eyes, tiny pebbles snuck in between his lashes, and he hissed. "Ah. Shit."

Quickly standing upright, using his one good eye, Damon searched for a source of water to flush out the debris. Tripping over the uneven ground, he grumbled. "Fucking Hades. This is just what I needed."

The crisp morning air caused every inch of Damon's dirt-covered skin to be riddled with goosebumps, and his muscles ached as though he had been running all night.

He unintentionally recalled the nauseating images from his nightmares, and his stomach flipped as he shivered in disgust.

Every night, his dreams were plagued by Brielle, and the acts he was forced to partake in were incredibly disturbing.

During one of the recurring nightmares, in the middle of a sandy desert, Damon and Brielle would tear a lion apart, from limb to limb. They would then laugh maniacally while eating the animal's entrails. As the lion's bright red blood dripped down their faces, they would fuck beside its dismantled corpse.

Reaching the shoreline, Damon jumped into the frigid lake, encouraging the mind-numbing cold to interrupt his tormented thoughts.

Slowly awakening, Quade peered over at Damon's empty sleeping bag and groaned as he stared at their unzipped tent.

The sides were flapping open with the gusts of wind, allowing bursts of cold air into the tent.

Quade grumbled and threw his blankets aside. "Not this again."

After dressing in several warm layers, he grabbed Damon's bag and stepped out of the tent. He passed by several lit fires and envied the Spartans sitting before the hot flames, each with a cup of coffee warming their hands.

"Damon!" he yelled. His friend's name bounced off the trunks of trees and scattered brush as he picked up the pace.

After jogging into the thick of the forest, Quade cursed as he fell over several interlacing fallen logs. "Ah, dammit." He brushed off his pants as he picked himself up off the forest floor.

"Of course, I'd be taken out by a fallen limb and not by an actual threat like the Frenzied.

Hearing a splash off in the distance, Quade's head jerked upright, and he squinted while shielding his eyes from the sun glints reflecting off Lake Michigan.

As Damon popped up out of the water, Quade flashed a sideways grin. "Gotcha."

Damon stood trembling, waist-high in the cold water, using the tips of his fingers to scrub the dirt from his skin.

Quade shouted over the sound of Damon's teeth chattering. "It is April in Benton Harbor, Michigan. It is too damn cold out here to be taking a bath in the lake! Your dumbass is going to get hypothermia."

Damon startled, then turned to face his friend. "Shit!" He laughed nervously. "We're in Michigan, right," he mumbled, quietly reminding himself. Walking to the shoreline, he shouted jokingly, "You sound like a mother scolding their child."

Quade slammed down the bag before unzipping it and digging through its contents. "Yeah, well, if I bring you home to my wife, dying, I think she might be a bit pissed off if your death is due to your own stupidity. Get out and dry off; I brought your clothes. Here's a towel." Quade held out a beach towel for Damon.

After snatching the cloth from Quade, Damon quickly dried off. His teeth chattered loudly as he thanked Quade. "Thanks, brother. You've always got my back."

Quade eyed Damon suspiciously as he sat down on the edge of a large rock. "What were you doing in there? It's not like you're taking a relaxing dip in the middle of summer."

Shaking his head back and forth, Damon pulled clean clothes out of the bag. "Uh, I had just gotten a bit dirty, is all."

Quade's eyes narrowed in quizzical suspicion. "Dirty? You went to bed before I did last night, and from what I remember, you didn't have a bit of dirt on you."

Damon chuckled without humor as he squeezed the water from his dark strands of hair. "Yeah, well, I didn't get dirty 'til the middle of the night."

Quade leaned back and crossed his arms. "What is that supposed to mean? What the hell were you doing in the middle of the night?"

Damon put on a pair of pants and socks, then exhaled. "It's hard to explain."

Quade clasped his hands together and stared intently at his friend. "Well, try. I've got time."

Damon shoved his feet into his black hiking boots one at a time before cocking his head to the side. "Uh, okay. You know how my memory has been for shit lately?"

Quade agreed with a tense nod. "Yeah. That's been worrying Sera and me. She wasn't sure if it was stress, a side effect from the worms, or something more nefarious."

Damon grinned mischievously. "Aw. You two have been talking about me? That's sweet."

Quade scoffed and rolled his eyes. "Shut it. You've been through a lot the last year, so, yeah, we're worried about you."

Damon closed his eyes, and unexpectedly, the memory of Brielle's lips separated in a sadistic smile with bright red blood dripping from them appeared before him. Damon's eyes snapped open as he swallowed the hot acid creeping up the back of his throat. "Nope, uh..."—Damon cleared his throat—

"I've just been having a hard time staying asleep. I've got so much on my mind with everything going on. My father, the Frenzied, Alessa ... So, I get up and jog around, practically in circles."

Quade raised his eyebrows in disbelief while pushing himself up off the large rock. "Okay, man. If you need someone to talk to, I'm here for you." He clapped Damon on the shoulder.

Nodding his head without looking up at Quade, Damon slung his pack's strap over his shoulder. "Ready to get back to your wife and son?"

"Am I ever." Quade grinned excitedly as he walked beside Damon. "And I can't wait to see how much our daughter has grown. Sera has got to be showing pretty well by now."

Damon grinned while looking down at his boots. "That's what happens when you're gone on missions hunting the Frenzied for months at a time."

"What do you think they decided to do about the doctor who implanted your faulty microchip?" Quade asked.

Unsure of how to respond, Damon cleared his throat nervously. "I'm not really sure. Last I heard, he was deemed innocent and put on medical probation, so all experimentation on the microchip has been put on hold."

Quade rubbed his hands together and blew hot air onto his cold fingers. "Do you believe him? That he had nothing to do with Brielle's elaborate plan to control you?"

Damon gripped his strap. "I do. She had some other doctor install the worms in my head before we even got back. Brielle is one crazy bitch who can manipulate the best—as evidenced by..." he pointed to himself.

Quade playfully elbowed Damon in the arm. "Hey, thanks

to you, we have some wicked tight security measures being taken these days."

Damon narrowed his eyes, and his face scrunched up in frustration. "I don't think that's anything to be proud of."

Quade tilted his head and raised his hands defensively in front of his chest. "Worse things could have happened." Quade rubbed his hands together, anxiously. "So, are you ready to see Alessa?"

Damon's heart stilled for a beat before he exhaled a controlled breath. "It's time. I've been toying with the idea of—"

"Hey, Quade! Damon! There you are," Carina interrupted. "You two good? Everyone back at the camp was looking for you—we didn't know where you had gone. The others have already broken down your tent. We're ready to get home."

With an excited hop in his step, Quade started to run back to camp. "Yeah, we're good. Let's head out."

Damon sighed and gripped his strap tighter, looking straight ahead. "Home."

With an exasperated sigh, Brielle leaned back in her computer chair, crossing her bare legs beneath her skin-tight, black leather skirt. *Oh, how I love getting a rise out of him. Making him squirm gets me so hot.*

Feeling herself slicken, Brielle rubbed her thighs together.

She was sitting alone in the control room, staring up at the large display which showed Damon's point of view through his eyes.

Sneaking around the corner, Cain unbuttoned his suit and

fanned out the sides before sitting down in the computer chair directly beside Brielle. "How was the night shift?"

"Shit!" Brielle exclaimed. Sitting upright, she pressed her hand to her chest and uncrossed her legs. "Could you have been any quieter? Nearly gave me a heart attack creeping in here like that."

"With the way you were staring up at that screen, I'm just glad you weren't touching yourself," Cain chuckled. Reaching behind his head, he loosened his silver and white decorative half mask.

"Liar. You'd love to see me doing that. And more." Brielle smirked wickedly over her shoulder, into Cain's sharp, grey-green eyes.

Ignoring her attempt at flirting, he removed the mask, exposing the healed scar that extended from his jaw up to his eyebrow. "You and I will never be intimate." He threw his mask onto the table and loosened his tie. "I have much ... darker tastes. I think it would be best for you if we kept things professional. Trust me."

Her eyes narrowed. "If you say so," Brielle said with a shrug.

Cain chuckled in amusement. "Oh, I am adamant, for your sake more than mine. Have you gotten any more information while I was away, *actually* working, or were you just messing with Damon's head the entire time?"

Brielle scoffed and pointed a finger at him. "Don't you dare make it look like I go against the requests of your uncle. I always do what is asked of me." She hesitated. "I only screw with Damon once the information has been successfully retrieved."

Leaning back in her chair, Brielle crossed her legs while she flashed a sarcastic grin. "So, Senator Cain, how is everything going with the proposed nationwide ban against women's rights?"

He groaned before plucking his dress shoes off and tossing them to the side. "Started off slow, like all proposed bills in the beginning, but it seems to be picking up speed. I expected some kind of push back, but so far it's been pretty easy to get the bill pushed through." Cain laughed to himself. "It's almost as if someone were whispering in their ears, prompting them to agree with me."

Shaking his head, Cain stood up and sauntered towards his already packed hiking bag sitting on a chair on the other side of the room. "Whatever it is, I am grateful. The next steps will make it much easier to gain control."

Keeping her eyes on Cain, Brielle straightened her back. "Where are you off to? Didn't you just get back?"

Cain shrugged out of his suit jacket and tossed it onto the countertop before he admired his reflection in a nearby mirror. "You are correct." He traced the noticeable scar left by Alessa. "But I'm needing to scratch an irritating itch. Nothing a good hiking trip won't take care of."

Flashing a sadistic grin, he reminisced about his victims shrieking as their blood splattered the trees near them. "I'll be back in a few weeks." He cocked his head to the side. "Best make it a month."

CHAPTER TWO

Nyx, the primordial goddess of the night, suddenly appeared in the middle of the underworld's field of yellow wildflowers.

She held tightly onto her blood red skirt as she ran excitedly to greet Kai. "Did you know?"

She was sitting alone, amongst the tall grass and flowers. Confusion was written across her face as she addressed Nyx's question. "My goddess, what are you referring to?"

Placing her hands upon her curvaceous, bejeweled hips, Nyx shook her head back and forth adamantly, while reassuring herself. "No, no. There's no way you could've possibly known."

Rubbing the dirt from her hands, Kai stood up. "Is there something I can help you with?"

Nyx stepped forward and wrapped her hands around the young woman's upper arms. "Is there any heavenly way you knew your sister is who they speak of in the prophecy?"

Kai's eyes scrunched in disbelief. "You mean to say Alessa is in an ancient prophecy? How is that possible? We weren't even born Spartans. We were a part of the general population until our parents were killed."

Nyx's eyes lit up as she clasped Kai's hands within her own. "The fates would have you believe that. They have an odd sense of humor; I should know, they are my daughters. But, I firmly believe your sister is the one I've been waiting for."

"How so?" Kai asked hesitantly.

"Besides being the mother of humanity's savior, the person of whom the prophecy speaks is also predicted to be strong enough to withstand my possession, allowing me to walk in the light of day."

Kai ripped her hands from Nyx's grasp. "Are you talking about possessing my sister?"

Nyx shook her head and closed the gap between Kai and herself. "It's nothing scary; not like humans make it out to seem. I wouldn't make her do terrible things. It would simply grant me freedom to walk in the sunlight, and it would only be allowed if she willingly agreed to it. I would never force someone to be possessed. My inhabiting her body would benefit us both."

Placing her fingertips on the side of her temples, Kai shook her head back and forth. "Did you say, 'mother of humanity's savior'? Alessa is *not* a mother."

Nyx grasped Kai's arm and wrapped it around her own before she stepped forward. "Yes, well, prophecies are poetic yet often riddled with confusion; they shouldn't be taken literally. It could be interpreted a thousand different ways. For example, maybe this new version of humans will be controlled by Alessa; ergo, she is their mother. Or it could mean something completely random that you or I couldn't even begin to fathom. You just never know with these things. My family has a sick sense of humor."

Kai nervously played with the beaded fabric sewn into her skirt. "Are these new versions of humans something they need to be worried about?"

As they walked down the hill beneath the false blue sky, Nyx patted Kai's arm. "Darling, I do not deal in the future. That is one of my daughter's gifts."

Looking into the stunning goddess's eyes, Kai granted her a tense smile. "You're correct, my goddess."

"And now you and I need to come up with a plan to help your sister. The first and most prevalent problem I predict for her will be Damon. Whether she chooses to befriend him or love him once again is completely up to her, but all I do know is, if she doesn't at least heal her heart, there's no chance of her championing the battle that is soon to come."

Concern crossed Kai's face, and she swallowed audibly. "That sounds ... not great."

The goddess of night inhaled deeply before flashing a reassuring smile. "Humanity would suffer a terrible fate. We are going to figure out how to help Alessa and Damon from afar."

Sitting atop his black onyx throne, Hades held out flayed human flesh to his giant three-headed dog. "Come here, my love."

He pursed his lips together and whistled while dangling the piece of meat in front of his eager pet. As the watchdog excitedly jumped back and forth, he threw the treat across the brightly colored throne room. "Go get it!"

The hound eagerly ran for the piece of meat, and the multiple heads fought over which mouth got to consume the flesh. Hades confessed to his pet. "Since Persephone has gone home, I've grown bored. I am annoyed by humans and their lack of ambition, which is why I have decided to partake in their downfall. The only ones I seem to have any interest in are the two they call Lucas and Cain. They are truly magnificently twisted human beings."

As the dog heads devoured the treat, they barked eagerly for more.

"Oh, alright. Hold on." Hades leaned over and instructed a trembling man to hold his arm out once more. "Cerberus would like more."

The tortured man shook violently from head to toe as silent tears ran down his face, but he did as he was told without so much as a whimper.

Grinning maliciously, Hades flashed his white teeth. "That's a good boy. You know how much worse it could be."

After slicing another layer from the man's arm, he tossed the piece of flesh high up into the air and laughed as two of his pets' heads grabbed each end of the meat, tearing it into two.

"Attaboy!" He joyously clapped his hands together. "We'll show my brothers who is truly the most powerful of all the gods. Isn't that right, Cerberus?"

Hades rubbed beneath the chins of two of the heads, and the giant dog used its rear leg to scratch behind its third head's right ear. "It is only a matter of time before the downfall of humankind on earth, and then my rise in status as the king of the underworld will be undeniable."

CHAPTER THREE

The Spartan warriors who had been sent on the mission to investigate the Frenzied were transported back home mid-morning.

Climbing out of the vehicles, they stretched their backs as the citizens of New Sparta went about their everyday lives.

Behind the statue, at the front of their city, was a flurry of people. Children were running around their teachers and elders, and the toddlers and babies were strapped onto their parents as they shopped the market, lining both sides of the broad street.

The families of those returning lined up beside the medical staff, who were waiting to evaluate the injured warriors.

Soren ran to his father, yelling excitedly, "Patēr!"

Quade dropped his weapons beside him, spread his arms wide, and caught his son mid-air. Wrapping his arms around the boy, Quade smiled widely. "Wow! You have been training well while we've been gone. I can barely hold you up anymore."

Soren's eyebrows lifted. "Maybe you are weakened from all of your fighting."

Damon laughed under his breath, and Quade glared over at his friend. "Your son has quite the sense of humor."

Seraphine held onto her extended belly as she ordered about the medical staff tending to the warriors' wounds.

Demanding Quade's attention, Damon pointed at the primary Spartan's physician. "Your wife is being quite bossy," he joked.

Quade's gaze softened. "There's no such thing as a bossy woman. Seraphine is in her element, and it is very sexy when she's in charge."

Damon clapped Quade's shoulder. "Okay, then. I was about to agree with you, but then you went somewhere beyond my scope as a friend."

Quade tilted his head toward his wife while flashing a mischievous grin. "Here she comes, and I'm going to tell her what you said."

All humor dropped from Damon's voice as he threatened Quade. "Don't you dare—Seraphine! You've been missed," he interrupted himself, flashing his teeth as he smiled.

She narrowed her eyes while giving Damon a hug from the side. "Mm-hmm. That's not suspicious at all." She rubbed her belly. "Oh, little one, wait your turn."

Quade set Soren down and moved toward his wife. "Did she just move?"

Seraphine reached for Quade. "Our daughter can wait her turn. I have lived without your touch for months. Come here, my husband."

Their bodies melted against each other, as much as her belly would allow, and Damon's eyebrows raised. "And that's my cue to exit." He peered down at Soren, who was glancing up at his parents with a scrunched-up nose.

Interrupting the kiss, Damon cleared his throat. "Is it okay if I steal your son? I'd like to spend the afternoon with my nephew."

Quade refused to take his eyes off Seraphine as he nodded his head in agreement. "That sounds perfect. You could drop him off at his grandfather's house after dinner."

Seraphine broke eye contact as Quade bent down to kiss her belly. "Doesn't that sound fun, Soren?"

The young boy's eyes grew wide with excitement, and he squealed. "I get to spend the day with Uncle Damon and Grandfather?" He grabbed Damon's free hand and dragged him down the main road. "Come on! Let's drop your stuff off at your cabin, and then I can show you all the things I've been learning from my elder."

Damon pulled on Soren's little hand. "You've already gotten an elder assigned to you?"

Soren scoffed and kicked at the small rocks along the paved road. "Well, yeah. I am the son of this compound's head physician as well as one of the best Spartan warriors of our time."

Damon smiled at his spunky nephew. "How did you get so smart?"

Soren shrugged his little shoulders. "Genetics, I suppose," he quipped.

Laughing loudly at his nephew's attitude, Damon froze in place as he caught sight of Alessa.

She was standing on the side of a building beside the main road. Her thick dark hair had grown past her shoulders, like it used to be, and the sharp curves of her biceps cut through the skin-tight arm bands beneath her corseted dress.

Flying through the air, Alessa's skirt fanned out behind her, and she kicked toward someone Damon couldn't see.

He watched as a small explosion occurred behind her, across the field.

"She doesn't have to look at the objects anymore to target them? That's incredible," Damon muttered to himself.

Blocking Damon's view, a tall blond man stepped in front of Alessa and pulled her into his chest.

Damon growled and took a step toward them as heat crept up the back of his neck. *Camden.*

Allowing himself to be pulled back by Soren, Damon talked himself down. *She's not yours anymore. You have no right to be jealous.*

The young boy grunted in frustration as Damon stood still. "Come on, Uncle Damon! You are so much slower than I remember," Soren complained while trying to pull the two-hundred-twenty-pound man.

Forcing himself to look away from Camden and Alessa, Damon closed his eyes and exhaled through pursed lips.

Realizing he needed to come up with an entire day of plans for the little guy, Damon directed his attention back to his nephew and forced a smile. "You up for a swim, little minnow?"

<hr>

Feeling the pull from an unseen force, Alessa glanced up to find Damon walking away, hand in hand with Soren.

Her body unintentionally stiffened, and her breath was taken away as a flashback of Alessa touching Damon's chest plate before they kissed flashed before her eyes.

Feeling her unease, Camden squeezed Alessa's shoulder with his good arm. "Are you okay?"

She plastered a false smile on her face and cleared her throat. "Uh, yeah. Yeah, I'm fine, just mentally exhausted."

Camden twirled her dark hair around a finger. "Maybe your hair growing long again is putting extra strain on your brain."

Alessa's face scrunched up as she rubbed her hand back and forth on the top of his head, tousling his light hair. "Speaking of hair growing out, are you going to cut yours any time soon?"

"Excuse me." Pretending to be offended, Camden pressed his freed hand against his chest. "I do not intend to cut my golden locks. Growing up in the Brethren, I was never allowed to have hair longer than two inches."

Camden slipped his free arm around Alessa and pulled her to his side before marching to Lexi. "I'd embrace you as well, but..." He tilted his head toward his stabilized shoulder, secured in the medical device.

Lexi smirked while lowering the book she'd been reading. "I'm good."

Camden's stomach growled loudly. "And that's my cue to call it quits. Lunch, ladies?"

Lexi closed her book and joined Alessa and Camden. "I could eat."

Glancing over her shoulder, Alessa watched as Damon disappeared into the treeline.

Noticing Alessa was distracted, Camden cleared his throat as they walked away from their outdoor session. "When do you think your elder will be back?"

"Um..." Alessa hesitated. "I honestly don't know. The fact that he's been gone for over two months has me a bit worried."

Holding the book in front of her chest, Lexi spoke up. "I hate to admit it, but I agree. I also feel like he should have been back by now. All he was doing was going to present your case to the Consilium, correct?"

Alessa watched her toes kick out from beneath her flowing skirt. "I mean, as far as I know, that's all he was going to discuss. But he does have a bad habit of not telling me everything."

"Maybe he's meeting up with an old friend or hooking up with someone," Camden joked, trying to lighten the mood.

"Yeah, maybe..." Alessa trailed off as she imagined herself being beheaded by the Consilium's tribunal.

CHAPTER FOUR

Sweat dripped down the middle of Damon's back as he shot arrows at the targets strung high in the trees. Spinning in a slow circle, he struck the center of each one, no matter how difficult their positioning.

Damon's world tilted and his vision blurred, suddenly feeling claustrophobic amidst the forest. Blinking furiously, he threw his bow.

He had been trying to work off his frustration for hours, but to no avail. *Of course, Alessa doesn't think about me. All I am to her anymore is the man who killed her sister, as the one who broke her heart, time and time again.*

Damon's self-hatred had begun to consume him, and most days, all he felt anymore was angry and confused.

Sprinting to the lake near his cabin, Damon jumped into the cold water, and using the last of his remaining energy, he swam to the middle.

Picturing the blonde-haired young woman Kai used to be, Damon broke down. Inhaling deeply, he filled his lungs with air before dipping below the surface. Opening his mouth, he released a gut-wrenching scream, and bubbles shot upwards.

As the last bit of air escaped from his lungs, Damon's head broke the surface, and he inhaled the night's chilly air.

Eyeing the shoreline, Damon moved his arms one in front of the other, his muscles burning as he swam back towards the sand. Crawling out of the water, he collapsed on the edge of the lake before falling into a deep sleep.

CHAPTER FIVE

At the front of the crowded intelligence center, Jareth, a lead Spartan warrior, stood with his hands clasped behind his back. Next to him was Carissa, a fellow Spartan warrior, who was in charge of putting together their current mission.

He pointed at the hologram showing pockets of violence that were being reported throughout the United States. "As most of you already know, the Frenzied were first discovered four months ago. They are known for their lack of empathy, their inability to communicate, and above all, their drive to kill. These humans appear to be transitioning into something dark and convoluted. Their violent attacks are becoming more widespread, now extending beyond the United States."

Using his fingers to zoom out, he expanded the map of the United States to a global view. The three-dimensional globe rotated in mid-air, displaying hundreds of glowing pockets of red where just last week there were fewer than twenty-five.

Camden, Lexi, and Alessa stood off to the side of the room, their backs pressed up against the wall. "Could there be a connection between the Frenzied and Ambrosia?" asked Alessa.

Carissa pointed at Alessa. "Excellent question. Some of the victims who have been attacked by Frenzied are friends or family members of those who had consumed the artificial sweetener. Other victims have been completely random. As you know, our scientists have been busy breaking down the chemical components of Ambrosia to determine exactly why the artificial sweetener was distributed in the first place. We don't have any answers just yet, but we are hoping to pin something down in the next few months. Also, I know the product is still on the market, but we have done a thorough investigation, and the night Lucas disappeared, the tainted sweetener was replaced by the non-harmful original sweetener. We assume this was to cover their tracks."

Rubbing his hands together, Jareth stepped forward. "At this point, we believe the general population is safe from future tainted Ambrosia consumption. And to answer the question I know you are dying to ask, Alessa, Lucas is still missing, but Cain, his nephew, remains in the spotlight. He's recently become a senator and, with his power, has introduced a new bill to limit women's rights to healthcare."

Alessa and Camden side-eyed each other as a feeling of dread hit them in the gut.

"We will continue to keep a close eye on Cain to find out if he gives up any clues as to where Lucas Greenfield is hiding."

Camden leaned over to Alessa and whispered in her ear, "Remind me again why we didn't just kidnap Cain and torture the information out of him?"

Alessa whispered, "Because he wouldn't budge an inch. He's the type who would enjoy the torture. As much as I want to fucking wring his neck, we need to go about this the smart way, or else we'll never find Lucas."

Standing tall, Camden crossed his arms while straightening his back. "Right..."

Carissa directed her attention to Lexi. "How's your investigation coming along?"

Glancing down at the book she'd been holding non-stop for the past few weeks, Lexi nodded. "We've been working on connecting the individuals involved in the first violent mobs to points of origin. We need to figure out any similar factors, places they had been, and people they encountered. It has been determined that whatever has occurred to make them aggressive is on a molecular level and is not contagious."

Jareth zoomed in on the United States. "Alright then. While Lexi and her team continue handling the back end of the investigations, we'll send additional cleanup crews around the country to address these mobs before they get out of control. Every compound is sending groups to various locations in their respective countries. We will be sending fifty groups of warriors, as will Alaska's compound. Once volunteers have signed up, we will split you up into your designated locations so we can take these fuckers out."

Carissa nodded enthusiastically. "And with that, we end today's meeting. May the gods show mercy on you."

As the three-dimensional board transformed into a sign-up sheet, the room buzzed with activity as every able-bodied Spartan made their way to the front of the room to enlist.

With racing thoughts, Camden peered down at Alessa with pursed lips.

Reading his mind, Alessa shook her head back and forth. She plucked her foot from the wall behind her and placed her hand on Camden's chest. "You can't come."

His muscles tensed below her palm. "I'm not letting you go alone."

Alessa leaned into him, standing on the tips of her toes. "I won't be alone. Cam, you can't possibly fight yet; you're still healing. Your getting in the way could very well get me killed."

Camden groaned and rolled his eyes in defeat. "I hate it when you're right."

Withdrawing her hand from his chest, Alessa approached the board to sign up as Camden and Lexi trailed close behind.

Alessa signed her name, and as it floated up onto the board, it fell below the rest of the Spartans listed under California. "See?" She pointed at the list of names. "I'll have Quade with me. Besides, Lexi needs all the help she can get, so honestly, you staying behind will help us get to the bottom of what's going on sooner."

Lexi shrugged while side-eyeing Camden. "She's not wrong. Having you here would be … nice. And once you get the okay from Sera, we can get your arm back into working order."

Unconsciously adjusting his shoulder sling, Camden huffed aloud. "Okay, okay. You two don't have to gang up against me; I'll stay. You have a good point about me not going into battle with one working arm."

Alessa and Lexi grinned as they turned toward the exit. "Let's get out of here and on with our day," Alessa suggested.

Stopping the group of friends from leaving, Jareth interjected with a raised hand. "Alessa, can I speak with you for a minute?"

Glancing over her shoulder at the lead Spartan warrior, Alessa dismissed her friends. "You guys can head out. I'll catch up with you later."

Standing firm, Camden's eyes narrowed at the approaching Spartan. "Are you sure?"

With an audible scoff, Alessa put her hands on her hips. "Would you stop it? It's not like I'm going to disappear; I'm just talking to Jareth." Alessa looked past Camden at Lexi, holding his good arm out to her. "Please, take him. He's probably due for physical therapy, anyway."

Wrapping Camden's arm around her elbow, Lexi smirked before tapping him gently on the tip of his nose. "Come on, young man."

Camden's face blushed red as Lexi dragged him from the room. "Did I just get booped on the nose and scolded all in the same sentence?" he asked.

Lexi laughed as they exited the building. "I believe so. But she does have a point—you are late for physical therapy. And the quicker you graduate, the quicker you can go back to fighting the assholes of the world."

Laughing at her friend's banter, Alessa turned around to face Jareth. "What did you want to talk about?"

Reaching a hand behind his head, Jareth rubbed the back of his neck anxiously. "Have you heard the rumors?"

Alessa's forehead scrunched in confusion. "Regarding what exactly?"

Stepping closer to Alessa, Jareth bent down and lowered his voice. "The Consilium's still at a loss for how to reprimand you for your act of insubordination."

Alessa's head jerked back incredulously. "That's still a thing? They don't have more important issues to worry about right now?" She threw her hands in the air and scoffed. "You mean my saving the world, yet again, is an issue for them? They're the ones who failed to take the threat seriously."

Alessa pressed the palm of her hand against her forehead and exhaled. "I don't understand; I thought we were over this. It's been five months since the incident. Warriors lost their lives; Camden's still healing. Why am I even in trouble for their inaction? This entire situation is—"

Jareth set his hand upon Alessa's shoulder in a comforting gesture. "I just needed you to know that the worst may not be over and to not let your guard down. Be careful who you trust."

Glancing off to the side, she bit her lip in frustration.

Suddenly, a disturbing idea popped into her mind, and she couldn't help but ask, "Jareth, is Damon's father, by chance, in charge of my punishment?"

Crossing his hands in front of his chest, Jareth stood tall. "He is."

Closing her eyes, Alessa released a scorned laugh. "Now, all this is making perfect sense. He's had it out for me ever since Damon and I were together." Alessa took a deep breath before running her fingers through her hair. "Thank you for telling me."

Turning on her heel, Alessa marched away with her head held high but tears in her eyes.

With the confirmation of Damon's father targeting her, her eyes flared red. Alessa was no longer afraid of the Consilium.

Jareth yelled out to her as she walked through the exit door. "Why do I feel like instead of warning you to keep your head down, I just sparked a flame?"

Alessa hollered back over her shoulder with a mischievous smirk. "Because that's what you did."

CHAPTER SIX

Seething with anger, Alessa jogged to her specialized practice field across the city, which had been set up to both accommodate and encourage growth in the development of her abilities.

The bottom of her skirt flew up around her knees as she ran through the tall grass, and upon reaching the top of the hill, Alessa exhaled in relief.

Electronics had been hidden throughout the course, behind trees over a half mile away, and dug into the ground; all of it designed for Alessa to hone her abilities.

She had learned through her training that she could feel electronics' vibrations and hear their slight hum, and as long as she targeted her anger, she could locate and destroy each one.

She closed her eyes and concentrated on picturing Brielle's face. Feeling her insides tremble, she opened her red irises.

Focusing on all the electronics within the practice field, she caused each and every one to explode simultaneously.

The fury inside Alessa dissipated, and her shoulders dropped in relief.

Slow clapping began from behind her, and with a sharp inhale, she spun around.

Damon's father was dressed in his traditional Spartan garb, which always put Alessa on edge. His maroon and golden cape lifted in the wind behind him as he slowly clapped his hands together. "Impressive. Those skills will surely come in handy."

Alessa arched an eyebrow while casting a glare. "If you decide not to kill me," she snapped.

"Why would we kill one of our most powerful warriors? Not only are you mastering your skills, but you have also shown that others will listen to you; you have the capabilities of becoming a great leader."

Alessa turned her back on him and chuckled. "If that's not the most gaslighting use of words I have ever heard. Don't try to persuade me of your or the Consilium's good intentions. I've already been warned of the truth."

Damon's father's upper lip quivered. "What have you heard and from whom?"

"I won't be telling you either of those things, but I can assure you that I have no intention of starting a rebellion." She looked the man dead in the eyes. "Unless you make me."

His smile did not reach his eyes as one eyebrow arched. "I think your volunteering for a mission is a great idea. It'll get you outside the city and in the real world for a bit."

Alessa's heart skipped a beat as she questioned her decision to leave. *He seems way too happy to have me gone.*

Feigning confidence, she cleared her throat and forced a grin. "Anything I can do to help the human race. My body is but a vessel."

Nyx gasped in excitement as she watched Alessa from the underworld. "Interesting choice of words, Spartan."

Damon's father cleared his throat as he held out his hand. "I will not stand in your way. May the gods be with you."

After a moment's hesitation, Alessa placed her hand atop Damon's father's calloused hand. Seemingly sincere, he pressed his other hand on top of hers and bowed before releasing her.

Watching the older man saunter away, Alessa rubbed the weird tingling sensation from her hand. "What the fuck was that all about?"

"Damon!"

Hearing his father's voice over the music playing, Damon stopped running down the path in the woods. He tapped behind his earlobe, pausing the music being played by his microchip. He turned his head from side to side, trying to locate his father.

"Shit," Damon mumbled under his breath as he set his hands on his hips, breathing heavily. "How did you find me?" Damon asked his father as he approached from a side path.

"As if I don't know where everyone does their training. Speaking of training, I need you to go with the volunteers tomorrow morning."

Damon lifted his knees up to his chest one at a time. "I just got home. Why so eager to get rid of me?"

His father swatted Damon's words away with a flick of his

wrist. "Oh, son, this has nothing to do with you. The Consilium needs you to keep an eye on Alessa."

Damon laughed, without humor in his voice. "I'm not sure if you noticed, but she hates me."

"That matters not. I need someone I can trust, who isn't under Alessa's control, to keep an eye on her and make sure she doesn't do anything"—he paused—"that might warrant her to be stopped."

Damon rubbed his hands together and scoffed. "So, you want me to babysit Alessa and report back if she does anything that she should be killed for?"

His father tilted his head to the side and shrugged nonchalantly. "Precisely."

Damon looked up at the sky exposed through the treetops. "What if I were to tell you that I may not be the best person for the job? I haven't been feeling ... quite right. I've been having these intense, crazy dreams, and there are complete moments in time that are missing since Brielle—"

Damon's father stepped towards him, his neck red and veins bulging. "Dammit, Damon. Would you stop obsessing over that crazy woman? She has no control over you anymore!"

Damon stood eye to eye with his father, and his stomach dropped. *Not even my own father gives a shit about me. It's all about control.*

Damon shook his head back and forth incredulously. "Any other requests of me, Father?"

His father stepped back and adjusted his cape. "Not at this time." He turned on his heel, shouting over his shoulder, "Be ready to leave in the morning."

Feeling the burning sensation from behind his eyes, Damon unknowingly activated, and his body stiffened as he was forced to run once more.

CHAPTER SEVEN

Quade entered the loud mess hall, searching for Alessa, and after finding her sitting at a table with friends, he pushed through the crowd. Touching her shoulder, he said quietly into her ear, "Can we talk?"

Bending next to Alessa, Quade kissed his wife on the lips. "Hello, my love."

Seraphine smiled after swallowing her mouthful of mashed potatoes. "You two don't spend too much time talking. You need to get a full belly before leaving in the morning."

Camden watched intently from his seat as Quade pulled Alessa away from the table.

Glancing down at his hand on her arm, Alessa's eyebrows furrowed. "What's so urgent?"

"Do you hate Damon?"

Alessa's jaw dropped as she recoiled in surprise. "Uh—I'm sorry, what?"

Dropping his arm, he placed both hands on his hips and hinged forward in an effort to keep their conversation as private as possible in the crowded room. "I understand you were hurt and confused by what happened with your sister, but I need to know, do you truly hate Damon?"

Alessa looked off to the side nervously, trying to spin Damon's absent ring around her finger. "Why are you asking me this right now?"

"Dammit, Alessa, answer the question," Quade barked.

Taken aback, she faltered before responding. "No, I don't hate Damon. Why are you demanding to know this right now?"

Relief flooded through him, and he exhaled while shaking his head. "I just found out that Damon is coming with us on the mission. And truth be told, I'm worried about him. I have been for a while, but he won't open up to me, and I wasn't sure you wanted to talk about him."

Alessa put her hands up in front of herself and stepped forward. "Quade, wait, slow down. What exactly are you worried about?"

"He looks like shit," Quade chuckled. "I mean, honestly, he is not looking good. Man hardly sleeps anymore; he says he craves exercise, or some bullshit. Damon's just not acting ... like himself."

Alessa peered down at the ground, and with a loud sigh, she rocked back and forth while crossing her arms in front of her chest. "I've been meaning to talk to him. I guess I could go now, so things aren't awkward between us on the mission."

Reaching out towards her shoulder, Quade flashed a sad smile as he stopped short. He balled his hand into a tight fist before dropping it down to his side. "I know it will be hard for you, but Damon needs us to look out for him. He's always had your back before."

Brielle's face flashed in her mind, and Alessa fought back the urge to scream. Squeezing her eyes closed, she bit down on her lower lip. "I get what you're trying to say, but I really don't need a reminder of how things used to be."

Quade held his hands up defensively in front of his chest. "Understood."

Alessa glanced behind her friend and urged him to turn towards his wife. "Seraphine's wanting to spend some time with you before you leave again. Go get yourself some food."

Meeting Camden's curious hazel eyes, Alessa felt the air escape from her lungs as she made her way back to the table. "So, there's something I need to go do."

Camden's back stiffened, and his knuckles blanched as he gripped the fork in his hand. "Like what exactly?"

She cocked her head to the side. "Cam, it's time he knows I forgive him."

Camden's chair scooted back with a loud screech as he stood up abruptly.

Lexi placed a hand on his muscular forearm, holding him firmly in place before addressing Alessa. "Do you need someone to come with you?"

The rest of the table turned away out of respect and pretended not to hear the conversation.

Shaking her head back and forth, Alessa exhaled. "This is something I need to do on my own."

Camden planted his hand on the table and leaned into her. "You can't—"

Alessa's forehead scrunched, and her eyebrows raised as she glared into the golden flecks in Camden's dark green eyes. "I can't what?"

Camden stood his ground but remained silent as his jaw muscles flexed.

Leaning further into him, Alessa stood her ground. "I understand your concern, but if I couldn't remain civil around

Spartan civilians, I would've been killed by now. You need to trust me."

Camden placed his hand upon Alessa's, gripping her fingers. "Just ... be safe."

She smiled sarcastically before removing her hand from the tabletop. "When aren't I? After I talk with him, I'll head back to the cabin to get ready. This shouldn't take long."

Seraphine stared at Alessa's back in concern as she walked away.

Noticing the look on Seraphine's face, Quade plopped down beside his wife. "What's that look for?"

She lowered her voice. "The last time Alessa went to tell Damon something important, they"—she shook her head and shoved her fork back into the pile of mashed potatoes on her plate—"It's really none of my business."

Alessa's chest grew heavy as she passed by the small lake near Damon's house.

The afternoon sun filtered through the leaves, casting streaks of golden light onto Damon's wood cabin.

Goosebumps spread up Alessa's arms, and she shivered while silently cursing herself for not having stopped to grab a sweater before she ventured over. The sleeveless, deep green dress she was wearing, though made of thicker fabric, was not all that warm once in the shade of the trees.

Picturing Damon's piercing blue eyes, Alessa's stomach flipped, and she turned around to walk away. *I can't do this. What was I thinking?*

"Alessa?" Damon interrupted her thoughts while standing motionless in the doorway.

Hearing the melodic sound of her name leave his lips, she froze in the middle of the path.

Damon hesitantly stepped forward, and his eyes narrowed. "Alessa, is that you?"

Tilting her head up toward the sky, she exhaled. It's now or never. "Yeah, it's—it's me." She turned around to face Damon.

He was standing shirtless in the doorway; his abs and chest as defined as ever, while veins bulged in his muscular forearms. Alessa forced herself to look away, and she closed her eyes tight. "Um, did I interrupt something?"

Taken aback, he stammered. "I—um, I was just heading out to go on another run. Are you okay?"

Clearing her throat, she made herself meet his deep blue eyes. "Yeah, can we talk?"

"Oh—um—yeah." He peeked inside his house. "Do you want to come in?"

"Actually, yes." She smiled gratefully, wrapping her arms tighter around herself.

Passing Damon, Alessa felt intense heat emanating from his body, and after walking over his threshold, she looked up.

Her eyebrows furrowed in confusion. "It looks—"

"Different?" he finished for her, shutting the front door behind them.

With her arms wrapped around herself, Alessa strolled forward with a curt nod.

"Yeah, well, I didn't want to keep anything that bitch may have touched," Damon said on the way to his closet.

"That's understandable," she mumbled, sliding her fingers across his new table near the front door.

As he rummaged around his closet, she glanced hesitantly around his home. Looking down at the new bed, she touched the corner of his black silk sheets.

Closing her eyes, she attempted to block out the traumatizing memory of Damon and Brielle together.

Re-entering the room, Damon saw Alessa frozen at the edge of his bed and knew exactly what she was re-living. "Especially that." He held out a sweatshirt. "Here, take this."

Fingering the soft fabric, she glanced up at him. "How'd you—"

Damon laughed while crossing his arms. "I'd have to be blind not to see the goosebumps covering your body."

"Thank you," Alessa said before sliding the warm shirt over her head.

A shirtless Damon walked in between her and the bed, blocking her view. "So, what did you come here for tonight? I assume it wasn't to judge my interior decorating skills and to borrow my clothes."

Alessa's heartbeat increased as she struggled to remain calm. "Um—I—um..."

Holding out his hand, he took a half a step forward before retracting it, as if he'd thought about touching her but had decided against it.

Damon ran his fingers through his dark hair and blurted out, "I'm sorry. I'm so sorry. If I could switch places with Kai and give you your sister back—"

Alessa closed her eyes, and a single tear escaped as she held her hand up. "Damon, stop. Please, just stop. Kai would never want that. And neither do I."

Damon's eyes glimmered with tears as he stood before her.

She nervously pressed her thumb against the empty space on her ring finger while debating what to say next. "These past few months, I haven't been kind to you. What I said to you after my sister died—that wasn't how I felt. Not truly. I was hurt and confused, looking for someone to blame. I lashed out at you, and I'm sorry for that. I realize I have been blaming you for things that were out of your control. Brielle, your memory loss, my sister's death, none of those things were your fault. Yes, the blade was yours, but I know it was ultimately Hades' decision which soul to take. He stole my sister from me, not you."

Alessa stepped towards Damon as he stood frozen in front of her. "What I came here to say is ... I forgive you."

With a painstaking groan, he dropped down to his knees and buried his head in his hands. His shoulder blades bounced up and down as he cried.

Her heart ached, and she dropped before him. Lifting his eyes to meet hers, they stared at one another, their apologies written across their faces.

As tears fell from Damon's eyes, Alessa wrapped her arms tightly around his neck and pulled him into a tight embrace.

With the release of his pent-up emotional pain, he stopped trembling, and she reluctantly let him go.

Sitting back, she wrapped her hands around her bent knees. Noticing the dark circles under Dmon's eyes and the paleness of his once-glowing skin, Alessa's eyebrows furrowed in concern. "Are you doing okay?'

He sniffled and wiped his tears away with a gruff laugh. "I will be."

She played with the place on her finger where his ring used to be. "I haven't seen you around much."

He copied Alessa's posture and bent his legs before intertwining his fingers. Placing his hands on top of his knees, Damon sighed. "I was trying to give you space. I took every mission I could to do so. I even contemplated going back home."

Her heart unexpectedly skipped a beat. "Home? This is your home, now. Isn't it?"

He rubbed his hands together and looked down at the hardwood floor. "I wasn't so sure anymore. It didn't feel that way."

Biting her lower lip, Alessa glanced over at the new bed beside them. "I'm sorry for that. It couldn't have been easy, what with the way I was treating you."

Damon smiled sadly. "It wasn't without reason."

She nervously cleared her throat and stood upright. "I heard you signed up for the newest mission."

Following Alessa, Damon stood up as well and rubbed his hands on his cargo pants. "I am being sent."

Her eyes dropped to his hands moving up and down his thighs, and with the threat of memories resurfacing from their time together, she backed up while trying to wiggle out of Damon's black sweatshirt. "Uh—I should be going. I'm glad things won't be weird between us anymore."

Damon touched the sides of Alessa's arms as his sweatshirt bunched up around her breasts. He pulled the bottom of the warm fabric down to her waist, over her deep green dress. "It's a good walk home; keep it. You can give it back later."

Her breath faltered with him standing so close, and she tried to collect her thoughts. "Okay..."

Turning back around, she walked toward the front door and froze as she recalled the last time Damon had stood behind her in a similar scenario.

Her face grew flush as she imagined his hand slamming into the door beside her ear before her back was pressed up against it in a passionate embrace.

Hearing the doorknob turn, Alessa's eyes opened, and Damon was standing beside her, shirtless, holding his hands out to escort her through the doorway.

Exhaling slowly, she grinned nervously. "Still going on your run?"

He closed the door before following her down the front steps. "Yeah. Lately, I've been running more than once a day; I can't seem to sit still. But, knowing you don't hate me anymore, maybe I'll be able to get some rest tonight."

She sighed. "I never hated you. My heart was shattered, and I dealt with it the only way I knew how. But I truly am sorry I made you feel..." She let the end of her sentence trail off, unable to bring herself to say the word unloved.

He looked down at the ground and put his hands on his hips as he anxiously stepped side to side. "Well, have a good night and get home safe."

Alessa hugged the warm fabric around her torso and smiled sadly. "We're in New Sparta. How much safer could I possibly be?"

Damon tapped behind his earlobe, triggering his microchip to start music only he could hear. "Take care of yourself, Alessa," he hollered back over his shoulder as he ran down the path.

Feeling lighter, Alessa exhaled into the dark woods as she activated her night vision. "Good night, Damon."

CHAPTER EIGHT

With a heavy sigh, Alessa hastily shoved clothes and toiletries into her black bag as Camden stood behind her, trying to justify why he should tag along.

"I need you to stop," she demanded.

Flailing his uninjured arm, Camden huffed. "I just hate the fact that I can't come with you because of this stupid fucking—" a trail of strewn-together curse words fell from his mouth as he tore at his shoulder sling.

Throwing her bag onto the bed, she stopped what she was doing. "Cam, listen to me." She grabbed his biceps and held him in place. "I'm going to be fine. I don't need you to be my keeper. Having you there, unable to keep up physically, will only distract me, and I need you here, someone I trust, helping Lexi with all the brainwork.

"Yeah." Camden chuckled, eyeing Alessa from the side. "I've always been interested in the behind-the-scenes portion of an investigation," he retorted sarcastically.

She chuckled, knowing he'd much rather be in the middle of any battle. "Well, here's your chance. Whether you like it or not." She wrapped her arms around his neck and pulled herself up onto her tiptoes. "I'll only be gone for, maybe, a month. Work your ass off while I'm gone, and maybe Sera will clear you to go to the celebration with us in Greece."

He pulled back and grinned. "I've never been to Greece before."

Withdrawing her arms, Alessa headed for the bathroom to grab the rest of her supplies. "Neither have I, but Quade and Seraphine tell me it's beautiful. Apparently, watching the waves crash against the cliffs is the most incredible thing to witness first-hand."

She returned with her toothbrush, a hairbrush, and dry shampoo. "I do hope you and Lexi dig up some good information while I'm gone. We need to catch a break in all of this madness. Maybe my elder will come home while I'm gone. If he does, you can get him caught up on everything that's happened."

She slung her bag's strap over her shoulder before heading for the cabin's front door. "Don't have too much fun without me."

He chuckled, following close behind. "And don't do anything I wouldn't do," he teased while opening the door.

Alessa wrinkled her nose as she turned around to face him. "Is there anything you wouldn't do?"

Holding back another smartass remark, he bit the inside of his cheek. "Okay, you got me there. What I mean is, don't die. You got it?"

She dropped the bag and threw her arms around his thick neck, burying her face against his warm skin. "I'll miss you."

"Me too, my fiery one," he said in his native Russian tongue.

"I wish I knew what you were saying when you spoke

Russian." Her eyes widened in excitement, and she gasped. "Maybe I can bring that up to the doctors with the new microchips."

Camden laughed while letting her go. "Go on, get out of here. The sooner you leave, the sooner you'll be back."

Dipping down, Alessa picked up her bag. "See ya," she yelled back as she ran up the path.

Damon stepped up into the back of the truck and sat beside Quade.

Having not yet completed any containment measures in the Northern California region, the warriors were unsure of what they would encounter upon their arrival.

The air was thick with anticipation as the warriors sat with their packed bags shoved to one side of the vehicle, and their weapons in hand.

As the doors were closing, a hand slipped around the edge, holding them open.

"Wait!" Alessa demanded as she pulled open the metal door and jumped into the back of the vehicle.

Throwing her bag onto the pile, she then plopped down and adjusted the weapons attached to her straps. With a loud exhale, she finally looked up.

Surprised to find Damon and Quade sitting across from her, she murmured awkwardly. "Hey."

"You almost missed the bus. What were you doing?" Quade asked.

Alessa shifted nervously in her seat. "I was ... uh ... just finishing packing and saying goodbye to Cam."

Damon pursed his lips. "Why isn't your Bodyguard coming along? I thought he never left your side."

Alessa's eyes narrowed as she stared at Damon defiantly. "It wasn't by choice. He's still got a few more weeks of healing before he can take off his sling. And he's not a Bodyguard anymore."

Damon glanced down at the ground and chuckled. "Not as strong as he made himself out to be."

Alessa aggressively leaned forward. "What the—"

"Okay, okay," Quade interrupted. "Enough. We're about to take off, and I need you two to shut the fuck up and focus."

"Got it." Alessa sat back against the cool metal of the truck.

Damon's lips separated in an aggravated grin. "Understood."

As the familiar vibration began, Alessa drew in a sharp breath. Before she fully exhaled, they arrived at their destination with a lurch.

Hearing ear-piercing shrieks outside the vehicle, every warrior in the truck reactively straightened their backs and raised their weapons.

Without speaking a word, Damon and Alessa's eyes met, as if to say, 'I've got your back'.

After the first Spartan warrior kicked open the doors, the rest filtered one after the other into the chaotic street.

Damon sprinted through the sea of bodies off to the side, to get to higher ground, while Alessa and Quade ran straight ahead into the thick of the battle.

At least a hundred of the Frenzied swarmed the bloodied street. Dead bodies were stacked one on top of another, littering the main road. Still, the Frenzied were unbothered by their presence, and they hastily climbed over them.

The creatures' mouths hung open at unnatural angles, as if stuck in a perpetual state of fear, and their eyes were wide and bulging.

Their skin was mottled and bruised, torn and cut; some even had the sharp ends of bones protruding.

Inhuman shrieks echoed across the landscape and were only silenced once they bit into human flesh.

Unable to comprehend the horror of what was happening, Alessa used her training to compartmentalize her emotions and focus on the battle. *They look so much worse than they did at the beginning of all of this. It's like they're not even human anymore.*

Realizing she needed weapons for hand-to-hand combat, Alessa swung her gun around the sling, onto her back. She grabbed her sword and reached back between her shoulder blades for her shield when she felt the breeze of a bullet fly past her neck. Thick black blood sprayed as it struck the eye of one of the Frenzied who had been lunging for her.

Her head whipped to the right and up the hill, where Damon stood a good two hundred feet away with a firearm aimed in her direction. Alessa's breath hitched as she saw his silver irises, and with a dismissing tilt of his head, she snapped back to reality.

Regaining her composure, Alessa withdrew the compressed sword and pressed the trigger, quadrupling the length of its sharpened blade. She stepped back, preparing for the rush of zombie-like creatures.

Having already withdrawn his compressed double-sided sword, Quade pulled the blades apart and stood with his back to Alessa, wielding a sword in each hand.

The Spartan smiled with reckless abandon. "Ready to play?" he asked Alessa.

Hearing the excitement in his voice, she glanced back into his activated irises that were glowing ice blue with a bright yellow ring around his pupil.

In response to her adrenaline rush, her own eyes glitched crimson red. "Body count game?"

An eager grin spread across Quade's face, and his eyebrows raised. "Twenty-four," he claimed as his final body count.

Lifting her sword up in the air, Alessa grinned wickedly as she sprinted forward. Swinging the blade around, she cut the arm clear off her first Frenzied. "I claim twenty-six!" she yelled back, upping Quade by two.

Alarmed by the Frenzieds' lack of reaction, Alessa's anxiety rose as she hacked away limbs and cut into the creature's broken bodies. Black sludge-like fluid leaked from their wounds instead of bright red blood, and it struck a nerve in Alessa. *Did my sister have a hand in creating these monsters?*

Extracting his sword from another Frenzied's back, Quade grunted. "Ten!"

Getting sucked into the depths of her trauma, Alessa started hallucinating, and as flashbacks of the battle between the Bodyguards and the Spartans appeared before her, the images disrupted her reality.

Blinking the memory away, Alessa blocked a bite from a Frenzied just before it reached her neck. She pushed the creature back and drove her blade into its eye while yelling over her shoulder at Quade. "Twelve!"

Turning around, Alessa grabbed the weaponized boomerang and tossed it into the Frenzied surrounding her. As it sliced through the creature's necks, black fluid spurted into the air.

Not realizing their bodies were failing them, the Frenzied continued attacking until the creature's veins were emptied of the thickened blood; at which point they fell to the ground, unmoving.

While looking down at one of the Frenzied who had just collapsed before her, Alessa's reality blurred, and she flashed back to the ballroom with Kai lying at her feet.

"No!" Alessa panicked, squeezing her eyes closed tight. "It's not real. You're not real."

Opening her eyes, Alessa yelled as she was knocked back.

Falling to the ground, her sword was kicked out of her hand, and as one of the Frenzied released a horrific noise from its mouth, the creature lunged at Alessa.

Unable to reach her weapons in time, she held her hands up in front of her face and braced for impact.

***

Watching from afar, Damon saw the moment Alessa was knocked down.

He jumped up, running as quickly as his activated microchip would allow. Dodging bodies left and right, Damon saw the Frenzied lunge for Alessa, and retracting his golden-hilted sword, he extended the blade with the press of a button on its hilt.

Alessa lay back against the ground with her arms covering her face as the creature bared its teeth and threw itself onto her.

Holding his sword high above his head, Damon leapt into the air, bringing the blade straight down into the Frenzied's upper back.

Hearing the impact of a sword being driven through flesh and bone, Alessa opened her eyes to find the creature hovering above her. Its face was contorted in a mix of anger and confusion as it glared at the blade protruding from the front of his chest.

Damon extracted a smaller, sharp blade from his arsenal of weapons and stabbed it into the base of its skull.

With the cessation of the Frenzied's feral growls, he tilted the creature to the side and kicked it off the end of his sword.

Standing tall above her, Damon extended his arm out for Alessa.

After she wrapped her fingers around his muscular forearm, he pulled her upright, and they held one another, breathing heavily, as the battle continued around them.

"Thanks," Alessa exhaled.

Damon flashed a crooked grin as he stared into her red irises. "Any time."

Sporting a cocky smile, Quade bellowed, "Twenty!" from over his shoulder.

After snatching Alessa's sword up off the ground, Damon handed it to her. "Your hand-to-hand combat is a bit rusty since you've been focusing all your energy on controlling your glitch, huh?"

They turned away, pressing their backs against one another.

Alessa answered with an audible huff. "Oh, shut up."

Standing back-to-back, Damon and Alessa held their swords out in front of them, prepared to fight.

He sliced his sword through the air, hacking the arms off a Frenzied before cutting the creature's head clear off its shoulders. "These fuckers don't by chance have microchips you could blow up, do they?"

Alessa grunted loudly as she kicked back an attacking Frenzied. "I've never thought about checking. Cover me."

She closed her eyes, standing still as a Frenzied sprinted for her.

Damon's eyes grew wide as he eyed the Frenzied lunging for Alessa, and he dove in front of her with his sword.

As Damon protected her, Alessa focused on expanding her ability to see electronics within those around her. But even with her increased range, she saw no microchips in the Frenzied; only the typical electronic devices one would find in a normal human being, such as a pacemaker or a continuous glucose monitor.

Releasing a heavy exhale, Alessa opened her eyes. "They don't have microchips for me to target."

Damon grunted as he held off another attack. "That's okay. Looks like we're about done, anyway." He pointed across the battlefield.

The Frenzied's numbers had significantly dwindled.

The dead and wounded Spartans, Frenzied, and those from the general population lay scattered amongst one another.

Damon inspected the area. "Looks like it's handled."

Pressing a button on the handle to retract the blade, he sheathed his sword before adding it to the arsenal of weapons secured to his back. "We'll be out here for a few weeks. I'll work with you."

Alessa unglitched, and her eyes returned to their blue hue as she stared up into Damon's silver eyes. "It wasn't just the fighting, I was"—she cleared her throat—"never mind."

Damon closed his eyes tight, forcing himself to deactivate, and when he opened them, they were back to their deep blue hue. "Okay, then, just let me know if you need anything."

Alessa ran towards the broken and bleeding citizens. "I need a medic bag and three volunteers," she called back.

Damon ran to one of their trucks, slung a medic bag over his shoulder, and grabbed three volunteers.

When he returned, Alessa was kneeling beside someone with a profusely bleeding neck wound who was staring off into the distance.

"She's gone," she declared before shaking her head in defeat and moving on to the next victim.

Hours into triaging and treating the wounded, Alessa and the medical team had stabilized the victims as best they could. At the same time, the rest of the Spartan warriors gathered up the bodies of the Frenzied.

After being piled high, an accelerant was poured on their bodies, and they were set on fire. Alessa hugged herself as she watched the flames rise into the air, chasing after the dark grey smoke.

Quade and Alessa stood side by side. "That's sad," he murmured. "Just a little while ago, they were all mothers, fathers, aunts, uncles, teachers, doctors..."

Alessa shuddered as the weight of his statement struck a nerve. "Yeah, well, they just took the lives of countless others who still had their humanity." Glancing off to the side at the small body of a toddler who lay with the dead, Alessa ground her teeth together in anger.

Clearing her throat, she wiped angry tears away with the back of her hand. "I blame the elders for this. Had they just listened—"

Quade painfully grabbed her arm. "You can't talk like that. There are still plenty of elder-sympathizers in this group who would love nothing more than to report you for speaking ill of the leaders. You'd be executed; watch yourself."

Alessa rolled her eyes and sighed. "You're right; I'm sorry. Let's just get these bodies burned and the local authorities on their way to gather the living. What's the bullshit story we'll be giving them?"

Quade cleared his throat as the smoke from the bodies tickled his airway. "We're making it appear as though a bomb was set to explode by a known terrorist group. We've already been wiping the survivor's memories. Should only be another thirty minutes at most."

"Good," Alessa sighed. "I need a shower ... and a drink."

CHAPTER NINE

Arriving at the rental houses, the Spartans took turns showering and grocery shopping for their first night in California.

After washing up, Alessa walked up to the rooftop, which had been set up as an entertainment space. The grill had been started, and the smell of cooking meat made her stomach growl.

Twinkling white lights were strung from one end of the roof to the other, attached to tall beams.

Off to the center was a fire pit surrounded by several oversized chairs, and just past the fire, water cascaded down from a decorative waterfall feature that hid a section of the roof behind it.

Alessa walked past the waterfall and leaned into the stone edging surrounding the rooftop. Tilting her head back, she closed her eyes and inhaled the warm night air while listening to the comforting sound of running water.

After cleaning the blood from his skin, Damon joined the other Spartans celebrating on the rooftop. Ascending the stairs, he felt a familiar tug in his chest.

Looking through the hazy waterfall, he saw Alessa standing alone.

Her soft cream dress was held together by thick champagne-colored ropes, and the light fabric clung to her curves as she pressed her back against the stone wall.

Damon moved slowly and quietly, taking in her beautiful form. It had been so long since he had seen her look relaxed and at peace.

Sensing someone close, she tensed before she spun around. Placing a hand upon her chest, she breathed. "Oh, Damon, it's you."

Walking past the wall of water, he grinned. "I was just coming up here to check on you. See if you need any food or anything."

"Today was..." she trailed off.

He walked up beside her and set his arms on the stone wall. "Yeah..." He peered over the edge at the people down below on the street.

They were oblivious to the zombie-like creatures in their world, dancing around with cups in hand, hollering and laughing.

"The pictures don't do the Frenzied justice. They look inhuman now. Like they're rotting from the inside out." Alessa stared off into the distance. "They weren't like that when this started. And are they getting stronger?"

Stepping beside her, Damon nodded. "You're correct, they didn't look this bad. Not at first. They seem to be ... decomposing. And yes, they are getting stronger. It's almost as if they are becoming desperate to survive. More aggressive."

She tilted her head in contemplation. "Have we ever seen them eat? How are they still alive?" She shook the image of the deceased toddler from her mind. "We need to figure out what's causing it. I know it has something to do with Ambrosia; it must. The timing is—"

"Too perfect?" He finished her sentence.

She glanced up at him. "Yeah."

"There was something else going on with you today," he suggested.

Licking her lips, she sighed and looked away. "Yeah. I'd rather not—"

Damon held up his hand for her to stop. "I recognized the look. It's PTSD."

Alessa's eyes darted from side to side. "Uh ..." She nervously laughed, not wanting Damon to figure out she had freaked out over a deceased Kai hallucination. "I think I would know if—"

He shook his hand back and forth, dismissively. "It's okay, I get it. No explanation needed, and I'm not going to rat you out for needing a moment. Just don't let it happen again, okay? You're lucky I got there in time."

She slowly nodded while absentmindedly rubbing her thumb against her ring finger. "Thank you for that."

"Next time you feel the urge to disassociate, it helps to use the Grounding Technique."

Alessa cocked her head.

Damon flashed a knowing grin. "It's where you name five things you see, four things you feel, three things you hear, two things you smell, and one thing you taste. Preferably as you continue fighting so you don't, well, you know..."

"Die." She shook her head as if to clear her mind. "Thanks. I'll try it. And you're right. I have been slacking on the physical aspect of being a warrior. I'm not sure if you noticed, but the elders, your father included, are pressuring me to hone my skills so they can pretty much make me a weapon."

He unintentionally balled his hands into fists. "Don't let them."

She scoffed while walking away. "Excuse me? I'm not some Wellborn who can just—"

Reaching out, he grabbed her arm, holding her in place. "No, you're not. You are Alessa Custos. The first of her kind. You are going to set the bar for what our people are capable of when the gods inevitably choose you as humanity's savior."

While being held in place, she looked down at his hand and glared up at Damon. "What are you talking about? I only became what I am because of what happened to you." Her face fell, and she swallowed the lump that had formed in her throat.

Seeing her in distress, Damon let go of her arm and shoved his hands into his pants pockets. "I choose to believe there is a reason for all of ... this." He glanced around the rooftop with a shrug before locking eyes with Alessa. "For what happened between us."

Her breathing hitched with the tightening of her chest. Staring up into his deep blue eyes, Alessa searched for answers. "Have you remembered anything yet? From the time Brielle stole?"

Looking down at the ground, his jaw muscles flexed. "Uh, no, I—I haven't. Sera said I probably wouldn't, so I'm not holding my breath."

She pressed her lips together and turned away.

He cleared his throat. "With the Frenzied, don't mess around with trying to cause them pain. It won't work. Just aim for the head to try to take them out as quickly as possible."

Alessa stared absentmindedly at her fingers. "The head. Got it."

Damon's shoulders sagged as he leaned back against the stone ledge. "One of the objectives on this mission is to bring home a Frenzied for our team to examine."

Her jaw dropped. "What, alive?"

He peered down at his hands while rubbing them together. "That's the plan. For us to determine the physiological damage and what parts of the body the disease, or the mutation, is affecting, they need a sample to study."

Damon exhaled an exhausted sigh. "Okay, that's enough of the heavy stuff. Have you eaten anything?"

Snapping back to reality, she blinked. "What?"

"Have you eaten dinner yet? It's ten o'clock at night, and I know how you get if you haven't had anything to eat all day."

Before she could respond, Alessa's stomach gurgled loudly.

Damon chuckled and grabbed her hand. "It's settled then. We need to get some food in you."

She felt at peace as the familiar warm electric shock spread throughout her with Damon's touch. They crossed the rooftop to the other side of the waterfall, where a group of Spartans were laughing with drinks in hand.

Quade raised his cup while manning the grill. "Alessa! Damon!"

Damon let go of Alessa's hand. "Oh shit. Who let this man have control of the food while drinking?" He jogged towards Quade. "I'll take that." Taking the spatula from Quade, Damon shooed him away.

"Alessa, I'm going to be a dad again!" Quade exclaimed sloppily.

She laughed as he haphazardly threw an arm over her shoulder. "Yes, you are."

"Isn't Sera the greatest? She's the best, right?" He took a swig of his drink.

"Oh, yeah. She's incredible. You did well," Alessa agreed while guiding him towards one of the oversized chairs surrounding the firepit.

Quade plopped down in the chair with a groan. "For me, it was always Seraphine."

Alessa's eyes darted to Damon, standing before the grill. She watched his muscular forearms flip the burgers while he talked with a few others.

"I'm so incredibly fortunate she said yes to spending her life with me. I couldn't imagine being here without her." Quade tilted his head back and finished his beer.

"Okay, we need to get some food on board. Damon!" she shouted. "Burger on a bun stat! And water. Lots of water."

"You got it." Damon prepared two plates: one with a single cheeseburger and another with two.

After handing off the spatula, Damon brought a plate to Quade and the other to Alessa.

"Why do I need two cheeseburgers?" she asked.

Damon grabbed one from Alessa's plate and sat in the chair beside her. "You don't." He shoved the burger in his mouth and took a big bite. "Oh man," Damon mumbled with a full mouth. "That's a damn good burger. Good job, drunk Quade."

Quade held up his burger in the air in a salute. "It is but one of my many talents."

Alessa laughed while Damon swallowed. "Alessa, we need to practice your combat skills tomorrow."

She nearly choked on her food before responding. "I know how to fight. I don't need—"

"Yes, you do," Damon interrupted. "I am well aware you know how to fight. If you don't recall, I'm one of those who taught you. You simply need a refresher course on how to get out of your head and how to move your body preemptively."

"You do need to get out of your head," Quade mumbled with a mouth full of meat and bread.

Damon pointed at Quade. "See? Drunk Quade agrees with me. Being able to control technology won't matter if they don't have a microchip."

Alessa took a bite of her burger and chewed as the wheels in her head turned. "You're right. But, I can control all types of technology, not just microchips."

Damon's eyebrows raised. "Didn't you say some of the Frenzied had pacemakers and um—"

Alessa slowly grinned in understanding. "Implanted glucose monitors. Yes. Yes, I did."

"Oh, shit, bro! That's a good one. Killing someone with their own pacemaker; that's diabolical," Quade chuckled.

Alessa half-grinned. "Actually, up until now, I hadn't considered taking someone out with the technology controlling their vital organs. I've always focused on bigger items on the outside or a single microchip. Huh. That's not a bad idea."

Relaxing into his chair, Damon tucked his hands behind his head. "I have good ideas from time to time."

CHAPTER TEN

Camden and Lexi had been at the library since sunrise, and he was growing impatient.

His stomach growled loudly as he stared at the back of Lexi's head.

She sat quietly in front of the computer screen, engrossed in her reading.

He watched as Lexi spun a few strands of hair that had escaped her braid around the tips of her fingers.

Leaning into her, he whispered. "You know I love how much you enjoy a good mystery, and I am fully aware how invested you are in your current research, but if I don't get some food in me soon, you might have to pick me up off the floor and drag me to the medical building."

Side-eyeing Camden, Lexi scoffed. "Yeah, okay. Let me just..." She clicked the printer icon.

Pushing back their chairs, they stood up simultaneously.

"What are you so interested in this morning?" he asked.

Grabbing her tablet, Lexi walked toward the printer. "With the information I've dug up, I've narrowed down the origins of the Frenzied. While we grab a bite to eat, I can continue reading about those who were the first to transition into a Frenzied. That way, we can pinpoint the exact locations and try to figure out the source."

He followed close behind her. "Locations? As in multiple? You don't think it came from a single place?"

Lexi tilted her head. "Alessa's been pretty consistent with her information thus far, so I've no reason not to trust her." She looked into Camden's hazel eyes. "Alessa believes Ambrosia is the cause of the change in behavior. Her hypothesis is the most logical of all the theories I've heard. You know what they say about the simplest explanation."

The pieces of paper spit out from the top of the noisy printer, laying one on top of the other.

He raised his arm and pressed the palm of his hand against the column behind Lexi, leaning over her. "It's likely the correct one."

Feeling the heat rise up the back of her neck, she swallowed before nervously glancing away. "Precisely." Her eyes locked on the busy printer as the papers piled up.

"What would that mean? If Ambrosia is causing the zombie-like symptoms in those who consumed it, would it be a disease? A mutation?"

The printer made a loud, disgruntled noise as the final paper landed atop the rest.

"That's a question I fully intend to discuss with Seraphine once I complete gathering evidence." Lexi picked up the stack of papers. "Oh, that's hot," she hissed before laughing to herself. "Duh, they just came hot off the press."

Camden wrapped his unsecured arm around her shoulders. "Oh, Lex. You are one hell of a beautiful nerd."

Did he just call me beautiful? If she were able to hide her blushing cheeks behind her long hair, she would have, but her red locks were secured in a thick single braid cascading down her back. "Thanks?" she chuckled as she held the pile of papers tight against her chest.

His stomach growled loudly once more as he glanced toward the library's exit. "And now, we eat."

CHAPTER ELEVEN

The first week they were in California, Damon and Alessa were too busy to see one another.

The Spartans took shifts, listening to the police scanner for any disturbances in nearby cities. As one location was cleansed, another experienced escalating violence that drew the Spartans' attention, and they moved on to another place.

The exhausted warriors fought around the clock to take out the Frenzied before the creatures had the chance to wipe out entire cities.

During the second week, Alessa had just gotten home and showered when she walked up the stairs to the new rental home's rooftop.

Damon sat on a rumpled blanket, leaning to one side. He was staring absentmindedly into the flames of a fire with a bottle of scotch in hand.

Concerned with which version of Damon she would encounter, Alessa hesitated. He didn't frequently consume hard liquor.

Moving slowly, she picked up the bottom of her skirt and approached guardedly. "Damon?"

Blinking slowly, the Spartan dropped the bottle from his lips and turned his head. He squinted through blurred vision. "Alessa, is that you?" he slurred.

Gathering her skirt, she sat down on the makeshift pile of blankets beside Damon while eyeing the bottle in his hand. "Watcha doing up here? Looks like you're having a one-man party." She directed his attention to the bottle of alcohol within his grasp.

Damon grinned sheepishly. "Oh, this?" He took a long swig before Alessa reached for the glass container.

"Okay, I think you've had enough." She grasped the bottom of the glass.

Damon rolled his eyes while reluctantly allowing Alessa to take the bottle. He fell clumsily back onto the blankets and scoffed. "Ugh."

"Yeah, well, we need you coherent if shit were to go down. I'd rather not have to worry about saving your ass while taking down the Frenzied."

Tears sprang to his eyes. "After everything I've done to you, after everything I've put you through, you would still save me?"

Her jaw dropped as she stared back at him, incredulously. "Of course I would."

Propping himself up on an elbow, he reached up towards Alessa. He tucked a strand of her thick brown hair behind her ear and smiled sadly. "I am blessed the gods sent me such a true friend."

Feeling as though she had been struck in the gut, she exhaled and pulled away.

Pushing her pile of blankets over, she lay down beside Damon.

He pressed his fingers into his closed eyelids. "Oh, thank you. The two of you were spinning around way too much, sitting up there."

Quietly laughing, Alessa pressed the back of her cool hand against the side of Damon's face, and after nuzzling into her touch, he fell fast asleep.

She watched his chest rise and fall, and feeling her walls break down, Alessa leaned into him. "I wish you had been the one," she confessed before curling up into his side.

Waking up in the middle of the night, Damon blinked as he slowly came to. Realizing his chest felt heavy, he looked down to find Alessa asleep in the crook of his arm, using the left side of his chest as a pillow.

As a wave of emotions hit Damon, he tilted his head back and closed his eyes. A collage of fragmented experiences between him and Alessa played back in his mind.

With a sharp inhale, his eyes flew open, and without waking Alessa, he carefully moved out from beneath her. After lying her head on the pile of blankets, he leaned down and gently kissed her forehead.

He watched her embrace a bundle of blankets, and a faint smile played on the edge of her lips.

Shaking the sleep from his foggy brain, Damon walked over to the edge of the rooftop. Pressing his thick forearms against the railing, he clasped his hands together. *This has to be the first time in months I've slept more than four consecutive hours.*

Looking up at the clear night sky high above, he located the Legend of Lyra amongst the stars. He sighed as the memory of him explaining their significance to Alessa all those years ago came to mind.

As the colorful sunrise kissed the edges of the dark sky, Damon glanced over at Alessa and sighed. "I wish I were deserving of you."

<hr>

"I love how we had to move again," Alessa grumbled as they trudged up the stairs to the new rental.

Quade laughed as he typed the code into the electronic lock on the front door. "How dare the Frenzied not give a shit about us getting a good night's rest?" he sarcastically remarked.

The door swung open, and the Spartans filed in, claiming beds, couches, and chairs to sleep in. Quade, Alessa, and Damon, as always, headed straight for the roof, where there would inevitably be hangouts for those vacationing in California.

"A pool? Yes!" Quade exclaimed as they ran across the rooftop.

Beelining for the lawn chairs stretched out in front of the small pool, Alessa pointed at the chair with the thickest pads. "Dibs!"

Quade sported a sideways grin and spoke to Damon out of the side of his mouth. "As always, she gets the comfiest spot." He plopped his gear and bag beside the end chair. "Guess this'll be mine."

Damon passed Alessa, looking to claim the chair on the opposite side of her. "And I'll sleep here, if that's okay."

Alessa felt her face flush, and she set her bag down beside the chair. "Of course. Camden would be glad to know I'm being protected on both sides."

Damon felt his insides clench with the sound of the Bodyguard's name. *Fucking Camden.*

"I'm going to get ready," Alessa announced.

Quade plucked weapons from his bag, setting them atop his temporary bed. "Good idea. We're going to hit up a local bar tonight."

"So, dress like a civilian?" Alessa asked.

Quade continued unloading weapons from his luggage. "Exactly."

She grabbed clothes out of her bag. "I think I can do that."

"Is she almost done in there?" Damon asked as he and Quade tucked their weapons beneath their clothing.

As if on cue, Alessa opened the bathroom door and stepped out into the hallway.

Her hair was curled in thick waves, cascading down just past her shoulders, and she had on her Spartan warrior corset top.

Wanting to feel sexy, she also wore skintight leggings with a buckle and a see-through mesh panel on one thigh.

Damon's eyes burned as he looked her up and down. Closing them, he pressed his fingertips into his eyelids, urging them to stay blue. *Don't you fucking activate. Don't you fucking do it.*

Catching on to why Damon's posture was so stiff, Quade pressed his lips together in a silent chuckle.

Oblivious to Damon's reaction, Alessa finished her outfit by tugging on black combat boots. "Ready to head out?" she asked while cloaking a few blades and devices with their advanced technology.

"Yeah, uh—let's get out of here," Damon responded as Alessa walked past him.

His eyes fell to her perky ass, and as Quade snorted, Damon punched his friend in the arm. "Shut the fuck up."

Quade couldn't hold his laughter in any longer. "Ow! The fuck, man? I'm not the one ogling."

Damon followed Alessa out the front door along with another group of Spartans.

"I said shut up," he threatened.

Wrapping his fingers around Damon's arm, Quade held his friend back as Alessa walked ahead to the waiting cars lined up along the street. "You know you two belong together. Just give her time."

"Quade..." Damon warned.

Retracting his hand from Damon's arm, Quade turned around to make sure the front door had locked. "I'm calling it now. You two end up together. You need to trust the process, bro."

"Yeah, right," scoffed Damon as he walked down the front steps.

Quade followed behind Damon. "No one can fight their destiny, not even you."

While getting into the passenger side of his car, Damon shook his head. "You're confusing destiny with fate. You can't fight your fate. With destiny, you still have a choice in the matter."

Quade started the rental car and looked over at Damon. "Whatever you say. All I know is, you can't escape what's meant to be."

CHAPTER TWELVE

Later that very week, to expand their coverage of the city, the Spartans separated into several smaller groups.

As Quade pulled up to the bar they had been assigned to patrol, Damon felt a familiar threatening hum, attempting to force his microchip to activate.

He walked in through the front door while rubbing the burning sensation from his eyelids. As his eyes locked onto Alessa standing at the counter, Damon was able to subconsciously shake off the hold Brielle had on his microchip.

Brielle furiously clicked the computer mouse, trying to reconnect with Damon's microchip. "Why isn't this damn thing working?" she growled.

Unable to gain access, her eyes flared. "I.T.! Something is wrong! I need you now!" she shouted into the microphone.

Back at the bar, the band played their rendition of "Maybe, I" as Damon approached the counter. "Two Jack and Cokes, please," he requested while holding up two fingers.

Alessa jumped at his proximity. "Oh, jeez, Damon!" She pressed her hand against her chest. "Sorry." Leaning into him, she smiled apologetically. "It's just so crowded and loud in here. I didn't know anyone was that close to me."

"You should probably be more aware of your surroundings. For more than one reason." Damon pointed at the men staring at her from further down the bar.

After turning her head, the men held up their beverages in hand as if to say 'hi'.

Alessa's eyebrows raised, and with an awkward grin plastered to her face, she tilted her head toward the men. Turning back around, she sighed. "I need to have some fun. Clearly, you're choosing to have some tonight as well, but your concern is warranted. Thanks." Tilting her head, she threw back a shot of tequila.

Trying to speak over the music, Damon leaned into her. "And yes, I drink from time to time. It's..."

She shook her head back and forth. "Whew!" she squealed. "It's what?"

He scoffed and anxiously licked his lips. "It keeps the nightmares at bay and my emotions in check."

She grabbed her glass of water from the counter. "So, it numbs you?"

He flashed a half-smile. "I guess so."

Alessa placed her hand against the side of Damon's face and stood up on the tips of her toes. "If you should need us, Quade and I will be there for you."

Looking into his deep sapphire blue eyes, she felt the heat start in the pit of her stomach, and her eyes fell to his lips.

"That'll be thirty dollars," the bartender interrupted.

Snapping out of the intimate moment, Alessa dropped her hand.

The bartender held out two drinks for Damon as the Spartan slid the cash across the counter.

With a drink in each hand, Damon looked at Alessa. "Be safe. That's an order."

Before turning away, he was shoved in the back by several inebriated men. Trying not to spill the full glasses balanced in each hand, Damon stumbled forward, smacking into Alessa.

Their chests pressed against one another, and he held his arms out to the side to keep the sloshing drinks from splashing onto her corset.

"Oh!" she exclaimed as she was pushed back against the counter.

Damon's eyes flickered silver as he growled over his shoulder at the jostling men. As they began shoving one another, Damon struggled to keep his rage in check.

Noticing his bulging neck veins, Alessa ducked down to the side and stepped up onto a barstool. "Hey, hey! I know everyone came here tonight to have a good time, am I right?" she asked in a false southern twang.

The crowd cheered and held up their drinks.

"Great!" She pointed at the men behind Damon. "I'm going to ask you five right here to calm it the fuck down, and if you behave yourselves, I'll buy you each a drink." Using her womanly curves, Alessa puffed out her chest while pouting her lips suggestively. "Deal?"

Their faces lit up in excitement as they agreed.

"All right then," she stepped down from the stool and watched Damon make his way back over to Quade.

After buying the men their drinks and refusing their advances, Alessa stayed at the counter.

Her head whipped back and forth as she kept a close eye on everyone, watching for signs of a Frenzied: blackened eyes, twitchy features, and blackened veins creeping up their bodies, extending up into their necks.

As the band started playing the song "I Believe in a Thing Called Love", Alessa looked to the front of the gyrating bodies.

Damon and Quade were hollering and gesturing for her to join them.

She pointed at the counter and mouthed, "I can't."

Quade shook his head back and forth while flashing an obnoxious grin. Bouncing toward her as Damon stayed put, he smiled widely before taking a drink.

Quade grabbed Alessa's arm and pulled her up out of her seat. "Come on, you know you want to. Just let loose for a few minutes. You're not the only one on call here."

Allowing herself to be dragged into the middle of the gyrating bodies, Alessa laughed. "You are the worst influence," she shouted over the loud music.

Grinning ear to ear, she bellowed the lyrics at the top of her lungs in the band's direction as Damon reached across her, handing Quade his drink.

The three Spartans bounced up and down to the beat of the music while belting out the lyrics.

Quade and Damon eagerly downed the rest of their drinks as Alessa whipped her hair back and forth to the beat of the music.

With the last line of the song, Alessa tousled her hair and threw her hands up in the air as the guitarist finished strumming.

Quade clapped his hands together, Alessa hollered, and Damon whistled at the band as the bar patrons went wild.

Quade tapped Alessa's shoulder. "I'll be right back. The bathroom is calling my name," he said breathily.

As Alessa watched Quade hurry away, the band announced their final song before karaoke.

The guitarist began slowly strumming his guitar, and the female singer began in on a cover of "You're the One That I Want".

Feeling eyes on her, Alessa turned around to find Damon holding out his hand. She placed her hand in his, hesitantly, and feeling the familiar electric jolt, she flinched.

The dance floor was thinning out as he pulled her into his chest. They swayed back and forth before he spun her in a circle.

Looking up at him, she noticed the still-present darkened circles underneath Damon's eyes. "How have you been doing?"

He scoffed and peered off to the side of the room, scanning for possible threats while contemplating his response. "It's hard to explain," he said.

Alessa stared at him, silently expecting an explanation.

He rolled his eyes with an audible exhale. "Okay ... I haven't felt like myself in a good while. Like, before you left New Sparta. There's just something ... I don't know. Different. Not quite right." He shook his head, clearing his mind of the violent images of Brielle and him together. Closing his eyes tight, he leaned his forehead against Alessa's.

Bringing Damon back to reality, she touched the side of his face. "Is there anything I can do to help?"

His smile didn't reach his eyes as he grasped her hand. "This is something I need to work out on my own."

He spun her outward, and their arms extended between them.

Colliding back into Damon's chest, Alessa gasped and was unable to bring her eyes back up to meet his.

"I have to live with what I did. To everyone, to you. I know I was under a spell of sorts, but it doesn't excuse the way I treated you and my friends," he explained.

Her features softened. "You need to stop blaming yourself over something you had no control over."

He looked down at her, his expression quizzical. "That's odd coming from you. You took the brunt of it."

"Exactly," she agreed. "So, if I'm telling you to move on, you should listen to me."

Damon stilled, holding Alessa's hand tight against his chest. "You want me to move on."

Licking her lips nervously, she dropped her hands. "That's not what I ... uh ... excuse me. I have to..."

Damon let her go, and she ran to the restroom.

Falling in through the door, Alessa stood in front of the mirror. Her fingertips gripped the sides of the sink as she stared at her reflection. After splashing cold water on her face, she watched the liquid drip down her chin as she fought with herself. "I want Damon to be happy. He deserves to be happy. It's not like he's a bad person. I used to want to be happy, too. What the fuck is wrong with me? Why can't I just let him go?"

Alessa's chest rose and fell as she continued staring into the mirror. Suddenly, she was interrupted by the beginning of 'Say You Won't Let Go'.

A familiar voice started singing the lyrics, and her head turned toward the door. "Damon?"

Exiting the bathroom, she stared at the stage. She saw

Damon sitting on a black, high-backed chair, his body illuminated by a single light above.

As if in a trance, she slowly sat down in an empty bar stool and listened to him sing the song in its entirety.

As the song ended, the crowd erupted in cheers, and a grinning Damon handed the microphone to the person working the karaoke machine.

Hearing an argument break out behind her, Alessa spun around, annoyed. "Hey, cool it!" she yelled without realizing the crowd behind her had begun backing away from at least ten individuals.

The newcomers were noisily chugging their alcohol, sloshing the amber liquid over the edges. As the liquid seeped down from the corners of their lips, it drew attention to the black zigzag lines creeping up their necks.

Alessa's spine stiffened as she looked past them, making eye contact with other Spartan warriors who were positioned at the ready. Leaning over the counter, she motioned to the bartenders who were staring slack-jawed at the people. "Hey, look at me. Come here; come here," she demanded.

While the bartenders slowly walked sideways towards Alessa, she silently counted the Frenzied. *Twenty-two. There are twenty-two of them.*

With a tilt of her head, she ushered the bartenders away from the Frenzied. "You need to get everyone out of here," she instructed as the creatures began climbing over the counter.

The bartenders looked at her, trembling. "We'll make sure they don't follow you. Get out as quickly and quietly as you can. Grab people as you exit. You have one minute at best. Move," she hissed.

The three bartenders darted out from behind the counter, and as they grabbed a person with each hand, they ran for the exit. Confused, the patrons looked towards the counter, and realizing what was happening, the establishment broke out into chaos.

The bald Frenzied closest to Alessa turned its head toward her at an unnatural angle. Its black pupils had expanded at least three times their normal size, and the creature's lower lip dangled from its face.

"Great," she grumbled, withdrawing weapons from her hidden straps.

Feeling a tug on her arm, Alessa was pulled back by Damon, who stepped protectively in front of her.

The Spartan warriors positioned themselves with weapons at the ready, glaring intently at the worsening condition of those overtaking the bar.

The newly turned Frenzied twitched as they threw down the alcohol simultaneously, and Damon's knuckles blanched white as he gripped his weapons. "Get ready."

CHAPTER THIRTEEN

A handful of the Frenzied lunged at Damon, Quade, and Alessa, while a third of the creatures stayed behind the bar. The remaining third attacked the other Spartans with a vengeance.

Preparing for the hit, Alessa bent at the knees and positioned her fists in front of her face.

As the first of the Frenzied dove for Damon, the Spartan's eyes activated silver. Pressing a button on his chest plate, protective arm guards extended down to his forearms.

Distracting the creature by holding out his arm as if it were an appetizer, Damon encouraged the Frenzied to bite his protected forearm.

With his free hand, Damon drove one of his small blades up through the creature's chin, impaling it through the skull. He twisted the blade before yanking it out with a loud grunt.

Standing beside Alessa, Quade blocked an attack with a swift kick to a Frenzied's chest.

Black liquid spewed from the creature's mouth as they soared through the air, shrieking in frustration.

Another Frenzied attacked Damon as Quade stood his ground with a sword in each hand.

The creature sprinted toward Quade, its arms flailing and its mouth gaping open. As the Frenzied fell onto the Spartan warrior, the clashing of blades echoed. Cutting through flesh and bone, Quade crossed his swords, slicing clean through its neck.

The creature's head fell back and bounced on the ground as its decapitated body fell to its knees. After a moment's hesitation, its body collapsed to the ground as well, unmoving.

Finally glitching, Alessa's irises shone bright red as she stared down an impending attacker.

Feeling the adrenaline hit, Alessa punched her balled up fist, adorned with her spiked brass knuckles, repeatedly, into the Frenzied's chest.

More annoyed than physically hurt, the creature stepped back with each strike but never faltered in its resolve to violently tear Alessa apart.

With one final punch to the face, Alessa spun around and sprinted towards the back wall.

The creature took chase after her, screeching loudly between its crazed grin.

Kicking off the wall, Alessa ran up the wooden boards and jumped over the Frenzied. Landing behind the creature, she drew her sword, extended its blade, and, as soon as it turned, Alessa drove the sharp blade into its stomach, pinning the Frenzied to the wall.

Watching in horror, Alessa's stomach flipped as the creature pressed forward on the blade of her sword. Its arms were extended and flailing as a spine-chilling scream tore out of its throat.

Pressing the heat-conductor button on the hilt of her sword,

Alessa pushed the heated metal up and back, curving it to hold the Frenzied in place on the wall.

Breathing heavily, Alessa declared, "Got one. Now the rest we can take care of."

Spinning through the air, Damon flipped over one of the creatures and landed between two more. Jabbing a dagger through an eyeball on each, he dropped them to their knees.

The other Spartan warriors in the bar worked together to subdue their attackers until the only sound in the large room was the karaoke music playing "Monster" by Skillet.

Quade nudged Alessa's shoulder while sporting an obnoxious grin. "That was probably the easiest we've ever had it."

Alessa directed her attention to Damon. "Why were they not that hard to take down?"

Damon's jaw flexed as he looked around at the dead Frenzied sprawled across the floor. "The only reason they went down that easily is that they were still adjusting to the change. Had they been a few days older, it would've been much more difficult."

The Frenzied that Alessa had saved hissed from its place on the wall. "Oh yeah, I have a present for you."

Glancing over at the corner of the room from his crouched over position, Damon stood up and approached the Frenzied. "Now we can head home. Thanks," he said without a glance in Alessa's direction.

She reached out for Damon, but he pulled his arm away.

Her eyes narrowed in confusion. "I thought you'd be happy. Wasn't this part of your mission? To bring one home?"

Damon looked down at the ground, and his irises deactivated from silver to blue. "It is. I'm sorry, I don't seem grateful. I'm just ... tired. But at least now we can return home, right?"

"Right..." Alessa dropped her hands and backed away.

"Hey, looks like we got another one for a sample!" shouted an excited Spartan.

One of the Frenzied that had been sliced through at the belly button still crawled around on the floor, their teeth gnashing.

"Stay here and help with the cleanup. I'm going back to the rental to gather our things and tell the others we're headed home. Then we can secure the two subjects and head out."

Alessa tried to look into Damon's eyes to get an idea of how he was feeling, but he had already turned away.

Once back at the rental, the Spartans moved fast, clearing out their belongings and cleaning the entire place from top to bottom.

After throwing Alessa and Quade's bags in the back of the truck, Damon stared up at the full moon hanging high above. *I wish I felt angry, happy, sad. Hell, I would give anything to feel something. I feel ... numb.*

"Ready to get home?" one of the Spartan warriors asked Damon.

Clearing his throat, Damon dropped his gaze. "Yeah, let's get back. They're waiting for us at the bar."

After securing the two Frenzied subjects, the remaining Spartans left the bar.

As the doors closed behind them, Alessa asked, "So are the rest coming home in the morning? Since we were split into groups?"

Looking straight ahead, Damon responded. "Those who were sleeping were woken up and will be going back at the same time."

She leaned into Quade and spoke quietly. "Why is it important we get back home so quickly?"

"The quicker we get the subjects back to Sera to study, the better. Time is against us," Quade explained.

"I guess that makes sense," she muttered, watching Damon suspiciously out of the corner of her eye.

Brielle groaned from her rolling computer chair. "Is it fixed yet?"

"Everything appears to be back online," one of Erebos's men confirmed.

"Well, what was wrong? I missed yet another night of gaining information." *Or should I say, fucking with him?*

A second man chimed in. "We can't say why it happened. This isn't exactly a common error; someone's implanted microchip not allowing our company access to their brain via hacking. It's kind of a learning curve for us all, but we're not worried about it."

Brielle scoffed and flicked her long nails. "Ugh, whatever."

"Just keep an eye on it, and if it happens again, let us know." The men walked out of the room side by side.

Brielle rolled her eyes while loudly smacking her gum and returned her attention to the screen. "Will do."

CHAPTER FOURTEEN

Hades towered above his trapped souls, who were swirling around one another in a never-ending dance in the cylindrical tube that extended as far down as the eye could see.

Groaning in frustration, he watched the battle at the bar play out inside of his basketball-sized glass globe. His eyebrows furrowed, and while scrunching his scarred eyebrow, he cursed aloud. "Dammit! How could she win yet again?"

Nyx appeared from out of the darkness, slinking towards the god in a midnight blue, skintight dress. "Maybe it is because she is destined to be humanity's savior."

Hades rolled his eyes at his counterpart and exhaled breathily. "You wish."

Gliding across the scorched ground, Nyx smirked as she continued to taunt the god of the underworld. "How else do you explain her continued victories? The situations Alessa has experienced since she was but a young child? What other human have you known, in the history of humankind, to be put through such trials?"

Hades pursed his lips in defeat, and his eyes flared as he stared down into his pit of souls.

"That is what I thought," the goddess of night purred. "And don't think I haven't been keeping an eye on you: whispering perverse thoughts and suggestions into the ears of those humans while Cain presents his bill to exterminate women's rights."

Hades grinned maniacally. "There is nothing in the rules about gods using the gift of persuasion to our benefit. Those weak-minded humans were going to agree with him eventually; I just gave them a little push."

Squatting down on the edge of the circular pool, Nyx watched the trapped souls spin around in an endless loop. She dipped her finger into the tears of the dead. "And why do you think he's attempting to get these laws passed?"

Hades grinned maliciously. "Do you think the god of the underworld wouldn't be keeping tabs on his most prized future possession?"

Withdrawing her finger, Nyx licked the salty tears off her skin. "So, you are aware they have every intention of destroying humanity as we know it?"

"Is it really all that great?" Hades guffawed. "I mean the wars, famine, rape, murder ... these are just a few of the things humans do on any given day. And to one another no less! Please, do tell me why the current state of humanity should be saved."

"You're not wrong. Some do those things. But not all." The goddess of night turned around to confront the god of the underworld. "Most are capable of kindness, warmth, love, and compassion. Humanity is worth saving. And thanks to Alessa, they have a fighting chance."

Hades leaned in, his upper lip curling in contempt. "We'll see about that."

Upon returning to New Sparta, an exhausted and filthy Alessa burst out of the back of the truck.

"Whew!" Quade exclaimed as he jumped out after her.

Seeing his beautiful wife atop the hill, Quade hit the ground running. "Sera!"

Seraphine extended her arms in an open invitation for her husband's embrace. "My love, welcome home." She grinned, falling into his muscular arms.

Soren whipped around the corner and ran for his parents. "Patēr!" the young child squealed, crashing into his father's legs.

"Oh, how I've missed you, my son." Quade picked Soren up and hugged him tight. "Have you been taking good care of your mother and sister?"

"Yes, sir. I am very excited to meet my sister. The gods will be bringing her to us any day."

Seraphine laughed and rolled her eyes knowingly, as if she would have nothing to do with the delivery of the newborn. "Yes, they will."

She redirected her attention to Damon as he approached. "Did you succeed in acquiring a subject?"

Damon's tired eyes looked up at the doctor while adjusting his bag's strap over his shoulder. "We did. Actually, we have two."

Seraphine gasped. "What? That's incredible! Where are they?" She glanced eagerly past the warrior.

"They'll be brought up in a minute."

"Wonderful job, Spartan," she congratulated him.

Damon peered down at Seraphine's baby bump. "When's the little warrior making her entrance?"

Seraphine placed her hand protectively upon her swollen belly. "Whenever she damn well pleases. I refuse to force her into this hot mess of a world until she is good and ready."

"Fair enough." Damon grinned. "I'm going to head home to take a hot shower and get some rest."

"I was about to say ... you stink, man." Quade quipped, punching his friend in the bicep.

"You smell pretty ripe yourself," Damon shouted back over his shoulder as he marched away.

Seraphine watched Damon from behind, concern etched upon her face. "My love, Damon, is he alright? I understand these past few months have been rough for him, but he seems..."

Quade nodded in agreement. "Off," he finished.

"Yes. Do keep an eye on him."

"I will when I am able. The elders have me running around like a madman these days."

"Oh!" Seraphine interrupted herself. "I only have a room set up for one subject. I need to get inside and ensure we have everything necessary for a second." She hurried away, leaving Soren and Quade amongst the returning warriors.

Strolling up beside the young boy and his father, Alessa laughed. "Did she see me and run?"

Quade smiled and turned around. "She had to get set up for the extra subject."

"Soren!" Alessa smiled as the young boy rushed into her arms. "You get bigger every day. Soon I won't be able to carry you."

Soren tilted his head. "That's what my patér said the last

time he came home. Aren't you supposed to be strong Spartan warriors, yet you can't even hold a child?"

Alessa's jaw dropped. "Oh! You have grown into quite the smartass while I was gone," she chuckled, tickling the young boy in her arms.

His entire body shook with contagious laughter. "Yield! I yield."

Glancing up, Alessa stopped tickling her nephew and noticed Damon walking away. "Is he okay?"

Quade pressed his lips together before responding. "Honestly, I don't know."

"I'll give him a day, and then I'll check on him," Alessa said.

"Great idea," Quade agreed.

Scooping Alessa up in his arms, Camden exclaimed, "Alessa!"

"Cam!" she giggled as he spun her around.

Putting her down, Camden held Alessa at arm's length, and she gasped before squeezing both of his forearms. "You have two whole arms again!"

Camden flexed his arm. "I graduated from physical therapy a few weeks ago, and soon after that, Sera said I could toss the shoulder restraint."

Wrapping an arm around Alessa's neck, Lexi pulled her in for a hug. "We've missed you. I, probably even more so than Cam. He's so excited about having the use of his arm back that he won't stop asking to spar. At first, I enjoyed kicking his ass, but now it's just tiresome."

Alessa smiled widely. "Oh, how I've missed you both. The entire experience was unnerving. Once I clean up and get some food in me, I'll debrief both of you."

"Why don't you two head back to the cabin, and I'll go grab us dinner?" Camden offered.

"That sounds great, thank you." Alessa pulled her pack's strap tighter on her shoulder.

Pulling her in by one arm, Camden kissed the top of Alessa's head. "Glad to have you back."

She glanced up into Camden's hazel eyes and smiled. "Me too." Breaking their eye contact, Alessa turned toward Lexi and slipped out of Camden's grasp. "I can't wait to hear all about your research. What all did you discover while we were gone?"

"Whew," Lexi breathed. "What didn't we discover?"

Alessa's eyebrows raised. "Well, let's start with Lucas and Cain."

Lexi walked alongside Alessa. "Lucas is still unaccounted for, but my people in intel have noticed a pattern in President Barnes' speeches that throws major red flags. He fully supports every decision made by Senator Bryant, I mean, Cain, no matter how crazy they seem."

"Like what?"

Lexi hesitated, licking her lips before continuing. "First was the abolishment of abortion, then there was bringing back capital punishment broadcast on air, and most recently, the government has been separating families and placing the parents in jail."

Alessa's face scrunched in disgust. "What? What could possibly be the justification for that?"

Lexi exhaled, and her shoulders dropped in defeat. "They claim the adults are here illegally, but after doing our own research on all those detained, every single one had a genetic disorder; whether they were showing symptoms yet or simply diagnosed. Thousands of those detained are unaccounted for." Lexi side-eyed Alessa nervously.

Alessa gulped. "So, they're dead?"

Lexi's gaze drifted to the mountains in the distance. "More than likely, yes."

Alessa's face paled, and she quietly gasped. "Shit. This has gotten so much worse—"

"There's more," Lexi interrupted.

Alessa stopped and grabbed Lexi's arm, turning her to face her. "What else?"

"The government announced today that there is about to be a radical increase in the price of medication."

Alessa stared past Lexi, realizing its implication. "Meaning the medications to treat those affected by genetic diseases would be nearly impossible to afford."

Lexi silently nodded.

"We have to do something," Alessa huffed, continuing down the path toward her elder's cabin.

Lexi hurried after her. "We are doing everything in our power to gather evidence and present our case to the Consilium, but that's not the only thing we're investigating. There are those assigned to researching the creation of the Frenzied, as well as what their ultimate objective might be."

As the exhaustion began to take hold, Alessa blinked exaggeratedly. "Have we learned anything helpful about them?"

"I've got a bit more to read up on tonight, then I'll feel more confident giving you an update." Lexi rubbed her hands together, silently contemplating how to bring up the topic of Alessa being the subject of an ancient prophecy. "I need to tell you something."

Alessa narrowed her eyes and grinned nervously. "Okay, what is it?"

Suddenly anxious about Alessa's reaction, Lexi chuckled. "Oh, um. Cam has really missed you while you've been gone."

Alessa grinned. "Is that really what you were going to tell me? That Cam missed me?" She snickered.

"Uh, yeah. That was it." Biting the inside of her cheek, Lexi followed Alessa to her elder's cabin.

CHAPTER FIFTEEN

The next morning, Damon awoke naked and dirty in the middle of the woods. "What the fuck? Not this again," he grumbled.

Brushing the loose dirt from his skin, he tried to pinpoint his location. "This didn't happen the entire time I was away. What was so different?"

After jogging back to his cabin, he took a quick shower before getting dressed in dark grey tactical pants and a black tank top. Feeling confused and angry, he sprinted for the outdoor training course.

Damon stood at the beginning of the run, examining the obstacles: a tall rock wall, a monkey bar apparatus, four balance boards he was meant to jump back and forth between, ropes he would hang and swing from, all before a long swimming pool he would free swim in.

Crouching down, Damon extended his legs and prepared to sprint.

The small box on the wall flashed a red light, scanned his

microchip to establish his best time, and then displayed it on the three-dimensional screen floating in mid-air, before him.

Smashing the button to his left, the Spartan took off. Climbing the wall with impeccable speed, Damon's eyes activated silver as his muscles demanded more oxygen.

Reaching the top of the rock wall, he grabbed the rope and swung down to the ground before climbing a ladder up to the monkey bars. After swinging between the dark blue metal bars, Damon jumped down onto the first of four balance boards.

He sprang effortlessly from one to the next, and as he hit the final board, Damon jumped for the rope. Holding onto the braided nylon, he rocked back and forth, reaching for the next rope in succession.

Swinging from one to the next, the veins in his arms engorged, and his muscles strained against his pale olive skin.

He shone with sweat as he dangled from the course ropes.

Releasing his grip on the final braid, Damon fell through the air into the swimming pool.

Splashing into the cool salt water, the Spartan pushed off the pool's wall and swam freestyle as fast as he could. Breaking the water's surface, he gasped for air, and the buzzer signaled loudly, announcing his crossing of the finish line.

Damon swam to the edge of the pool to read his results, but as he lifted himself up out of the side of the pool, he stood face-to-face with Alessa.

Standing before her, the salt water dripped from Damon's hair and clothes.

Alessa stared up at the beautiful man. "Damon..." she said as all other words escaped her mind.

His eyes scrunched up in curiosity. "Alessa." He moved to the side and marched past her. "What are you doing here?"

Finding her voice, she followed close behind. "I came here to talk to you."

He flashed a sarcastic grin. "Well, you've succeeded."

Glancing at the floating three-dimensional screen, he laughed to himself. "Huh. Shaved five seconds off my best time. Not bad." Closing the screen, he turned to face Alessa.

He stared silently at her while running his fingers through his wet hair.

Nervously licking her lips, she stared into Damon's eyes. "I —I..."

He dipped his head toward her impatiently. "You?"

She sighed in frustration and threw her hands up. "I'm worried about you, okay?"

"You're worried ... about me?" Damon scoffed before grabbing a white towel off the rack. He rubbed the large cloth through his dripping hair. "Weren't you the one who was finding it difficult to fight the Frenzied?"

"That's not fair. I was distracted—" she grumbled under her breath.

"From what I recall, I didn't have any issues taking any of them down," he interrupted.

She watched as he rubbed the towel further down his body. "I'm not concerned with your ability to win a fight."

Damon glared at Alessa. "What then? What are you so concerned with?" he demanded in a harsh tone.

She fought against the sudden urge to step back. "Your mental health. Your physical health. I mean, you're suddenly stand-offish, and you look physically ill. You have dark circles underneath your eyes, you admitted to barely sleeping anymore, and you seem—"

He stepped forward, his shoulders squared. "What do I

seem like? Please tell me since you've been around me so much lately," he scoffed.

Her expression softened. "You seem confused. Like you don't know who you are anymore." She held her hands up toward him. "This isn't you."

Damon aggressively threw the white towel into the hamper. "That's great. I'm so glad you've kept such close tabs on me when it was me who was supposed to be watching you."

Alessa stilled as a cold chill shot down her spine. "What is that supposed to mean?"

He shook his head and stepped towards her, pointing his finger angrily. "My father sent me on that damn mission to keep an eye on you and make sure you didn't do anything that would require your dismissal."

She looked up at him in disgust. "My dismissal?" she asked, her voice shaking. "My dismissal?" she yelled. "You mean my death?"

Realizing what he had just confessed to, his jaw dropped.

Her eyes narrowed as she backed away. "Here I was worried about you, when you were secretly sent to keep tabs on me? You were going to report me if I did something that made me dangerous enough to be killed, weren't you?"

Damon peered down at Alessa, his eyes pleading as he stepped toward her.

"Well, what do you think?" Her voice cracked as she shoved him back. "Have I done anything to warrant my death sentence?"

Unable to meet her eyes, Damon looked away and shook his head back and forth.

"Well, that's good ... I suppose." She exhaled breathily. Pressing her fingers against her lips, Alessa thought about what to say next, but couldn't bring herself to speak aloud. Turning around, she held back tears as she walked away. *After all this time, how does he continue to make me feel this way? Why do I allow him to have so much control over me?*

"Alessa!" Damon yelled.

She froze in place but refused to face him.

He wrung the towel nervously, and his voice wavered. "I'm sorry for lashing out at you. I—I don't know what's wrong with me. Thank you. For caring."

Hurrying up the hill, Alessa remained silent as tears streamed down her face.

He slammed down the towel as his eyes flickered silver. "I would never betray you. You have nothing to worry about!"

CHAPTER SIXTEEN

Cain slammed his bag on the desktop before plopping down noisily into the computer chair next to Brielle. "Well, that was refreshing."

She jumped as his chair rolled closer to her. "Seriously? Ugh. Could you not announce your presence like a normal human being? I feel like you're one giant jump scare."

Leaning over the arm of his chair, his grey-green eyes were vibrant and wide with excitement, behind his white-and-silver mask that covered half his face. "Maybe there's a reason for that."

Brielle rolled her eyes and scowled. "Crazy radiates off of you."

Cain leaned back in his chair and clapped his hands together. "You're one to talk. A guy rejects you, and you end up kidnapping him, erasing his memories, sexually assaulting him, hijacking his mind—"

"Okay, okay," she snapped. "I get it. We're both a little fucked up."

Sporting a wicked grin, he leaned back in his chair with a wink. "If you only knew the half of it. But now that my battery is recharged, I can focus on the government takeover once again."

Her right eyebrow arched as she glared at him. "You really enjoy camping ... or whatever you did, don't you?"

He flashed a sideways grin as he pictured the blood pouring from his victim's wounds.

Two sisters had made friends with the wrong man.

"Or whatever. Yes, when I need to recharge my battery, I find the wilderness is the perfect spot to do so." He glanced around the bland room, full of monitors. "Do you ever leave this area? I mean, there are acres of building to explore, and I only ever see you in here, staring at your obsession."

She scowled. "For your information, I had just gotten back from taking a tour around the pregnancy crops."

He tilted back his head as a laugh escaped from his lips. "Crops? Is that what you're calling the giant room full of women in various stages of pregnancy?"

She shrugged callously. "Well, that's essentially what they are. I'd hardly call them human after all the drugs your uncle has them pumped full of, to keep them catatonic."

"You're not wrong." Cain tilted his head and pressed a finger to his lips. "Have they gotten any closer to a successful super soldier being made?"

Brielle examined her deep red fingernails. "Not yet. Your uncle is very displeased with the scientists. I try to stay on his good side by continuing to collect information from my sugar bear."

Cain cringed at her use of Damon's nickname. "Gross. Anyway, I have a surprise for you."

She crossed her legs and narrowed her eyes suspiciously.

"You got me something? Like, from the woods?" she asked, her voice hesitant.

He laughed, shaking his head. "I said a surprise, not a gift. We have the go-ahead to get rid of the asset. Damon has given us all the information we need to move on to the next phase. You had mentioned wanting to be the one to take him out."

Brielle froze, unsure of how she felt. Possibly, hesitant and slightly sad, with a touch of excitement. "So, I can do—"

Cain grinned widely with a satisfied sigh. "Whatever you wish with no repercussions."

She turned to the large screen, where she was able to see through Damon's eyes as well as watch the scenes Brielle forced upon him, play out in his mind. Excitement swelled within her as she pictured all the ways she had imagined torturing him, up until her watching Damon take his final breath.

With a crack of his knuckles, Cain concluded, "The only thing my uncle asks is that you not drag it out more than a day or two, and no matter what, he cannot survive."

Watching Alessa's outline disappear on the screen before her, Brielle grinned wickedly. "I shouldn't need more than a day. Oh, the visions I have planned for you, sugar bear."

***

Camden and Lexi sat atop a picnic blanket, side by side, while eating breakfast in the courtyard.

"Hey!" Alessa jogged towards them, the bottom of her thin, dark violet skirt dancing in the wind.

Camden smiled after taking a bite of his egg and bacon burrito. "Good morning."

Lexi lifted her gaze from the thick pile of papers held together by a black spiral coil. "Hey! Where have you been?"

Alessa sat down beside Camden, and he playfully elbowed her in the arm. "When I got up this morning, you were already gone."

"Yeah, I had to check on something, and then I went on a walk ... to clear my head," Alessa lied. Reaching for an apple, she rubbed the fruit on the skirt of her dress.

Lexi brought her warm cup of coffee up to her lips. "Mm-hmm," she said in disbelief, before taking a drink.

Alessa side-eyed her red-haired friend while taking a large bite to keep from answering any further questions. With her mouth full, she pointed at Lexi's makeshift book and raised her eyebrows.

"What am I reading?" Lexi asked.

While chewing, Alessa nodded.

"Lex printed a bunch of anecdotal evidence and is reading through all of the personal takes on the Greenfield Farms taste testing events and such," Camden answered.

Alessa swallowed loudly before leaning in. "Are any of the stories overlapping or—"

"Yes! Actually, quite a few." Lexi scooted closer, invading Camden and Alessa's personal space.

"Oh," Alessa giggled as Lexi leaned across Camden's lap to get closer to her.

Camden leaned back and kept eating. "You get used to it." He shrugged nonchalantly.

Lexi glanced back at Camden unapologetically. "Shh. Now, I haven't conferred with Seraphine yet, but I really think you're onto something, thinking it's the artificial sweetener."

Alessa tilted her head. "Really?"

"Here." Lexi flipped through the book until she found the

page she was looking for, then pointed at the words. Mrs. Richards was one of the first cases that I could find. Dr. Richards said his wife had attended the artificial sweetener taste test one month before her change in behavior. She had been enjoying a girls' weekend with her friends, and when she came home, she slept for two days straight. Then it was a downward spiral into madness, including unprovoked attacks, night terrors, hallucinations, until eventually…"

"What?" Alessa asked. "Eventually what?"

His interest piqued, and Camden leaned forward.

"Her husband came home from work to find her eating the flesh from one of her friends he had called earlier to come over and check on her," explained Lexi.

Camden swallowed noisily and set his burrito down. "And just like that, I'm done eating."

Alessa pressed her lips together. "Hmm. Okay, so why isn't everyone who tried the artificial sweeteners becoming like this? No kids have been affected, right?"

Lexi lifted her gaze. "That is correct. There has to be a trigger. Now that Seraphine has subjects to study, hopefully she'll be able to figure it out. Or, maybe, the answer is in one of these articles. Strange enough, the only connection I've found so far seems to be alcohol consumption."

Camden covered his belly and laughed. "Alcohol is Greenfield Farm's downfall? That seems strangely comedic."

Lexi looked up at him as she lay across his legs. "I assume it has to be a high enough level. Alcohol is present in foods and medications, so it seems that only those who ingest above a certain alcohol content are affected."

Alessa scrunched up her legs and wrapped her arms around both of her knees. "We really need to get this figured out sooner rather than later. We've got the trip to Greece in less than a week, and no one attending will be in any state to help with this investigation."

Lexi readjusted, lying down on her stomach so she could keep reading comfortably on the checkered blanket.

Alessa's gaze landed upon Damon from across the courtyard. He was still in his workout gear from this morning and appeared to be talking to himself as he walked among the plants. *I would have thought he'd change after getting soaking wet.*

"And you're sure the elders are cool with an ex-Bodyguard attending their celebration?" Camden asked hesitantly.

Alessa watched Damon's face contort as he held his hand up to his ear.

"Um, yeah, I'll make sure they know you're going." Alessa squinted. "Are you guys seeing this?" She directed Camden and Lexi's attention to Damon.

The Spartan was nervously pacing back and forth between two trees in the distance.

Camden shrugged and took another bite out of his burrito. "The man looks like he's working off some steam."

"His behavior has been rather bizarre lately," Lexi agreed.

Damon stormed off as Alessa watched him, concerned. "His mood swings would give anyone whiplash," she murmured.

"Is that who you were checking on this morning?" Camden asked in a clipped tone.

Unable to meet Camden's eyes, Alessa stared at the apple in her hand. "Yes, Cam, it was." She stood up and brushed the grass from her dress. "I need to talk to Sera."

"Just don't do anything stupid," Camden warned.

Alessa flashed a sarcastic smile. "But I do stupid so well."

Camden threw up his hands and hollered after her, "You

know what I mean!" He turned to Lexi, who was glancing at him out of the side of her eye, disapprovingly. "She knows what I mean."

"I don't think she does, and you essentially called a female Spartan warrior dumb. That's pretty much a death wish, sir," Lexi chuckled before continuing to read.

CHAPTER SEVENTEEN

Breathing heavily, Damon gasped as he dug his heels into the dirt, nearly colliding with the trunk of a tree. Looking around, he realized he was running through the woods near his cabin. *How the fuck did I get here? I was just in Philly.*

Since his encounter with Alessa at the obstacle course that morning, his hallucinations had taken over completely.

"Shit!" He was slammed back into Brielle's apartment, sitting upright on her couch. Wearing only a black lace push-up bra and blood-red stilettos, she straddled Damon.

His fingertips glided across her exposed, warm beige skin, and he traced her collarbone with his lips. "Wait, wait, what's going on?" he mumbled as if in a drug-induced stupor.

Brielle leaned in and whispered into his ear, "We're reconnecting, sugar bear."

"No. No. I don't want this." He shoved her away. "I don't want you."

As she stood before the Spartan in her deep red stilettos, Damon's head bobbed to the side, and his eyes widened in disbelief.

Alessa was sitting with her back propped up against the back of the couch. Her eyes were open and unblinking while her neck was cranked to the side in an unnatural position, as if she were being forced to watch them. Across Alessa's neck there was a bright red slash, and her colorless face was expressionless.

"No. No. Baby... What the fuck?" Damon panicked, scrambling to get to her.

Brielle laughed maniacally as she stood before them. "Look what you made me do. Look what you made me do. Look what you made me do," she repeated as her heels clacked across the hardwood.

Damon reached for Alessa, and as her cold body fell into his arms, he sobbed. "Sydämen liekki ... I'm sorry. I'm so sorry."

He held Alessa tight against his chest.

"Oh, Damon," Brielle cooed.

Distraught, he looked up to find Brielle bringing down an axe on both him and Alessa.

Shielding Alessa, Damon yelled, "No!"

Opening his eyes, he found himself alone, kneeling in a pile of dirt on the forest floor.

Rocking back and forth, he held his head in his hands. "It's not real. None of it is real."

Lifting his gaze, Damon was suddenly staring at Kai, and he jumped back in alarm.

Her grey skin hung loose around her sallow, sunken eyes, and her fatal wound was actively seeping dark red liquid down the backs of her arms, dripping down her fingers onto the dirt.

"K—Kai?" He stammered in shock, his eyes filling with hot tears.

"How could you do this to me?" she demanded sharply.

Shaking his head back and forth, Damon sat back on his heels. "I—I didn't mean—I could never—"

Kai clenched her teeth behind pale, cracked lips, and she leaned into him. Her face was mere inches in front of the Spartan warrior when she growled, "You what? Didn't mean to kill me?"

The black-red blood began oozing from between her lips as she smiled cruelly. "But you did. You were like a brother to me, and you killed me. You've ruined everything."

His entire body started shaking with the shock of seeing her.

She bent forward with a sinister grin. "I can never come home. Alessa will never forgive you. Nothing will be as it once was."

Rocking back and forth with his eyes squeezed tightly shut, Damon's fingers trembled while he held his head between his hands.

Her blood-soaked teeth were just inches from his face, Kai growled. "You should be here. You deserve to be dead, not me."

"It's not real. She's not real. Kai can't be real ... she's dead. Kai died," he whimpered, trying to block the unwanted visions.

Alessa jogged through the medical building, trying to find Seraphine. "Sera!"

From inside a spare medical office, Seraphine heard her name being called and turned around, nearly knocking over a small table with her pregnant belly. "Shit," she swore, moving unnaturally fast to catch a falling microscope in mid-air.

"Sera!" She giggled. "I see pregnancy hasn't slowed you down," Alessa complimented as she walked into the room.

Seraphine huffed while flashing a sarcastic grin. "It isn't the pregnancy that gets you. It's after they're born and they hate to sleep, that's when you really feel like shit. We're lucky we have such a large village; I don't understand how people have children otherwise."

Alessa's eyes widened. "You are much stronger than I am."

"What are you doing here?" Seraphine exhaled, turning back towards the computer.

"I need to know what you've got so far on the Frenzied."

Seraphine's eyes narrowed. "Why do you sound so worried?"

Alessa shook her head with a shrug of her shoulders. "I can't pinpoint it. I just have a bad feeling. A terrible, earth-shattering, heart-achingly bad feeling."

Seraphine turned around, facing Alessa, and placed her hand protectively on her belly. "About what exactly?"

Alessa paced back and forth, biting her lower lip. "The cause of the Frenzied, Cain's motivation for being a part of the government, where Lucas is hiding, where Brielle disappeared to, Damon's change in personality..."

Seraphine's eyebrows raised in alarm. "Okay, that's quite a lot. Let's tackle one thing at a time. I'll start by showing you what information we've gathered over the past few days." She sat down in the elevated computer chair. "These are scans of their brains."

Alessa pointed at the three-dimensional image of the scans. "What is that part in both that's lit up like fireworks?"

"That's the amygdala."

Alessa leaned towards the floating picture. "What's its purpose?"

Seraphine rubbed the sore spot in her belly where her

daughter had just kicked. "It plays a crucial role in processing emotion."

As realization hit Alessa, her face fell. "The anger, the fear—"

"Yes." Seraphine nodded in agreement. "It's as if a hot poker has destroyed that specific section of their brains, allowing all of their emotions to go unchecked."

"Which is why they are so strong and out of control," Alessa murmured.

"You got it." Seraphine hissed and rubbed the side of her stomach. "Ouch. Little one, be careful stretching. You are running out of room."

"Did she kick?" Alessa smiled.

"Our little one is a Spartan warrior before she is even born," Seraphine chuckled. "Would you like to feel her?"

Alessa walked towards her friend, allowing Seraphine to place her hands on her swollen belly.

Feeling the strange sensation of a foot from inside her friend's stomach, Alessa jumped. "Wow! That must be weird, feeling that on the inside."

The women smiled at each other as the two Frenzied loudly slammed into the glass separating them from the Spartans.

"Shit!" Alessa's pulse raced as she sprang back. Her fists raised in front of her face as she instinctively prepared to fight.

Seraphine waddled towards the glass barrier. "The anesthesia must've worn off. Don't worry. They can't break through."

Alessa's shoulders rose and fell as she caught her breath. "You put them in the same room together?"

Seraphine approached the glass. "We needed to find out if

they would recognize others with similar traits as their own or whether they would be violent."

Alessa rubbed her hands together nervously. "How do you think this change in the chemical makeup of their brains was introduced?"

"It could be a mutation, but the likelihood of multiple adults suffering from the same unprecedented mutation would be improbable. Unless it were from some type of chemical that targeted that specific area of the brain."

With her hands on her hips, Alessa rocked back and forth. "Like an artificial sweetener? Ambrosia?"

Seraphine shook her head. "Yes. But the thing I can't figure out is why Lucas would want this; to create a group of people that violently attack."

"Maybe to distract from something else he has planned?" Alessa suggested.

"Or the intended effect was botched by an interfering substance. Hear me out," Seraphine began. "We've already established their amygdala is lit up like a Saturnalia tree. What if Ambrosia was meant to target this segment of the brain to make people more susceptible to suggestion, but something interfered with its binding mechanism? This could have amplified the chemicals, causing permanent brain damage."

Alessa stared, slack-jawed, before glancing nervously back and forth between the creatures clawing at the glass and her friend. "Holy Hades. Sera, you are a genius!"

Seraphine tilted her head. "You think my hypothesis could hold any bearing?"

"Why not? It makes the most sense. I also came here to tell you Lexi's findings are pointing towards alcohol as being the interfering substance. But it needs to be a certain percentage of alcohol."

"Oh, wow. That's an interesting take," Seraphine agreed. "I will definitely look into that. Now, what else were you worried about? Cain's motives? I'm sorry, but I can't help with that. I am clueless about that man. You know more about him than I do," Seraphine confessed.

Alessa watched the Frenzied repeatedly smack into the glass, trying to reach them. "All I know for sure is, he's one sadistic fuck. I wouldn't doubt that he has a much darker side than we know about."

Seraphine chuckled but stopped when she saw Alessa's serious expression. "What would give you that idea?"

Alessa placed her hands on the back of a chair and leaned forward. "Anyone who could scare my sister the way he did is not a good man. And his entire demeanor is just ... eerily calm and violent. As far as where Lucas and Brielle are, Hades, we may never know." She stared off into the distance as if she were lost in a daydream.

Placing a hand on her lower back, Seraphine turned to face Alessa. "As far as Damon goes, I've noticed for a while that something's been off."

Attempting to spin the non-existent ring around her finger, Alessa groaned in frustration. "His mood swings have been rather intense. When we were on our mission, we actually had ... fun ... but when I went to check on him this morning, he jumped down my throat. I'm giving him the day to cool off."

Seraphine placed her hand on Alessa's shoulder. "Quade's sleeping right now, but I'll have him check on Damon after he gets off his guard duty shift. I think he's on until four in the morning."

Alessa patted the back of her friend's hand. "Thanks."

Seraphine's arm dropped with a sad smile. "We both know Damon would do the same for you if the tables were turned."

Alessa backed away from her friend, heading to the exit. "I hope you're right. I'll see you later."

One of the Frenzied slammed itself against the glass, and a tooth clattered to the floor.

Alessa jumped and grimaced while staring at the creatures. "Take care of yourself and my niece. Don't underestimate those things." She nodded at the Frenzied clawing at the glass, smearing the black fluid leaking from its mouth with its fingertips.

Walking in through the front door of her cabin, Alessa sensed another's presence and stilled partway through the entryway. "Elder?" she called out.

Turning the corner, she saw him sitting in a kitchen chair, with his back to her. "Elder?"

With a jerk of his head, Alessa's elder responded, "Oh, I'm sorry, I didn't hear you come in. Please, have a seat." He held out a hand, directing her to sit in the chair opposite him.

Alessa's momentary relief was replaced by concern as she noticed the dark circles beneath his eyes and his exhausted appearance. Reaching across the table, she placed her hand upon her elder's. "Is everything alright?"

Exhaling loudly, he forced a fake smile. "No, my little Spartan. I don't think it is."

Alessa's stomach dropped, and her back stiffened. "Tell me. Whatever it is, I can handle it."

Withdrawing his hand, her elder rubbed the stubble along his jawline. "I will go into more detail once I have rested and my head is clearer, but I will say I feel unease after deliberating with the Consilium." He paused, taking a drink of his hot tea.

"I believe we are correct in fearing they are going to try to use you as a weapon."

Alessa's jaw dropped, and she sat back in her chair. "They said this to you?"

"It wasn't what they said, it was how they said it: mentioning your abilities, how they can be used to their advantage, ways to control you..."

"Ways to control me?" Alessa scoffed and stood up. With her hands on her hips, she paced back and forth. "I'd like to see them try."

He wrapped his hands around his warm mug. "I wouldn't get too hung up on it right now. They have too much on their plates to even consider how to use your powers to their benefit. While I was there, new hordes of the Frenzied had begun to strike."

Alessa stilled. "They finally got to the secluded parts of Europe?"

Her elder nodded before taking another drink. "It seems so. But I'm not sure if it's a good thing or a bad thing, for you, that is. I mean, at least it distracts the leaders from focusing on you."

"It won't last forever." Alessa went to her room, picked up a large bag full of weapons, and swung it over her shoulder. "I'm gonna go practice."

Alessa's elder inhaled deeply. "That is a great idea. Just be careful who you put your trust in."

CHAPTER EIGHTEEN

Later that afternoon, Camden and Lexi were sitting beneath the bright sun, at the base of a tall tree on top of a secluded hill. His head lay in her lap as she silently read her bound papers.

He played with a lock of his own blond hair, absentmindedly twirling it around a finger while she turned another page.

Camden exhaled, loud and exaggerated. "I ... am ... bored. Not just a little bored, but an overwhelming ache of boredom has seeped deep inside my bones, making itself at home."

Lexi lifted an eyebrow and shifted her papers so she could cast a quizzical look down at him.

Camden looked up at her chocolate brown eyes, and his pulse quickened.

Lexi's vibrant red hair was typically held back by a thick braid, but for whatever reason, today she let it hang loose. Its unruly curly locks were gently being blown about, and the scent of lavender wafted off her skin.

The neckline of her light blue dress exposed the tops of her breasts, which bounced with every breath. While peering down at Camden, Lexi pressed her peachy-pink lips together to keep from laughing.

"You're bored?" she quipped.

Staring up at her, Camden nodded his head in her lap. "Yes, very much so."

She scoffed and rolled her eyes. "You know you could be helping me research. I could use the help figuring out what these things are. It is the reason you stayed behind."

"I was forced to stay home because of my stupid injury." Sitting upright, he pulled a foot in and wrapped his arms around his knee. "Besides, if I discover the answer to our problem, then everyone would automatically assume it was the man who deserves the credit."

She smacked him with the back of the bound pages. "You know it wouldn't kill you to pick up a book every now and then."

Chuckling, Camden brushed the grass off his legs. "I'm more physical than intellectual." He wiggled his eyebrows. "If you know what I mean."

Lexi's cheeks blushed red as warmth spread throughout her body. "Wow ... just, wow."

Leaning to the side, she looked off into the distance, past Camden. "Alessa?"

He turned to the side to find Alessa jogging down the path towards them.

"You two were really hard to find," Alessa called out, breathily. While placing her hands on her hips, she arched an eyebrow at Camden. "Do you do anything besides lie around anymore?"

Camden scoffed. "Trust me, I hate it as much as you do, but I already did my training for the day, and I am under strict orders not to train too hard for at least another week. Besides, it's a perfect day to be lazy."

Lexi's forehead scrunched in disbelief. "Maybe for you it is. I've been researching non-stop."

Alessa directed her attention to Lexi. "About that, I need to ask you some questions."

"Okay." Giving Alessa her full attention, Lexi placed her pages down in the grass beside her. "Ask away."

Rubbing her hands together, Alessa nervously paced back and forth in front of her friends. "I spoke with Sera, and she thinks Ambrosia was originally used to target people's amygdala, but when ingested in conjunction with a high percentage of alcohol, as you had theorized, it had the unintentional side effect of causing their emotions to go haywire. It would explain the aggression, their reduced ability to register pain—"

Lexi's eyes lit up in excitement. "The Frenzied's lack of fear. It's a compelling theory." She bit her lower lip before sighing aloud. "Alessa, I've been meaning to tell you something—"

Exhaling loudly, Camden rolled his eyes while interrupting her. "Not this again."

Lexi glared at Camden. "She has a right to know."

Alessa's forehead scrunched up in confusion. "What do I have a right to know?"

Lexi pulled Alessa down beside her, in the grass, before she began. "When I first met Camden, and he told me your and Damon's story, I felt as though it wasn't my first time hearing it."

Alessa laughed uneasily. "What does that mean?"

Lexi pulled her bound stack of papers and flipped to a page where the corner had been folded to mark its place. "Fear not the one soul split in two, for they are destined to save this realm. Both bathed in blood and consumed by fire, absolution must be at the helm."

Alessa sat in silence as her insides vibrated with an eerie sense of familiarity.

Lexi continued, "One of the two souls forgotten, the other believed to be dead. Their lives painfully intertwined yet distanced by fated bloodshed."

"Where did you find this?" Alessa laughed uneasily while trying to grab the book out of her hands. "What are you reading from?"

Ignoring her questions, Lexi dodged her and continued reading. "Violence and rage shall threaten the world in the guise of a humanlike creature while a deception most keen must be severed unseen to secure the twin flames' future."

"Stop. Just stop," Alessa interrupted. Standing up, she put her hands over her rapidly beating heart. "Where did you find that?" Tears sprang to her eyes, and her lower lip trembled.

"It's written in the scrolls." Lexi pointed to the passage written on the page. "The Oracle of Delphi predicted these events over two thousand years ago."

"But how could that be?" Alessa swallowed. Inhaling a shaky breath, she stared at the book in Lexi's hands. "How can a prediction that was made—you said over a thousand years ago?"

"Two thousand," Lexi corrected.

"Oh, okay. How can an oracle have predicted what sounds like my life? I wasn't even born a Spartan." Alessa looked up helplessly at Camden, as though he could stop the madness.

Camden's hands balled into fists as his anger bubbled to the surface. "I knew you shouldn't have said anything."

"There's still one more passage, but it was not included," Lexi explained.

Alessa's eyes locked on Camden's. "Wait, you knew? You knew this could be about me, and you didn't say anything?"

His face fell, and his lips parted. "Alessa, there is nothing that mentions your name. It could be anyone—"

"What do you mean, Cam? Did you not hear what she just said? About the fire, one being forgotten and the other believed to be dead?" Alessa demanded.

Camden shook his head apologetically. "Alessa—"

"No!" She held out a hand to stop him from getting any closer. "I only need one thing from you right now."

He stilled. "Anything."

Holding back tears, Alessa's voice cracked. "Make it make sense. I feel like I'm losing my mind."

Camden dropped his hands in defeat and looked back at Lexi for help.

Alessa stared off into the distance as Lexi set the book beside her, on the ground. "Okay, so let's think about this logically. It sounds like the Frenzied were meant to be, but 'a deception most keep must be severed unseen?' Who is that about? Who's being deceived, and how do you sever something you can't see?" Lexi asked.

Alessa stepped back as if struck by an invisible object. "To secure the twin flames' future..."

Lexi sighed. "I just wish we had the final line to the prophecy. It might have been able to help you figure things out."

"Where is it?" Alessa asked while still staring off.

"The part of the tablet it was originally recorded on was missing, so it was not included in the written scrolls."

"Okay." Alessa sighed and looked up at the white birds

flying high above her. "What does that mean? My future is set in stone? How can this prediction be about me? I'm not even a Spartan by blood." Her eyes widened, and her lips parted in shock. "So, if I make the wrong decision, all of humankind will suffer? Is that what you make of this as well?" Her eyes darted back and forth between Camden and Lexi.

Not knowing how to help, Camden dropped his head and glanced down at Lexi, who pursed her lips and slightly shrugged in a silent response to his unspoken question.

Tears streamed down Alessa's face as she stepped backward. "I—I—um..." Tripping over her skirt, she licked the salty tears from her upper lip.

Camden reached for Alessa, and she dodged his touch. "No, I—I need to be alone right now. I have a lot to think about." Pressing her fingertips against her lower lip, Alessa turned around and walked away as if in a daze.

Camden gripped Lexi's biceps. "Why did you have to say anything?"

Glaring at Camden, Lexi said through clenched teeth, "She had a right to know."

Realizing how tightly he was grabbing Lexi, Camden released her, and with an exasperated sigh, he jumped up.

Watching Alessa stagger away, he ran his hands through his hair in frustration and growled, "Fuck."

CHAPTER NINETEEN

Exhausted and overwhelmed, Alessa fell into a restless sleep as soon as her head hit the pillow.

She dreamt of Hades and Nyx in the underworld, fighting over humanity's future.

"Your brothers will put an end to this," the goddess of night threatened while standing before Hades.

His lips curved up at the sides as his fingertips dug into the arms of his throne. "I'd like to see them try. It's too late for them. The seeds of doubt have already been planted in the minds of the weak, and soon, Cain will have gained enough votes in the United States government to overtake women's reproductive rights. From there—" the god whipped around, staring straight at an invisible Alessa.

"Who's there?" he demanded.

The goddess of night turned to see where he was looking. "You feel that as well? It's as if someone is watching us," she remarked with an intrigued smile.

"I do not appreciate being spied on," Hades growled in a deep voice.

Holding his hand open in the air, a ball of fire appeared within his palm, and he threw it forcibly at Alessa's invisible form.

As the flames overtook her vision, Alessa screamed in her mind.

Sitting straight up in bed, Alessa gasped. As her hearing returned, she recognized the sound of pounding on her front door. "What in Hades is that?" she mumbled aloud, dragging her half-awake self out of bed.

Discombobulated, Alessa ran to the front door while rubbing the sleep from her eyes. "I'm coming! Just hold on a second," she announced, unlocking the wooden door.

As the door swung open, Quade fell onto the hardwood floor.

Alessa's jaw dropped as she saw how badly beaten he was. "Oh my gods! What happened? Who did this to you?"

He spat a mouthful of blood onto the floor. "Damon."

Kneeling before the injured Spartan, she struggled to comprehend what he had said. "What about Damon?"

Quade wiped the blood from his lip and looked up at her from his swollen eye. "Damon's lost his mind."

Alessa's eyes widened as she gasped. "Are you saying Damon did this to you?"

Quade nodded his head while groaning aloud.

"H—How did you get here?" She stammered.

He hissed as he touched a deep cut on his upper arm. "I had to warn you."

She placed a hand on his shoulder. "Where is he?"

"I'm not sure." He groaned in agony as he lifted his shirt

and touched his bruised side. "I for sure have some broken ribs. Ugh."

"Okay, where did this happen to you?" She swallowed. "Where exactly did Damon attack you?"

Quade inhaled a shaky breath. "I had gone to his cabin to check on him like my wife asked of me, but his place was trashed, and he was yelling at people that weren't there. Then he activated. When I tried to calm him down, he attacked me."

Alessa ran to her hall closet, where she kept a first aid kit. "Here. Let me..."

Quade brushed her hand aside. "You don't have time. I'll survive. But Damon won't."

She shook her head in confusion. "What are you saying?"

He swallowed painfully. "I came to warn you. I heard on the com that they're sending a unit to take him out. You're the only one who can save him now."

Alessa's adrenaline spiked, and her microchip glitched. With blazing red irises, she demanded, "Where is he?"

A deep voice projected from Quade's wristband. "Code Black. All available warriors report to the arena for eradication."

Quade's and Alessa's heads jerked upright, and their eyes met, wide in a panic.

"Go!" he urged.

Jumping up, she flew out the front door; her thin blue nightdress flying behind her.

Sprinting across the large field, Alessa's bare feet squished into the wet grassy fields as Lexi's words echoed in her mind.

"Fear not the one soul split in two, for they are destined to save this realm. Both bathed in blood and consumed by fire, absolution must be at the helm.

"One of the two souls forgotten, the other believed to be dead.

Their lives painfully intertwined yet distanced by fated bloodshed.

"Violence and rage shall threaten the world in the guise of a humanlike creature while a deception most keen must be severed unseen to secure the twin flames' future."

Seeing fellow warriors' bodies litter the ground, Alessa gasped. "What have you done? Please be alive, Damon," she pleaded desperately.

At the top of the hill, the enormous, beige, oval-shaped arena appeared in front of the breathtaking sunrise. The bright colors seemed out of place compared to the tragedy about to unfold.

Her chest rose and fell with her sharp intake of air as she reached the top of the hill.

Her breath caught in her chest as she leaped over several bodies lying across the entrance to the arena.

Damon was in the middle with both of his hands on his head, shouting to himself incoherently.

The Spartans surrounded Damon with their weapons at the ready.

Their leader yelled, "Take aim!" and every warrior surrounding Damon cocked their weapon.

Alessa raised her arm, and with a flick of her wrist, the weapons flew from the warriors' hands, landing in a messy pile on the edge of the arena.

"What the fuck?" the lead Spartan demanded as Alessa strolled across the arena towards Damon. "What's she doing here?"

Alessa watched Damon pace back and forth.

He mindlessly babbled to himself while punching the sides of his head, and unhinged laughter escaped from between his moving lips.

"You can't be here," the woman addressed Alessa as she was instructing the warriors to brandish their swords. "Everyone, grab your blades. We have our orders."

Keeping her eyes locked on Damon, Alessa cautiously approached the belligerent Spartan warrior.

"You'll have to get through me first," Alessa challenged.

"So be it. Take your mark!" the lead warrior commanded.

Alessa breached the circle of warriors and imagined the electric torches' flames encircling her and Damon. Lifting her hands in the air, she sent her intentions to the flickering firelight.

As the fire swirled around them, Damon and Alessa became trapped in a tornado of flames.

Her skirt whipped about wildly as the wind from the hot fire kicked her deep blue fabric up into the air, and she exhaled shakily. "Damon?" she called out above the roar of the quick-moving flames.

His silver irises bore into her as if he hadn't realized there was anyone else in the arena with him. "Alessa?" he asked, his voice full of disbelief.

As the image of Alessa flickered back and forth between her and Brielle, flashing a demented grin, Damon whimpered. "No, no, that—that can't be you."

Brielle laughed maniacally as she watched the scene unfold on the large screen before her. She was getting to see in real time how frightened Alessa was of Damon, and she was loving every second of it.

Alessa put her hands up in front of her as she moved towards him. "Yes, Damon. It's me, Alessa. Listen to my voice…"

He shook his head violently back and forth. "You're not Alessa! It's all your fault!" Damon bellowed, aggressively pacing back and forth.

The flames licked at the hem of her skirt, billowing in the middle of the vortex created by the spinning fire. "Do you remember telling me about the constellation Lyra? Or about your mother?"

Spit flew from between Damon's lips as he held his head in his hands and shook. He watched a disjointed image of a half-naked, bloodied Brielle jaggedly step towards him. "You're the reason I lost her—"

Alessa continued to talk to him as she got closer. "What about playing Capture the Flag for the first time? And then we spent the night together?"

Damon tilted his head, and his eyes flickered blue as Brielle's grip lessened.

"What the hell was that? What just happened?" Brielle swore while furiously typing commands on her keyboard.

Damon struck the sides of his skull, and the tendons in his neck strained against his skin. "I killed Kai. I killed Alessa's Kai. I don't deserve to live. She wants me dead. I should be dead, not her."

Alessa stilled and gasped in response. "Kai would never…" She swallowed before continuing towards the distraught

Spartan. "Damon, Kai loved you. She loves you. She would never, ever want you to take her place."

Alessa stared at his head and noticed the tiny green dot at the base of Damon's skull glowing in conjunction with several writhing lines. "Brielle," she gasped. *Fuck. She's still controlling him.*

Directing her attention to the glowing in the base of Damon's brain, Alessa focused all of her energy on destroying each of the electronic worms. The raging flames whipped around them, encroaching on their remaining oxygen, and as sweat dripped down their cheeks, they faced one another, gritting their teeth against the intense heat.

As she got closer, Damon lashed out. Wrapping his fingers tight around Alessa's neck, his eyes flared as he glared at a hallucination of Brielle. "You're the reason I lost the love of my life!"

He squeezed tighter, and through clenched teeth, he snarled, "You have to die!"

While making Damon see her instead of Alessa, Brielle ground her teeth together, excited by the possibility of Damon killing the Spartan.

If that happened, he would for sure end his own life, meaning Brielle's plaything would no longer be a loose end for Lucas and Cain, and she would have won. Finally.

Alessa dug at his fingers while continuing to direct all her energy towards the illuminated worms in his brain.

"I never loved you." He squeezed tighter. "It was always Alessa. It will always be Alessa."

Hearing Damon's confession, Brielle hissed.

Then, unexpectedly, a sharp *crack* sound was heard, followed by a spiderweb of fractures spreading across the large screen.

"What was that?" Brielle shrieked as those working for Lucas and Cain stood silently behind her.

As stars threatened to overtake her vision, Alessa felt a snapping sensation as one of the worms was destroyed. At the same time, Damon's grip lessened, and a scream ripped from his throat.

Releasing Alessa, he fell backwards and shook his head back and forth in confusion.

Alessa's throat burned as she noisily inhaled the cool morning air through her crushed trachea. With her vision returning, Alessa refocused on the additional worms.

As each one dissipated, it felt as though a tiny glass vase was breaking inside Damon's skull.

Shrieking in agony, Damon grabbed the sides of his head and fell to the ground on his knees.

CHAPTER TWENTY

"What is she doing?" Brielle demanded. Leaning into the screen, she smacked it with her open palms.

"No, no, no, she can't do this!" Brielle shrieked while pounding her bloodied fists repeatedly on the cracked screen. "He is mine to do with as I please. Not yours!"

As the last of the worms imploded inside his brain, Damon collapsed onto the palms of his hands.

Wanting so badly to comfort him, Alessa moved slowly towards him while staring at the tiny green glowing dot at the base of his skull. She watched it vibrate back and forth until Damon looked up at her, his silver irises meeting hers.

Both determined to save Damon and terrified he was about to attack her, Alessa clenched her jaw as she stood her ground. *I will save him from whatever hell he is being put through. No matter what the cost.*

Finally able to recognize Alessa through the fog, Damon

sprang to his feet and, while placing a hand on either side of her neck, he pulled her in.

Her body stiffened as she braced herself for the assault, when suddenly Damon's warm lips pressed against Alessa's, and her defenses fell.

The flames rose high into the air, swirling dangerously close to them.

Their tongues danced as Damon's hands caressed the side of Alessa's face and neck, and his desperate kiss deepened.

The tiny dot in his brain glowed even brighter until it finally burst, completely evaporating and releasing Damon from Brielle's grasp.

Brielle's screen submerged into darkness as Damon's microchip disconnected from Erebos.

"NO!" she shrieked at the top of her lungs. "You can't have him! You fucking bitch!" Brielle swiped the keyboards off the tops of the tables. Screaming loudly, she snatched every object within her grasp and threw them violently about the room.

Her deep brown eyes glared into the blacked-out screen, as if she could still see Alessa's face, and she snarled, "He is MINE."

With the painful sensation of a rubber band snapping in the back of his head, Damon felt an immediate wave of relief.

Pulling away, his deep denim blue eyes locked onto Alessa, and his lips relaxed into a smile. "Silence," he sighed. "I hear ... nothing."

Alessa's eyes filled with tears as an exhausted smile tugged at her lips.

Placing his hands on either side of her face, Damon pulled her in for another kiss.

Desperate for her touch, his lips moved urgently against Alessa's, parting her lips with a flick of his tongue.

Her body instantly melted against his as the spark of familiarity ignited their suppressed passion. Running her fingers through his dark hair, Alessa pulled Damon closer.

This kiss felt different, not unhinged like the previous one. It felt like home.

Reluctantly pulling away, he bent down and pressed his forehead against hers. Between heaving breaths, Damon's voice wavered as he whispered, "Thank you."

Tears welled up in his eyes as he beamed, and wrapping his arms around her waist, Damon lifted Alessa into the air and spun her around in circles. "Thank you. Thank you so much." He laughed before setting her back down on the ground. "For the first time in as long as I can remember, there are no voices in my head."

Coinciding with Alessa's exhaustion, the fire surrounding them dissipated, and all that was left was black smoke.

The twenty or so Spartan warriors stood around them in a circle, just outside of the scorched ground, confused and intimidated by what they had witnessed. After the lead warrior gave them permission to move with a nod of her head, they rushed in.

Alessa sighed in relief while rubbing his fingerprints from her bruised neck. "I'm glad I got to you in time," she said in a raspy voice.

"How did you know—" He wrapped an arm around her waist, holding her in place, while his other hand caressed the visible spots on her neck. "Oh shit, babe, I'm so sorry. I didn't mean—"

Damon's hands were tugged behind his back as he and Alessa were forced apart. Held in place, he was bound with glowing handcuffs.

The lead Spartan spoke. "Damon, you are hereby detained for questioning regarding the violent attack against, well, a lot of Spartan warriors. It is unknown at this time if there are any survivors."

Alessa struggled to push past the warriors separating them. "He was clearly not himself. Damon can't be held accountable for his actions while he was obviously forced to do only Gods knows what—"

Damon's eyes widened in concern. "I'm so sorry. I didn't know what I—"

"Save it for the Consilium," the lead warrior interrupted. "They'll be very interested in hearing your side of the story, but for now, you may want to keep your mouth shut. The only reason I decided against killing you is your Wellborn status."

He looked at Alessa with regret in his eyes. "I didn't mean to hurt you. Or anyone else. I had no idea what I was doing. It had to be the secondary microchip we implanted. That and maybe the worms were amplifying Brielle's hold on me."

Alessa was forced to stay back. "I had no idea you had another one implanted."

Damon struggled against his captors. "Talk to Seraphine."

Alessa pushed against the Spartan warriors standing between them. "I'll have a medic team sent to evaluate those you unintentionally injured. Then I'll find your father."

"I'm sorry!" he proclaimed as he was hauled away to the holding cells. "I'm so sorry."

"We'll get all of this sorted out. Don't worry," Alessa yelled.

Pushing back against the guards standing in her way, she grumbled, "Don't worry, I'm going."

Alessa pointed at one of the guards. "You, make sure you contact Sera immediately. Tell her she needs to go to my elder's cabin first."

Strolling past the arena's entrance, she addressed the stationed Spartan. "Where can I find Damon's father?"

The weapon-wielding Spartan puffed out his chest. "He was told to seek shelter in his quarters."

Alessa laughed to herself as she marched away. "Sounds about right, the fucking coward."

Approaching Damon's father's protected door, Alessa barked at the warriors standing guard. "I need to speak to him."

"Not until we hear Damon's been put down," retorted one of the guards.

Alessa glared. Forcibly grabbing his arm, she spoke into his wristband. "Is Damon a continued threat?"

Snatching his arm back, the man scowled before a voice responded through his com. "That's a negative. He has been detained and is sitting in the cells awaiting trial. It is all clear."

"Happy?" Alessa grinned sarcastically. "The chicken shit can come out of hiding now."

As the guards remained in front of the door, she growled in frustration. "You are dismissed."

Controlling their microchips, Alessa forced them away from the door with a turn of her head. *Training so vigorously over these past few months has really started to pay off.*

The guards marched away, backs stiff, as Alessa tried the front door's handle. *Dammit, it's locked.* She groaned before focusing all her attention on the electronic lock hidden inside the door.

With the glitch of her eyes, Alessa willed the lock open, and it clicked before its release.

Slamming the door open, she found Damon's dad sitting on the floor of his room, before his bed.

With tears in his eyes, he glanced up at Alessa. The distraught look on his reddened face gave away the fact that he had been crying, and Alessa unglitched as she shut the door behind her.

"Is Damon—?" he asked, afraid to hear the answer.

"Dead?" Alessa finished for him.

Closing his eyes, Damon's father let his head fall in defeat.

"No, he's not. No thanks to you." She strolled across the hardwood, her wet feet leaving footprints on the white tiled floor.

"Wait..." His father struggled to stand up. "I was told he was unsavable. That he was too far gone."

Alessa leaned her back against an ornate dark wooden dresser, facing him, and shrugged. "Well, I did it. I saved your son. Now, you owe me."

His father's face fell. "What do you want?"

"I want you to call off my witch hunt. I am not interested in taking over the Spartans. I have no alternate agenda. I just want to live my life in peace. Well"—she laughed to herself—"as much peace as a Spartan warrior is allowed by the gods."

The older man glared at Alessa, disdain written across his face. "Done."

She rolled her eyes and shook her head. "I know this isn't what you wanted—me surviving, but clearly I am in the gods' favor." Knowing how much this gutted him, she smirked. "How else can you explain my innate inability to die, no matter how many dangerous situations I put myself in?"

Fuming, he pursed his lips together and glared at Alessa from the side of his eyes.

"And you'll want to work your magic to get your son out of trouble. It would probably help if you made sure every Spartan he attacked while he was under their control survives."

His father nodded in agreement. Turning around, he gripped the bed's footboard before grumbling, "Maybe Damon was right in choosing you to be his wife."

Alessa's lips parted, and she froze in place. "What did you just say?"

"Before you went missing, Damon had declared his intention of asking you to be his wife." He turned his head to the side. "Surely he told you this when you got your memories back."

Alessa cleared her throat, and the room tilted sideways. "Mm-hmm," she mumbled as she stumbled towards the exit in shock.

Damon's father stared at Alessa's back as she walked unsteadily towards the door. "I truly am grateful for all you've done for my son. Thank you for saving his life. Again."

Trying not to pass out, she inhaled deeply before opening the door and stepping out onto the small porch. Moving to the side so she could no longer be seen by Damon's father, Alessa closed her eyes and slid down the side of the house.

Conflicting emotions bombarded the Spartan as she sat on the front porch with her back against the wood siding.

Tired of trying to figure out how everything fit in her heart, Alessa painfully dug her fingernails deep into her palms, and through teary eyes, she watched the colorful sunrise spread across the dark blue sky.

CHAPTER TWENTY-ONE

After picking herself up off the floor of Damon's father's porch, Alessa staggered alongside the path towards her cabin.

She was met by stares and whispers as fellow Spartans stayed far away from the disheveled warrior, even going as far as crossing the road if they were walking down the same side.

Her deep blue nightgown was torn, burned, and filthy, and her morale wasn't much better off.

Feeling the adrenaline dump from her veins, Alessa struggled to keep her eyes open. *You can do it. You're nearly home.*

Running up behind her, Camden recognized Alessa and yelled her name. "Alessa!"

Turning around, she stumbled onto the light grey pebbles. "Cam?" she exhaled as her vision swam, and she fell forward.

Running and dropping to his knees, the ex-Bodyguard slid and caught Alessa just as she was about to hit the ground. "Shit, Alessa!"

Shifting her body weight in his arms, Camden lifted her up

and held her against his chest. He looked to the side before heading towards the small lake.

As the intense wave of anger and relief struck Camden, he marched into the chilly water while still holding Alessa.

With the shock of the cold water, she inhaled sharply. "What the fu—"

As she emerged from the surface of the water, sputtering, Camden got in her face. "How could you do this? I mean, he could have killed you—"

She slicked back her wet, dark hair as she stammered. "I— I—"

Camden's arms thrashed about. "From what I was told, he was out of his mind. Which, clearly, you were as well—"

Alessa's jaw dropped as her brain began working again, and she shook her head back and forth. "I wasn't—"

"That's right, you weren't thinking," Camden interrupted. "I can't believe you risked your life once again—"

"I didn't have a choice!" Alessa cried while digging her toes into the tiny pebbles at the bottom of the lake.

Camden stood silent as the water moved around them in small waves.

She exhaled loudly. "Quade showed up at my doorstep, badly wounded, and told me what Damon did—"

"So, what, seeing your childhood friend nearly killed by your ex inspired you to—?"

"I had to try!" She breathed. "I had ... to try." Her shoulders dropped. "I don't expect you to understand, but I knew in my heart if I didn't try to bring him back—" Tears sprang to her eyes as she shook her head with a shrug. "I had to try, or I'd never forgive myself."

Camden stared down at Alessa, the water dripping from

the blond hair hanging in front of his eyes. "You should've come to me. I would've helped you."

She shook her head with a shrug of her shoulders. "There wasn't time. I barely made it before—" She shivered as the image of the warriors positioned in a circle around Damon came to mind.

She fell into Camden's chest and wrapped her arms around him, sobbing. "I'm sorry. Cam, I'm so sorry."

He embraced Alessa, placed his hand on the back of her head, and leaned in to kiss her forehead. "Don't ever scare me like that again."

They held each other in the water before Camden led Alessa out of the lake. "Let's get you home so you can get cleaned up. I need to find Lexi to discuss some things."

Lost in her thoughts, she absent-mindedly nodded her head in agreement, allowing Camden to lead her back home with his arm wrapped tightly around her.

***

Two hours later, Camden found Lexi sitting beneath her favorite tree.

He pointed his finger at her upon approach. "She almost died because of what you told her!"

Lexi's head whipped up to see Camden charging towards her, and she swallowed. *Here we go.* "I heard," she said.

He stood tall before her, sitting on a blanket in the tall grass. "But by the will of the gods, she survived."

"I heard that as well." She closed her book.

Camden's eyebrows furrowed in anger. "Is that all you have to say for yourself? 'I heard,'" Camden mimicked.

Standing upright, she glared defiantly into his dark green

and golden eyes. "Alessa is a grown-ass woman who has every right to make her own decisions. I merely presented her with the facts; she's the one who chose to risk her life."

"Yeah, but—"

Lexi threw her book to the ground and forced Camden backward. "Had I not told her everything I had discovered, every single line of the prophecy, or at least as much as we know, she would not have been given the proper chance to determine her own destiny."

He pressed his lips together in a hard line and clenched his jaw. "That's bullshit."

"Cam, I know you have feelings for Alessa; it's blatantly obvious, but you need to understand this is her life, not yours. You have no right to take away her free will."

Fuming, Camden turned away from Lexi and placed his hands firmly on his hips.

She cocked her head to the side. "Do you honestly think she would have forgiven either one of us once she found out we had withheld the truth?"

He laughed without humor. "Her name isn't written anywhere in the prophecy; you can't possibly know for certain it is about them."

Lowering her head, she smirked. "You're right. It doesn't explicitly have her name written into the prophecy." She threw her hands in the air. "You're right." Lexi huffed while picking up her book. "But I don't care. Because of my informing Alessa last night, she was able to figure out what she wanted, and she followed through."

Camden rolled his eyes with a huff as Lexi shrugged her shoulders.

"She saved Damon, and for that, I'm not sorry. Yes, she could have died, but that would not have been my fault. Alessa is the only one who can choose her own destiny. Not me, not you, not even Damon," Lexi explained.

Camden's blood boiled in his veins, and his irises flashed gold as he struggled to keep his anger in check. Turning away from Lexi, he pumped his fists.

Seeing his muscles flex, she stood tall. Tossing her book back onto the ground, she flashed a mischievous grin. "Fight me."

He scowled and peered over his shoulder at the Spartan woman. She was standing behind him, her leg peeking out from between the fabric of her violet skirt.

"What? No," he shook his head, as if to convince himself.

"Listen to your own advice and channel your anger. If you don't get it out, you're damn well going to explode." Lexi stepped forward and smacked Camden upside the head, twice.

"The fuck was that about?" Camden demanded.

"All you ever talk about is Alessa! Did you not have a life before this woman? And what's your obsession with Damon? Do you also find him attractive? Because he's next on the list of things you talk about non-stop."

Camden's jaw dropped, and as pure rage coursed through his veins, his hands pumped.

Lexi stepped forward, her stance tall and strong. "Do you even like me? Genuinely, as a person, or am I just someone to complain to?"

Surprised by her question, he shook his head. "Of course I like—"

"Then what's my favorite song? I hum it all the time." She paused, awaiting his answer.

He ran his hand through his sandy blond hair. "Um ... I haven't really paid that close attention—"

"Have you ever asked about my likes? My dislikes? No, you haven't. Because deep down, I'm just the backup."

His eyes furrowed. "No, you're not—"

She held up her hand, and her cheeks burned red. "Yes, I am. I always have been, but I'm sick of it. Just once I'd like to be someone's actual friend."

Camden's shoulders dropped. "Lex, I'm sorry I've made you feel that way. That was never my intention."

Her eyes filled with hot tears as her palms flexed in frustration. "Just shut the fuck up and show me how you're feeling. I'm through with talking. Fight. Me."

She bent her knees into a starting position before Camden, and as she stood at the ready, Lexi waved her fingers as if to say, 'come and get it.'

"Now," she proclaimed in Greek before lunging forward.

Her arms chopped through the air, and she smacked him upside his head.

Camden's head cranked to the side from the force of her hit, and with an audible grunt, he cracked his vertebrae back into place.

Lexi wiggled her eyebrows, and her lips curled up in a smirk. "If that were a blade, you'd already be dead. Come on, already. Fight me like a woman."

He flashed a half-smile. "Don't you mean fight like a man?"

Her right eyebrow arched, and she huffed. "I said what I said."

Pressing his lips together in a straight line, Camden closed his eyelids. Upon opening them, his irises had activated gold.

"Finally," Lexi sighed. With a blink of her eyes, her irises shone a vibrant violet. "Stop holding back."

He bent at the knees and raised his fists. "Let me know if I get too rough."

She chuckled. "I think you forgot we've been sparring for a while now."

Camden bounced back and forth between his feet. "Yeah, well, I haven't exactly been going full strength."

Her eyebrows lifted in excitement, and she glanced behind him. "Oh, Alessa, hey!"

While he turned his head, Lexi charged forward. Stepping up onto Camden's thigh, she stuck out her foot, and as his neck began twisting back around, she kicked the side of his face, whipping his head to the side.

Lexi grinned wickedly as he wiped the blood from the side of his mouth. "If you think I haven't been taking it easy on you, you're sorely mistaken."

Both impressed with Lexi and aggravated with himself for letting his guard down, Camden stared the Spartan down. "That was low."

She shrugged as they encircled each other. "No, that's called finding your weakness and using it to my advantage."

"Touché," Camden replied as Lexi threw a punch.

Fifteen minutes later, Camden lay on his back in the tall grass with his fingers digging at Lexi's legs that were wrapped around his neck.

She panted, squeezing her thighs tightly together. "Give?"

With his vision fading, he held up his fingers for the universal sign, and Lexi squealed in celebration. "Yes!"

After she unwrapped her legs from around his neck, Camden gasped for air.

Bringing his legs to his chest, Camden tried to hide the massive bulge he had gotten during their sparring.

"Thanks for not going easy on me." She wiped the blood from her ear before popping a finger back into place. "I really needed that, and I could tell you did as well."

"If you only knew," Camden murmured to himself.

"What was that?" Lexi asked as she picked up the book from the ground.

He sat upright with bent knees. "Oh, nothing."

She brushed blades of grass from her torn dress. "Wanna go grab something to eat?"

Wiggling his hips back and forth, Camden cursed himself for being a man. "I do, but I just—uh—need a minute. You go on ahead; I'll catch up."

He intently watched her hips bounce back and forth as she walked away. "What the hell was all that about? And why did I enjoy it so much?"

CHAPTER TWENTY-TWO

Damon stood in the shower, beneath the hot running water, replaying his time together with Alessa in the arena.

He could still feel the heat from Alessa's breath as their lips collided and their tongues teased each other playfully, as though no time had passed.

Damon blinked furiously, trying to clear his blurred vision.

"You doing okay?" Seraphine asked from the other side of the curtain.

He shook the water from his dark hair before turning off the shower. "Uh, yeah, I'm good."

She reached forward from the other side of the curtain. "Here's your towel."

"Thanks. So, what are they saying about me?" he asked while rubbing the water droplets from his body.

Seraphine held the bottom of her pregnant belly while sitting on the closed toilet seat. "Well ... I had to convince the elders to let me show them evidence regarding your mind-control; they wanted to sentence you without any defense. But once you were given the sedatives, I took several images of your brain; all of which showed proof that your worms were eliminated by Alessa."

Damon wrapped the towel around his waist and secured it in a knot. "What did the physician who implanted the second microchip say?"

She swallowed. "He jumped off a bridge."

Damon's eyebrows raised. "Seriously?"

She nodded and sighed. "He was clearly in on everything Brielle had planned."

Peeking his head out from behind the curtain, he stepped onto the cold tile floor. "So, Brielle never really left my head?"

"Unfortunately."

"Huh," Damon huffed, moving over to his medical cot. He fingered his black tactical pants and navy blue form-fitting T-shirt. "Have they decided my fate?"

"A decision has been made, yes." Seraphine exhaled.

Sliding his shirt onto his head, Damon pulled it down over his defined abs. "Well, what's to become of me?"

Seraphine groaned as she stood up and waddled out of the bathroom. "Your life is to be spared. Believe it or not, your father fought with the others, stating that your being saved was proof you are in the gods' favor."

He tugged on his briefs and pants. "My father? You're sure about that?"

She absentmindedly rubbed her belly while looking away. "I was informed of the decision directly from the Consilium."

His eyebrows furrowed. "It typically takes a few days to deliberate something as serious as my transgressions were. How long was I out?"

Knowing he'd be upset, Seraphine hesitated. "More than three days."

He nearly choked on his saliva. "Excuse me? You said what now?"

"Damon, you needed to rest. You had gone far too long with your brain being stimulated non-stop. Your body was beginning to shut down; your organs were on the verge of failing."

Remembering what he had done to Quade and all the others, Damon gasped. "Oh shit, Sera, I didn't mean to hurt Quade. Is he—"

She held up her hand, silencing Damon. "He was in bad shape when we found him, but with my help as well as our technology, he's already back to his usual headstrong self."

"Great. That's great. Did I kill anyone?" he asked hesitantly.

"No. By the grace of the gods, it's as if you knew, even in the state you were in, that you shouldn't kill a fellow Spartan. You and I both know when you put your mind to something, you're more than capable of achieving it."

He pulled on his combat boots. "Where is Alessa?"

Seraphine shook her head, scrunching her face in disapproval. "Damon, you need to continue resting. You shouldn't be up and moving so soon after waking. Your body is still healing."

"I spent too long not living. Now that I can see clearly, I need to speak with Alessa. I need to know..." he trailed off.

Seraphine touched Damon's arm, and he jumped. "What do you need to know?"

Staring into her deep brown eyes, Damon cleared his throat. "I need to know if anything between us has changed or if she still feels the same. Because, Sera, that kiss ... my gods, that meant something to me. But if it didn't mean anything to Alessa, I will reluctantly let her go. For good."

With a sigh, she lifted her hand to the side of his face. "May the gods be with you."

Damon placed his warm hand on Seraphine's. "Thank you."

"Go in peace," she encouraged with the flick of her wrist. "But, I beg of you, please listen to your body. If something doesn't feel right, come back and see me."

"Will do, Doc!" Damon yelled over his shoulder as he ran out of the medical ward.

***

Breathing heavily as he sprinted down the side of the path to Alessa's cabin, Damon froze upon finding Alessa and Quade sitting beside each other on her small cabin's front porch.

Seeing her easy-going smile, his heart clenched.

Just as Damon was about to turn away, Quade placed his hand on Alessa's upper knee and patted her leg. After a quick squeeze, Quade stood up, and she followed.

Standing on her tiptoes, she wrapped her arms around Quade's neck and pulled him in close for a hug.

Damon couldn't help but feel jealous. He laughed to himself, thinking how much of a creep he was being, watching their interaction from a distance. *Couldn't get much lower than this.*

Alessa leaned back, grinning at Quade before she slapped him playfully on the shoulder.

Biting her lip, Alessa's shoulders raised and dropped with a sigh as she pressed two fingers against her lips. Watching Quade run down the path, Alessa walked around the exterior of the cabin before disappearing into the woods.

Damon jogged behind Alessa's cabin, and as he recognized her body's outline within the forest, he stilled.

Touching the tree beside him, panic set in, and he exhaled. *Feel the ground beneath your feet, the rough bark of the tree standing tall beside you. This is real.*

Letting go of the tree bark, sticks cracked beneath Damon's boots as he walked towards Alessa.

She spun around and raised her arms defensively in front of herself. "Damon?" she gasped. Glancing around the woods, she slowly dropped her fists. "When did you wake up?"

"Less than an hour ago," Damon responded, his gaze intense. "You're the first person I wanted to see. Besides Sera, of course."

"Wow, that's not long at all." She paused. "You didn't think to speak with your father first, before coming to see me?"

He moved a branch out of his way. "This couldn't wait. I needed to talk to you."

"Oh?" She nervously played with the nonexistent ring that used to be around her finger. "You shaved…" she said.

One step at a time, Damon slowly closed the gap between them. "What were you and Quade talking about just now?"

Alessa felt the sexual tension rolling off of him as he slowly approached, and she exhaled slowly. "You, actually."

His eyebrows raised in surprise. "Me?"

She silently nodded, her head jerking up and down as she felt the heat spreading through her.

Encircling Alessa, Damon asked, "What about me?"

Watching him from the corner of her eye, she straightened her back. "He forgives you, you know? For attacking him."

Strolling behind Alessa, he confessed, "He's next on my list of people I need to personally apologize to. And was that it?"

Why does it feel like Damon knows I was talking to Quade about my conflicted feelings about him? "Mm-hmm."

His eyes narrowed in disbelief. "That's all you two talked about? Was his ability to forgive me?" He stepped around to the front of Alessa, standing tall before her.

Struggling to catch her breath, she looked up into Damon's ocean blue eyes as he stared down at her.

Staring at his lips, she imagined them frantically moving against hers. "No, that wasn't all…"

Damon stepped forward, minimizing the space between their bodies, and Alessa felt the invisible pull. "Um—I talked to Quade about the secondary microchip you had implanted. He got me caught up on that."

Taken by surprise, his demeanor changed. "I'm sorry for everything; for not believing you, for betraying you. Most of all, I'm sorry for killing Kai."

She stepped forward and placed her hand on the side of his face. "You have got to stop blaming yourself. Kai wouldn't want you to live like this."

Damon gently touched her throat, moving the tips of his fingers against her invisible bruises. "I'm so sorry for hurting you."

She glanced away and dropped her hand. "It wasn't so bad."

He gently grabbed beneath Alessa's chin and turned her head, demanding her attention.

Leaning into Alessa, Damon's eyes darted back and forth between her blue eyes and her rosy lips. "I'm sorry for every single way I have hurt you. If you'll let me—"

Her breathing hitched as his mouth hovered above her own.

Just then, a familiar man's voice bellowed, "Alessa, I need a word."

Blinking furiously, she inhaled and stepped back.

Released from Damon's trance, she looked around the tall, muscular Spartan warrior and saw her elder. Shaking the heat from her face, Alessa grabbed the bottom of her skirt and ran to him. "Yes, Elder."

Her elder eyed Damon and tersely tilted his head back at the warrior. "Damon."

"Good evening, sir," Damon said through gritted teeth.

"I'm sure you have plenty of other things to do," Alessa's elder suggested.

Nodding in silent agreement, Damon cleared his throat, and turning on his heel, he walked beside Alessa.

Lifting their gazes, they stared into one another's blue eyes as he passed by.

"Alessa," Damon acknowledged before marching out of the woods.

Her elder's back stiffened. "You have never been faced with such scrutiny by the Consilium. You need to get your head out of romantic endeavors and focus on saving your life," he chastised before walking back to their cabin.

"What are you talking about? I already know the Consilium has it out for me. Is there something else you haven't told me?" Alessa followed behind, stepping over fallen logs and avoiding the patches of poison ivy. "I will practice, study, and train, but I *will* continue living. Or what's the point? Besides, where have you been for the past few days? I haven't seen you since the night you returned."

Her elder exhaled slowly. "Join me for a drink. It's time to tell you more about my conversation with the Consilium."

They walked in silence to the cabin, and as they entered the kitchen, Alessa turned her head. "Tea?"

"I may need something a bit stronger," he mumbled under his breath.

Taken by surprise, she froze. "Whatever you're about to tell me can't be good."

Her elder pointed at a cabinet on the kitchen wall. "The bourbon is on the top shelf, behind the coffee mugs. Make sure to grab yourself a glass as well."

Pressing her lips together, Alessa opened the cabinet doors. After grabbing two coffee mugs and the bottle of liquor, she sat down on the couch beside her elder.

Taking the bourbon, he yanked the cork from the bottle's opening, and the lip clanked as it tapped the side of the mug.

After filling the first mug, he handed it to Alessa.

"You know I don't really drink," she laughed nervously. *Neither does he. What is so bad about what he's about to tell me?*

"You may not want to be completely sober when you hear what I'm about to tell you," he confessed. Smacking his lips together after taking a big swig, her elder exhaled noisily while taking a seat on the couch.

"Once I was approved by the Council of Elders to go to and speak with the Consilium in person, I believed it would be rather easy to get them to see the truth about the Frenzied; about everything, really. But I'm afraid they've become untrustworthy and corrupt, caring only about their personal ambitions and not giving a damn about humanity anymore." He took a long swig from his mug before shaking his head.

"What exactly did they say?" She asked before taking a sip of the amber-colored liquid.

Her elder stared into his mug. "There is no credible link between the Frenzied and Greenfield Farms, and my hunch wasn't good enough, so they aren't going to pursue Cain. They're afraid that if they push him into hiding, they'll never find Lucas and are foolishly hoping Cain will still give up clues as to where his uncle is."

He held out his mug towards Alessa. "You and I both know he will never slip up like that."

She nervously bit her lower lip as she sat down in the chair on the opposite side of the coffee table.

"And then there were the non-stop questions about you."

Alessa nearly choked on her saliva, and she set down the mug on the wooden coffee table. "What did they want to know?"

"We'll talk about that in a minute. First, I want to hear about Sera's pregnancy. How's she feeling?"

Caught off guard by his change of subject, she shook her head. "Oh, um, her daughter is growing big and strong. I think Sera's cherishing these last few weeks without having a newborn."

"And Camden? If my eyes weren't playing tricks on me, I didn't see him with you and Damon out back in the woods."

Clearing her throat, Alessa grabbed her mug and brought the liquor back up to her lips. "Uh ... yeah. Some things happened while you were gone, but that's going to have to wait until you sober up. It's a whole thing."

Her elder's eyebrows raised. "Oh?"

Swallowing the burning liquid, Alessa nodded. "Yep. But, uh, Camden is doing great. He's healed and has been working closely with Lexi and Sera, trying to figure out the origin story of the Frenzied and how to slow them down or, hopefully, how to stop them altogether. Quade went on a mission with Damon and me"—she paused, recognizing her elder's curious glance—

"and an entire group of Spartans to take out more Frenzied along the West Coast."

"Will you be attending the Hyacinthia festival?" he inquired.

She licked the liquor from her lips. "Oh, yeah, I had completely forgotten about that."

Her elder chuckled. "It's only held every year, at the same time."

She ran her finger along the top of her mug. "Will you be going?"

Her elder clucked his tongue. "Oh, no. I have been away from home for far too long. I am peopled out. Besides, parties are for the young." He took a swig of his liquor. "You should go, though. Sounds like you need a proper break from all the craziness."

She shook her head while glaring at her elder incredulously. "Now, you know I attract trouble wherever I go. Always have. It's a curse."

Lifting his mug, her elder stuck his lower lip out in contemplation. "Can't disagree with that."

Holding the mug between her hands, she impatiently bobbed her legs up and down. "Now, please tell me what the Consilium wanted to know."

Her elder sighed before continuing. "They asked how your training is coming along, what your abilities allow you to do, and if I felt you could be kept in check." He looked over his mug while finishing his drink.

"Excuse me? The fuck kind of question is that—them asking if I can be kept under control?" Alessa's face dropped as the realization hit. "They want me training for something specific, don't they?"

He sighed heavily. "That was the impression I was given."

Her jaw clenched, and she stood up, angrily pacing back and forth. "Those fucking ... I had a feeling they might try to use me in the future, but less than a year after I developed these ... abilities?" She pressed her tongue against the inside of her cheek as she shook her head back and forth. "Any idea what it would entail?"

Her elder fell back against the plush couch cushions. "All I know is they had mentioned something about the Frenzied."

With her hands on her hips, Alessa turned to face her elder. "The Frenzied don't have anything to do with technology. I can't help with eradicating them any more than any other Spartan can. My skills are *only* helpful when it comes to dealing with *technology*. Did you tell them this? Are they aware?"

Her elder closed his eyes and nodded. "Yes, I told them to kindly fuck off and then promptly left before they could throw me in jail."

"You did?" She asked, shocked that he would speak to his superiors so brazenly.

Finishing the last of his drink, he looked down into the bottom of his mug before setting it back down on the table. "You mean more to me than life itself, and I will protect you until my dying breath. But there will come a time when I won't be here anymore. You need to strengthen your abilities and trust in your friends to have your back."

Keeping the prophecy to herself, Alessa plopped back in her chair with her head hung in defeat. "What if I choose the wrong person, or people, to trust?"

Her elder closed his eyes once more and leaned back, sinking into the cushions. "That's for you to find out."

CHAPTER TWENTY-THREE

Quade grunted as he leapt from one edge to another on the rock wall.

Ascending from below him, Damon grinned as he pushed up behind his Spartan friend.

"You know, if this is too hard for you, we can head back down," Quade suggested from above. "You did just wake up from a three-day coma after being possessed by a psychopath."

Damon snickered. "This is exactly what I need." He pushed up and over, grabbing onto the next secure spot in the rock.

The Spartan men clung to the vertical rock wall, a good forty feet in the air.

"Besides, after what I did to you, I gotta give you the chance to take me out, and no one would think twice if I fell from this height," Damon replied.

Quade shook his head, peering down at his friend. "I already told you, it's all good. You didn't know what you were doing." He reached for his next holding place and groaned. "Besides, your attack wasn't all that bad. We both know I would've kicked your ass if I hadn't taken pity on you," he joked. "It only took two days to heal. I'm fine now."

Quade dipped his fingers into the chalk bag hanging around his waist. "The question is, are you fine?"

Damon chuckled. "What the fuck do you think?"

"That's what I thought. Why couldn't we have had this discussion on the ground?" Quade re-adjusted his grip with his powdered fingertips.

Damon followed suit, moving his fingers through his chalk bag, coating them with the sticky white chalk. "If I sit still, what I did to Kai comes rushing back to me, and I feel like I'm going to lose it all over again."

Damon's hand flexed where he held onto the rock. Letting go, he flew horizontally, landing gracefully a few feet to the left. "I went to see Alessa."

Quade's jaw dropped, and he turned to face Damon. "And?"

Damon grunted, the muscles in his arms straining. "There's definitely still something there."

Quade recognized the signs of Damon's body getting tired. "Hey, man, I feel a bit shaky," he lied. "Mind if we start our descent?"

"Yeah, sure," Damon grunted.

Quade nodded stiffly. "Okay, you first, I'll follow. So, what happened? What did you say?"

Looking down, Damon found his footing. "I apologized for Kai, for hurting her, for everything."

"That's a good start," Quade encouraged.

The sweat dripped down Damon's forehead, stinging his eyes. "Yeah, well, we were about to kiss when her elder showed up."

"What?" Quade exclaimed. "You got caught like high schoolers about to make out?" Quade taunted.

"Shut up," Damon laughed, digging his fingertips into the rock.

Quade stuck his foot into the side of the wall. "Has she said she's forgiven you yet?"

"Yeah, um, she said she forgave me before we left for California," Damon groaned as he swung to a new ledge.

Quade reached down for another position in the rock. "And have you forgiven yourself?"

Damon's head jerked upright. "What?"

"Have you forgiven yourself for what happened to Kai?"

Exhaling loudly, Damon turned his attention back to his careful downward movement. "I'm not sure I ever will."

"You're going to have to work on that, brother. The guilt could end up eating you alive, and I don't want to see that happen."

Knowing Quade was right, Damon scowled and rolled his eyes. "It isn't as simple—"

"Yes, it is," Quade interrupted. You must know in your heart that you didn't cause the blade to move. Alessa told me a while ago, it was Hades."

Damon's head jerked upright in surprise. "You knew?"

"Of course I did, but you isolated yourself during the past few months, and not knowing it was because you were being possessed, I gave you the space I thought you needed. Won't be making that mistake again," Quade chuckled. "I'm going to haunt your dreams."

Damon dropped further down the rock, groaning as his fingers painfully gripped into a sharp edge. "I'm gonna hold you to it, but how do I go about making this right with Alessa? I mean,

I took away the one person she loved more than life itself. I'm not sure how we move on from that." Damon glanced down at the ground and pushed off the rock wall, landing with his knees bent.

Following suit, Quade pushed off the wall and hit the ground before standing upright to look Damon in the eyes. "Take one day at a time."

He patted Damon on the shoulder before pulling him in. "I want the best for both of you. But before you pursue Alessa, you've got to get your shit straight. Got it?"

Damon swallowed before breathing shakily.

Quade unbuckled the pack from around his waist and threw it in with the pile of others. "You're coming to Hyacinthia with us, right?"

Knowing he'd have to get on an airplane to attend the celebration, Damon's tanned face paled. "Um," he cleared his throat. "I'm not sure if I should. Or if I'm even allowed."

Quade's face scrunched up in disbelief. "That's ridiculous. You've been cleared both medically and psychologically; you're not being held responsible for any of your previous actions. You're a direct descendant of a king, and this is one of the first years you're not on a mission, so I can only assume it's expected of you."

"Fuck," Damon grumbled under his breath.

Quade took a big swig from his water bottle. "You okay? You're not looking so good."

Damon blinked exaggeratedly and pressed his hand against his forehead. "Uh, yeah, I think I'm just dehydrated and tired. I should probably head home and get some rest."

"Make sure you're feeling better by the time we need to leave in two days. You're my plus one since Sera is due any day." Quade winked. "Can't risk the mother of my children giving birth forty thousand feet in the air."

Damon threw his pack on top of Quade's. "Oh, brother. That's the last thing we need." He directed his attention to the top of the rock. "Have you ever reached the top?"

Quade looked up at the flat edge. "Not yet. But someday I will. I bet the view is amazing up there."

"One day we both will," Damon agreed, smacking his calloused hands together.

As Cain presented his proposed bill on the Senate floor, Hades hid behind the senators. Jumping back and forth, he danced to music only he could hear.

Whispering in the humans' ears, Hades persuaded them to side with the bill preventing women from legally obtaining abortions throughout the entirety of the United States.

The chair called for a vote. "All in favor? Those in favor say 'aye'."

"Aye," echoed the voices of every person sitting in the large room.

"All those opposed? Those opposed will say 'no'." The room sat in silence as everyone's lips remained sealed.

"Alright, looks like the bill has passed and will be sent to the House of Representatives," the chair said before dismissing the members for the day.

Watching a young woman approach Cain, Hades smiled cruelly while leaning against a far wall.

"Senator Cain? Do you have a moment?" the bleach-blonde asked.

Plastering a sickly-sweet smile on his face, behind his white-and-silver half mask, he turned to face the woman. "Yes, what can I help you with, Miss—?"

She could barely contain her excitement as her hands flew before her chest. "Oh, um. It's Miss Jackie." She shook her head, and her cheeks blushed in embarrassment as she held out her hand. "I mean, my name is Miss Baker. Jackie Baker."

Watching the young woman fumble over her words, Cain shook her hand firmly.

Looking down at their touching hands, the woman's breath hitched. "I just wanted to say thank you from the bottom of my heart for introducing this bill. It has been a long time coming."

His visible eyebrow lifted in curiosity. "Oh, really?"

"Most definitely." She nodded fervently while trying not to stare at his alluring mask. "We, as a nation, need a leader like you to take charge and help save the lives of the unborn."

Hades squinted as he took in the effect Cain had on women. "Impressive. If only she knew what she was agreeing to," he said to himself before disappearing from the human realm.

Cain's eyes drifted up and down the woman's expensive clothing.

His gaze stopped at her partially unbuttoned top, exposing the top of her breasts, and thinking about her bright red cherry blood spilling over her pale skin, Cain unintentionally licked his lips as he became aroused.

Chasing the image from his mind, Cain shook his head before clearing his throat. "Um, yes, thank you." *If only she knew the truth about the bill's purpose, perhaps she'd change her mind. Or, maybe all the women who were about to become forcibly impregnated by their Bodyguards, yet unable to obtain an abortion thanks to the new laws, wouldn't even matter to her.*

Letting go of the woman's hand, Cain watched her ass shake back and forth as she walked away. About halfway across the room, she turned and smiled flirtatiously at Cain. *Oh, definitely the latter. She couldn't care less about anyone other than herself.*

Cain shoved his hands into his pockets and rocked back and forth on his heels. Watching her leave the room, he flashed a condescending sneer. *For my entertainment, perhaps I should put her name on the list of volunteers to be targeted and impregnated by our Bodyguards. It might be good for her to feel empathy for another person before she is cast aside like the disgraceful human being that she is.*

Cain laughed at the idea of Miss Baker's dead body being tossed to the side of the room, after being used for their experiment. *Let's face it, our scientists are no closer to figuring out how to grow the super soldiers successfully in a womb without the fetuses developing deadly mutations. It also doesn't bode well that they end up tearing apart the mother from the inside out during birth.*

Cain sighed aloud as he walked confidently out of the large room's door. His back was straight, and an easy-going smile was plastered upon his face. "As the proverb goes, 'If at first you don't succeed, try and try again.'"

CHAPTER TWENTY-FOUR

A ten-year-old Damon sat across from his mother and his sister on the airplane.

To pass the time, his mother was teaching his five-year-old sister, Calliope, a handclap.

"You're going too fast," Calliope half-giggled, half-whined.

Their mother held her hands up to Calliope with an encouraging smile. "I'm sorry, my love. Let's try again."

Focused on her mother's hands, Calliope squealed as she wriggled with excitement. "Okay."

One of Damon's older brothers, Theo, was reading a book a few aisles closer to the front of the aircraft. His feet were scrunched up, and his knees were drawn up underneath his blanket.

Damon's oldest brother, Zachariah, punched the side of Damon's upper arm before he sat down in a seat across the aisle. "You're up."

"Zachariah..." their mother chastised while shooting a warning glance.

Rubbing his arm, Damon groaned as he trudged down the aisle. "Damn."

Once inside the tiny restroom, Damon shut and locked the door before holding his arm up in the mirror to get a good look at the red mark his brother had left. "Someday I'm going to kick your ass," he grumbled.

Without warning, there was a loud explosion, and the airplane jerked to the side, throwing Damon off balance. "What was that?"

The floor beneath him vibrated as the aircraft tried to maintain altitude.

Unbeknownst to the passengers, the propeller had torn through the bottom of the plane, and they were going down.

Slamming open the bathroom door, Damon emerged just as everything began violently bouncing up and down, including the passengers who weren't strapped in.

Falling to the floor, he landed on his stomach with a loud grunt. "Ugh."

Pulling himself up, Damon's legs shook as he clung to a headrest. He stared into the terrified faces of his family and prayed to the gods for the nightmare to end.

His mother was clasping a crying Calliope tightly against her chest, and as their eyes met, Damon recognized the terror written across her face.

Theo had dropped his book, and a panic-stricken screech escaped between his lips while Zachariah clung to the arms of his chair, his lips moving in silent prayer to the gods.

Above all the noise, he heard his mother shout, "Damon! Buckle up!"

Looking down at the seat he was clinging to, Damon pulled himself into the seat, and by the grace of the gods, he secured the buckle.

Immediately after pulling the belt tight across his lap, the aircraft fell into an uncontrolled nosedive.

Everyone aboard screamed, and as the lights flickered on and off, the oxygen masks fell from above. The yellow plastic pieces dangled in front of Damon and his family and they frantically grabbed for the straps.

Light-grey smoke filled the cockpit, obscuring the pilots' vision.

Pulling up on the yolk, the pilots struggled to see through the thick smoke as they tried to correct the plane's rapid descent into the Colorado mountains.

Accidentally activating their tannoy for the passengers to hear, the first pilot grunted, "I'm not sure we're going to make it out of this one."

The co-pilot coughed up the smoke from their lungs. "It's been a pleasure serving beside you in this life. See you on the other side."

Hearing the pilots talk of their mortality, Damon hyperventilated from behind his mask while looking at his mother for comfort.

Her arms were wrapped tightly around Calliope, and tears streamed down her face.

"Mother!" Damon yelled just before the aircraft crashed into the valley.

When Damon finally awakened, the sun had set, and the only light provided in the valley was the bright flames licking towards the sky from what remained of the aircraft.

With every inhale, a sharp pain stabbed through his upper right side. He gingerly poked at his ribs. *At least one is broken.*

Damon realized his left kneecap was dislocated while he was assessing his injuries.

Struggling to grip his patella, Damon exhaled loudly as he focused on maneuvering his kneecap back into place. "Ah, shit," he cursed with the sound of a *pop*.

He took a second to catch his breath before releasing the tight strap still in place across his lap. Falling sideways out of the chair, he took in the devastation surrounding him.

The aircraft had broken into four parts, the front of which had been destroyed upon impact. Dark smoke billowed high into the sky, sucking the oxygen from the air while casting a searing-hot ring around the objects that were still aflame.

Touching the side of his aching skull, Damon searched for his family. "Mother! Calliope!" he yelled over the sound of crackling fire. "Theo! Zachariah! Where are you?"

Damon climbed over a large metal part of the plane when he saw the first of his brothers.

Theo was lying on his back beside the demolished aircraft.

"Theo! Theo, don't move! I'm coming!"

As Damon hobbled closer, he saw a large object cutting into his brother, separating his torso from his legs. Theo's head was tilted at an unnatural angle, turned away from Damon with unblinking eyes.

Tripping over debris, Damon leaned to the side and vomited beside his brother's dead body.

With tears welling up in his eyes, he cried out for the rest of his family. "Zachariah? Mother? Calliope!"

Limping towards a section of the broken aircraft, Damon saw a darkened silhouette against the bright orange flames. "No. No. No…"

Zachariah never made it off the plane.

His charred remains hung halfway out the open doorway;

only recognizable because of the ruby gemstone embedded in yellow gold that still clung to his right ring finger.

Damon's heart raced, and his vision was overcome with black dots while he struggled not to pass out. He stumbled over his feet in a disassociated daze.

The ten-year-old scanned the terrifying scene before him, desperate to find his mother and sister.

In a fleeting moment of hope, Damon saw what looked like a woman sitting with her back against a detached part of the aircraft. "Mother," he breathed, sprinting over.

As he got closer to the woman, Damon collapsed. "Mother?" he asked cautiously, reaching out towards the two bodies.

His mother was propped up against a piece of the plane. Her head hung limp to the side, and her lips were parted with dried blood that had stained her chin.

The small girl was curled up in her mother's arms, lying across her lap. Half her face had been seared, and the arm that was closest to Damon was missing.

Damon's bottom lip quivered. "Calliope? Oh my gods, no." His hands hovered above his sister. "What do I do? What do I..." he cried out.

In her dream, Alessa stood alone in the middle of a dark valley.

Everything was black apart from the stars up above, and the dancing light spread across the valley. *What is this? Where am I?*

Walking hesitantly towards the bright flames, Alessa approached the wreckage. "Oh, shit."

Looking at a detached wing of an aircraft, she covered her mouth in horror. "That's an airplane. Or at least it *was* one."

Rounding the corner, Alessa realized there was a small child sitting on the ground, rocking back and forth with their head in their hands. Tiptoeing up behind him, she looked past the boy and saw a deceased woman and what Alessa could only assume was her child, cradled in the woman's arms.

Inhaling sharply, Alessa unintentionally alerted the child to her presence.

The boy jumped up and stumbled backwards.

"Oh, um." Alessa stepped forward, her hand held out to him. "I'm not going to hurt you."

"Who are you?" he demanded in a shaky voice.

Recognizing the boy, Alessa shook her head in disbelief. "Damon?" she asked, her voice just above a whisper.

Continuing to back away, he asked, "What did you say?"

Glancing down at the woman and child, the boy's entire body began to shake, and his legs gave out from underneath him.

Amidst the smoke and flames, Damon transformed into his adult self and lay his head down against his trembling arms.

***

"Shit!" Damon exclaimed, sitting upright in bed.

Breathing heavily, he stared at the sheets. Damon grabbed fistfuls of the fabric to ground himself. "You're safe. You're in the cabin. You're in your bed. It was just a dream; just a memory."

Damon exhaled before swinging his legs over the edge of the mattress. After grabbing an empty glass from his bedside table, he poured alcohol from a bottle into the glass.

After downing the liquid courage, he coughed due to the burning sensation. "I gotta see Sera about some pills, or I'll never make it."

While brushing his teeth, Damon stared into the mirror, suddenly confused.

Hold on ... was that Alessa in my memory?

Alessa's eyes sprang open, and she gasped while sitting upright.

Glancing around her room, she struggled to get her bearings. "What was that?" she asked while pressing a hand against her chest, in an attempt to calm her fast-beating heart.

With a shake of her head, Alessa stood up and, upon approaching her full-length mirror, she spoke to her reflection. "Was that real? It couldn't possibly have been. That would mean Damon was on the plane when it crashed, and he told me he and his older brother, Cassius, were away at training camp."

Convincing herself she had been hallucinating, her eyebrows raised, and she laughed under her breath. "There's no way that was real."

Staring at her reflection, she suddenly grew serious. "Right?"

CHAPTER TWENTY-FIVE

Alessa marched in through the double sliding glass doors into the medical ward, and then, after bypassing the empty patient beds, stepped into the sectioned-off room and froze.

Quade and Seraphine were leaning into each other, speaking in hushed tones.

Seeing her friend standing upright and healed, Alessa could not hold back her excitement. "Quade!"

Looking past his wife, he smiled. "Hey, you!"

Running up to Quade, Alessa wrapped her arms around his neck, and he picked her up. "Hey, me," he laughed.

"You look great. Are you ready to go to the festival?" Alessa asked while pulling away.

Quade scoffed and rolled his eyes theatrically. "I don't know what the big fuss was all about. He just nicked me."

Alessa raised an eyebrow, and the edge of her lips lifted in a sarcastic grin. "If you say so." Redirecting her attention to Seraphine, she pointed at her friend's swollen belly. "May I?"

Seraphine smiled. "Yes. Maybe you can encourage her to stay in until her father returns from the festival."

Alessa placed her hands on her friend's firm stomach and leaned in. "Hey, baby. This is your Auntie Alessa. I'm going to be your best friend once you make it earthside. I promise to always be here for you and to keep any secrets you tell me in confidence." She peeked up at Seraphine, who was glaring down at her. "Except if your mom needs to be clued in, of course." She leaned in and whispered to Seraphine's belly, "We'll talk more about that when you get here."

As Alessa stood upright, there was a knock on the doorframe.

They all three turned their heads to find Damon leaning up against the door. "Um, hi." He ran his fingers through his dark hair as he stood, unsteady, at the room's entrance.

Alessa's vision became hazy as an image from last night's dream resurfaced: Damon, as a young boy, was sitting amongst a broken airplane, surrounded by smoke and fire.

Breaking eye contact with Alessa, Damon looked at Seraphine. "Sera, you got those meds we talked about?"

"Oh, yeah." She hurried over to a wall-mounted cabinet and snatched a small bottle of pills off the shelf. "Only take one every four to six hours."

He grabbed the small orange bottle and turned to leave. "Got it."

Seraphine gripped his thick forearm, holding him in place. "I'm serious. Or else you risk putting yourself into a coma."

Damon scrunched his forehead while looking at her. "It's going to take more than a little alcohol and these to put me down." He held up the bottle before marching away.

"Do NOT drink alcohol with them!" Seraphine yelled at Damon as he hurried away.

"Ugh, that man is maddening," Seraphine huffed.

Alessa and Quade eyed each other suspiciously.

"What was that about?" Alessa asked.

Seraphine shrugged. "You know how Damon is with airplanes, and he wants to attend the festival, so—"

"He's drugging himself up," Alessa interrupted.

"Oh," Quade laughed. Smacking his hands together, he rubbed his tongue against the inside of his cheek. "This could be a fun airplane ride. You know how he gets when he drinks, especially when you mix drugs with the alcohol."

Alessa side-eyed Quade. "I know exactly how he gets. Sera, how could you think this would be a good idea in his frame of mind?"

Seraphine tilted her head, and shrugged nonchalantly. "I'm sorry, but I am not his keeper. Damon is a grown-ass man, and if he needs medication to help him deal, then so be it. I can only educate him on the side effects and how to take the medication properly. He's already been evaluated by psych and approved to go."

Quade wrapped his arms around Seraphine, holding her belly from behind. "It's okay, babe. Alessa and I will keep an eye on him. Right?" He stared hard at Alessa.

Absentmindedly, Alessa ran her finger along the space Damon's ring used to sit. "Do either of you know much about the way Damon's family died?"

Seraphine shook her head as she ran her hands up and down Quade's forearms. "Not any more than anyone else. Just that they died in a plane crash when Damon was a young boy."

Alessa bit her lower lip in contemplation. "And Damon wasn't in the wreck with them, right?"

Quade laughed incredulously, his arms bobbing up and down. "Of course he wasn't. He and his oldest brother were away at camp."

Intertwining her fingers with Quade's, Seraphine eyed

Alessa suspiciously. "Why do you ask? I thought you knew all of this already."

Alessa turned away from her friends, who were snuggling one another. "No reason. I—I should get back to the cabin and pack," she stammered.

CHAPTER TWENTY-SIX

The first newscaster flashed their pearly white teeth as they smiled widely. "In the past few weeks, there has been a decrease in reports of violent mobs in the United States."

A second newscaster adjusted themselves in their chair, behind a large wooden desk. "Some believe it is due to the containment efforts put forth by the government. Others speculate it is more sinister than that, and the mobs are mobilizing to strike—"

The first newscaster cleared their throat, interrupting the speaking individual's sentence, while glaring at them. "Which has proven to be nothing more than a speculation."

The second newscaster looked off to the side, behind the cameras, and their back straightened. "Uh, yes. I am—uh—Excuse me," they said nervously.

Rushing off the stage, they knocked into one of the cameras.

As it fell to the floor, the camera showed an angled shot of the reporter. Their muffled voice begged for mercy as they were manhandled by several large individuals in silver suits.

One of the silver suits lifted a pistol with a silencer attached and shot the newscaster straight through the forehead.

The bullet lodged into the camera's lens, and the image displayed the broken, spiderwebbed glass as the men frantically ran about, trying to end the broadcast.

"Kill the feed! Kill the—" was the last thing listeners heard before their television screens displayed colorful, noisy static.

CHAPTER TWENTY-SEVEN

Alessa, Camden, and Lexi marched towards the airplane with their luggage in tow.

Camden eyed the large aircraft. "Exactly how many Spartans are coming?"

"I was told about three hundred from our compound," Lexi responded.

"I'll take those." Camden grabbed hold of each of the luggage handles before approaching the Spartan who was standing near the exterior compartment at the rear of the plane.

Lexi looped her arm through Alessa's. "Is this your first time attending?"

"Surprisingly, yes," Alessa responded as they made their way towards the stairs to board the plane.

"Why is that? I've gone nearly every year; what with living so close and my father being a part of the—oh, I'm sorry. I didn't mean to sound like I was bragging," Lexi stopped talking.

"You don't," Alessa reassured her. Turning around to face Lexi, Alessa explained, "I guess I've either been on a mission when it's being held, or if I'm being perfectly honest"—Alessa's eyes darted between Camden and Damon staggering up behind him with a bottle of liquor in his hand—"I've never had a reason to go before."

Lexi eyed Alessa suspiciously. "Well, what's your reason now?"

Damon snuck up behind Lexi, and she could smell the alcohol on his breath before she heard him speak.

Damon smiled lazily at Alessa. "Hey, you."

"Do you have a second?" Alessa let go of Lexi and stepped off to the side, gesturing for Damon to follow.

He pointed at his chest with the bottle, pushing his chin down toward his neck. "Me?" he mouthed.

Tilting her head, she urged Damon to follow her. "Yes, you. Come here."

Wavering back and forth, he pursed his lips, trying to decide whether to follow Alessa or not.

Not giving him a chance to avoid her, Alessa grabbed Damon's muscular forearm and pulled him behind her.

"Whoa, there. There's no need to be aggressive." He half-grinned, tripping over his feet beside Alessa. Gripping his bag's handle, Damon tossed it onto his back.

Stopping a short distance away from those boarding the plane, Alessa glared at Damon. "The fuck are you doing?" Her eyes narrowed as she looked him over from top to bottom. "I have never seen you like this. Even when you were possessed, your appearance was never this disheveled. What's going on with you?"

Smacking his lips together, Damon shook his head. "Yeah—yeah. No, I'm okay. I just needed something to take the edge off." He glanced at the airplane.

Alessa followed his gaze. "Is it because of what happened to your family?"

Clearing his throat, Damon peered down at the ground. "Hmm—yeah, my family."

He tilted his head back and took a swig from his bottle.

Chewing the inside of her lip, Alessa glanced off to the side. "Damon," she sighed. "You weren't by chance on the plane with them—like, when it crashed, were you?"

Unmoving, Damon stared at Alessa, his face suddenly serious. "I've told you I was with my brother at camp. Why would you ask me—"

"Oh, um, I had this dream." She shook her head back and forth, dismissively. "It was bizarre of me to ask. Just—never mind."

Dropping his glass bottle to the ground, Damon reached forward and firmly grasped Alessa's wrist, pulling her close. "What dream?"

Camden appeared from behind Damon and smacked him hard on his upper back. "Hey, buddy. How you doing?" He walked around Damon as the force of his hit shocked Damon enough to let Alessa go. "You're not looking too hot," Camden pointed out. "You sure you're feeling good enough to go?"

Damon glared at Camden as the fist holding the handle of his bag pumped. "I'll be fine once we get there."

As Alessa and Camden made eye contact, she darted her eyes quickly to the right, signaling Camden to move off to the side.

Understanding her hint, Camden distracted Damon by taunting him a bit more. "You think you might be better off staying here? I'm sure Sera could use the company."

Damon dropped his bag and aggressively stepped towards Camden. "Where Alessa goes, I—"

Balling her hand in a tight fist, Alessa struck Damon in the neck just below the jaw, knocking him out cold.

Falling to the side, Camden caught Damon's head as it nearly struck the ground. "Damn!" he chuckled nervously, setting his head gently on the grass. "You knocked him the fuck out."

Alessa knelt beside Damon. Pressing her fingertips into his neck, she felt for a pulse. "Okay, he's good."

Quade ran from the plane. "What did you guys do to him?"

Camden put his hands up in front of his chest, defensively. "I didn't do a thing but prevent him from smacking his head on the ground."

Alessa shrugged. "He was getting belligerent thanks to him mixing alcohol with your wife's prescriptions, so I helped him take a nap. I still don't know what she was thinking."

Quade hollered back at several men from the plane. "I'm going to need some help!"

"Besides, Damon will do much better being unconscious for the ride there. Trust me, he'll thank me later," Alessa huffed.

Quade and the additional men lifted Damon onto a gurney. "Yeah, but couldn't you have knocked him out once he was already on the plane? This is going to make it significantly more difficult for me."

Alessa frowned. "I'm sorry. I saw an opportunity, and I took it. Cam, grab Damon's bag."

Camden's eyebrows scrunched, and he bent down to grab the handle before slinging it over his shoulder. "Like I'm tellin' you 'no' after seeing Damon hit the ground like a bag of rocks." He exhaled before walking back towards the plane. "We'd better get going. Lexi's saving us seats."

In her dreams, Alessa sat at the counter in a mom-and-pop restaurant, next to her sister, Kai.

The white-tiled walls were decorated with hundreds of vintage logos and smiling faces. The floors were laid in a black-and-white checkerboard pattern, and the cherry-red booths were filled with customers sporting poodle skirts and leather jackets with retro slicked-back hair.

"Mmm. This strawberry milkshake is delicious!" Kai exclaimed, wiping the pink drink from her lower lip.

Alessa cringed in disgust. "Any fruit and the word 'milkshake' do not belong together. Chocolate, vanilla, or peanut butter are the only acceptable options."

Shaking her head back and forth, Kai swallowed and smiled. "I'm starving, aren't you? I'm going to order us a couple of burgers and fries."

Suddenly ravenous, Alessa's stomach rolled and gurgled. "Uh, yeah, I guess so."

Looking around the restaurant, she realized the other customers' lips were moving, but no sound was coming out. "Kai, there's something strange going on."

Turning back around, Alessa gasped as her eyes landed on the worker behind the counter. His left eye was dangling from his eye socket, and the entirety of his right cheek had decomposed, exposing rotting teeth and jawbone.

Kai shrieked as he lunged across the counter, his teeth chomping together. Knocking him to the ground, she stomped the heel of her boot into his face, crushing his skull.

"What was that?" Kai asked, her chest heaving as she kicked his brains from her shoe.

Every patron in the restaurant was eerily straight-faced, pointing and staring at the kitchen window.

Alessa stood up from her chair and walked behind the counter, towards the large kitchen window.

"Alessa?" Kai hissed.

Slowly pushing open the swinging doors, Alessa peered in.

Near the freezer on the far side of the room, the kitchen staff was crouching on the floor.

Alessa tiptoed slowly towards them while holding her breath.

Noticing their heads bobbing inhumanely as they tore into something, she swallowed nervously.

The staff's animalistic noises echoed off the walls of the small metallic room, and a look of horror crossed Alessa's face as she held back the urge to vomit.

The restaurant staff were hunched over a human body lying on the cooler's floor. The victim's abdomen had been ripped open, and their intestines were being fought over.

The attackers' jaws hung, unnaturally wide, as they screeched at one another.

Alessa covered her mouth as she inhaled noisily, holding back the urge to scream.

The staff whipped around to face her. Blood dripped from their open mouths, and black spots were scattered throughout the whites of their eyes. "The Frenzied," she gasped.

Looking past the creatures, Alessa's jaw dropped as she recognized the victim. "Kai!"

She peered out the large kitchen window, where her sister had just been standing a few seconds ago, but she was gone.

Horrified, Alessa's head snapped back towards the group of Frenzied, and her mortally wounded sister was somehow sitting up, her guts spilling onto her lap.

Lifting her arm, Kai pointed ominously at Alessa and whimpered, "They're coming."

CHAPTER TWENTY-EIGHT

The veins protruded from Hades' neck as he shouted. "Nyx!"

Appearing out of thin air, Nyx stuck her leg out of her jet black, skin-tight skirt's slit and arched an eyebrow. "You summoned me?"

"Dreamsharing, are we?" Hades huffed, his fingers digging into the handles on both sides of his throne. "You're allowing Alessa to dreamshare with her dead sister?"

Scratching behind one of the three-headed dog's ears, Nyx shrugged. "And?"

Struggling not to lose his cool, Hades scowled. "You overstep. That has to be against the rules ... somehow."

Nyx's bright red lips separated as she laughed. "Since when are you concerned about rules? I know you've been whispering in the ears of the weak-minded, influencing their decisions to take away women's rights."

Hades flashed a wicked grin. "Indeed, I have."

Nyx's eyes narrowed, and her voice sharpened. "You do realize what this could mean for women? For humankind? You know what he has planned for those poor souls."

"Yes." He rubbed his hands together excitedly. Hades approached the stunning goddess of night in her black skin-tight dress. "It doesn't matter how it happens: with either the women's deaths or those resulting from the experiment's success, fewer souls will inevitably roam earthside, and more will be down here, making my job the highest-ranking position. My dominion will be the most coveted, and I will finally be the most powerful of all my siblings."

Nyx rolled her eyes and exhaled loudly. "All of this is over a power trip? Are you sure you're not a human man? Because you are one pathetic excuse of a god."

Hades growled, and his eyes flared. "How dare—"

The goddess of night glared at the god, smiling wickedly. "If you think I'm going to let the possible savior of humankind go down without a fighting chance, you are sorely mistaken. I will give her all the help I am allowed to give."

Alessa awoke with a start, and her eyes flew open as she sat up straight with a gasp.

Beside her, Camden and Lexi were playing a card game next to the window. "Shit!" Camden laughed nervously as he and Lexi jumped back.

Alessa stood up and pressed her hand against her chest. Feeling her rapidly beating heart, she stared suspiciously at her fellow Spartans sitting in their seats as she trudged down the aisle. Her nightmarish visions flashed before her, and she closed her eyes tight. *It was a nightmare. It isn't real.*

Feeling a firm tug on her elbow, Alessa spun around, prepared to fight.

"Are you okay?" Camden asked, his fingers holding firmly onto her elbow.

Alessa nodded her head disjointedly as she relaxed her balled fists. "Mmm-hmm. I—I, uh, just need to use the bathroom." Fighting back nausea, she licked her lips, willing the terrible visions from her mind.

"You sure?" Camden eyed Alessa, not believing she was okay for a second.

Prying her arm out of Camden's grip, Alessa headed down the aisle to the rear of the plane. "Yeah, I'll be right back."

Reaching the bathroom, Alessa locked the door before leaning against the sink. "You're not crazy. You're not crazy," she repeated to herself while wincing at her reflection in the mirror.

As the image of her sister's exposed abdominal cavity came to mind, Alessa bent over the toilet and vomited.

Wiping her mouth with a piece of toilet paper, she flushed her stomach contents into the belly of the plane.

She stared at her reflection and mumbled to herself, "The fuck was that about?"

"Alessa? Are you okay in there?" Camden pounded on the bathroom door.

Snapping back to reality, she grimaced. "Yes, I'm just, uh, using the toilet. Do you mind?"

After another minute, Alessa opened the door to find Camden standing with his back up against the wall and his arms crossed in front of his chest.

"What was that about?" he demanded.

Rolling her eyes, Alessa let the door slam behind her and turned away. Walking down the aisle to their seats, she huffed. "It's nothing, really. I mean, at least I hope it's nothing."

Lexi watched in confusion as Alessa and Camden's body language intensified.

Alessa tried to sit down, but Camden grabbed her by the elbow, holding her torso awkwardly in place as her bottom hovered above the seat.

"Ow. Damn, Cam. Let me go." Alessa glared up at him.

Camden's grip loosened a bit. "I will if you promise to tell us what the hell that was all about."

Quade snuck up behind Camden and squeezed in beside Lexi. "Well, this looks interesting. What did I miss?" He clapped his hands together, excitedly.

Sighing loudly, Alessa gave in. "Fine," she snapped, yanking her arm out of Camden's grasp.

Camden plopped down in the seat beside her, impatiently awaiting her explanation. "Well?"

Her three friends stared at Alessa as she tried to figure out a way not to sound certifiably insane. "Earlier, I was having a nightmare."

"We all know by now your dreams aren't without meaning," Quade remarked.

Lexi cocked her head to the side. "What was it about?"

"Um..." Alessa dug her fingertips into her temples. "My sister and I were at a restaurant when a waiter attacked her. After she fought him off, I went into the kitchen." Alessa paused, trying not to picture the gruesome dream's contents.

"And then what happened?" Quade asked.

Alessa swallowed before breathing in through her nose and then exhaling through pursed lips. "A bunch of the Frenzied were eating someone on the floor of the cooler." Alessa swallowed. "The victim turned into Kai."

Lexi's hand covered her mouth in disgust. "Shit, that's horrible."

Alessa snickered humorlessly while opening a bottle of water. "That's not all." She took a swig of the cool liquid.

Looking into Quade's eyes, Alessa found the strength to continue after a pursed exhale. "Then she sat up, looked straight at me, and said, 'They're coming.'"

Camden's head jerked to the side. "What kind of fuckery is that?"

Alessa's legs bounced up and down as her lips separated in a silent apology.

Quade reached forward, setting his warm hand on Alessa's forearm. "Do you know who she's warning you about?"

Alessa shook her head back and forth. "At this point, it could be anyone: Hades, Lucas, Cain..." Alessa tilted her head and deeply inhaled. "I mean, it could even be Brielle or—"

"The Frenzied," Lexi finished for her.

Camden's face scrunched up in disbelief. "There's no way those creatures are being controlled by something. They aren't capable of following instructions, right, Quade?"

They all turned their heads to look at him.

The Spartan sat back, putting his hands up defensively. "Whoa. I know nothing. Sera's only had the two in her custody for less than a week. That's not nearly enough time to gather enough evidence to say one way or the other. Let's just make sure we stick together and stay alert while we're in Greece."

"Agreed," said Lexi.

Quade winked at Alessa before changing seats to be beside her. "Could you try not to have any more doom and gloom premonitions?" he jested with a half-smile.

Camden switched seats to sit across from Alessa, and Lexi rested her head on the top of his shoulder before she closed her eyes.

Wrapping his arms around Alessa's shoulders, Quade

pulled her into a comforting embrace. "Take slow, deep breaths. We'll only be gone a few days; what could possibly go wrong?"

"A lot," Alessa scoffed.

CHAPTER TWENTY-NINE

Alessa awoke to the overhead announcement of their plane's landing in Greece. "Please wait until we come to a complete stop, at which point you can grab your personal effects and exit the airplane."

The sun shone brightly as the Spartans deboarded the aircraft. Camden and Lexi grinned enthusiastically as they playfully shoved each other back and forth while descending the stairs.

A traditionally dressed Spartan stood at the bottom of each of the airplane's stairs. "Welcome, fellow Spartans," their male Spartan greeter announced. "We look forward to spending the next week celebrating with all of you. First, regarding your sleeping quarters: everyone has an assigned bedchamber, which you can find on your wristband. Secondly, it is encouraged that you stay within the boundaries, as we don't want to bring unnecessary attention to the Official Fortress."

He scanned the gathering crowd of Spartans before continuing. "You have the day to do with as you wish, as the first day of the Hyacinthia Festival isn't until tomorrow.

There will be a constant supply of food and drinks, music and entertainment, and the scenery is ... well ... incredible." He nodded towards Alessa. "Soak it in while you're here. Enjoy."

Stepping to the side, he held out his hand, encouraging the incoming Spartans to move past him.

Camden peeked over Quade's shoulder at the projected three-dimensional image on his wristband, showing his room number and roommate's name. "Oh man, looks like you and me get to be roommates," he held up a hand for Quade.

"It's like they knew you'd need a babysitter." Quade laughed as he high-fived Camden. "I won't be able to party hard the whole time because I'll be working the second night, but the third night—it's on."

"Wanna check out our rooms?" Camden asked, excitedly.

"Sure," Lexi agreed. "We can drop our luggage off and then grab something to eat."

"It's like you can read my mind, Lex." Camden ran towards The Fortress, with bags in hand.

"Hey, wait up!" Quade yelled before chasing after Camden.

"You coming?" Lexi asked Alessa.

Biting her lip, Alessa looked at the water off in the distance. "Um ... I think I'll be up in a bit."

"You need some time alone?"

Alessa swallowed her emotions and, with tears in her eyes, nodded. "I think so."

"No explanation needed. Just know we're here for you." Lexi turned around to follow the men. "Say hi to your sister for me," she hollered back over her shoulder.

Wandering alone down a stone walkway, Alessa set down her luggage as she came to the edge of a cliff. She stared off into the distance, across the seemingly endless body of water, and she felt peace for the first time in a long time.

Tilting her head up towards the sun, Alessa allowed the heat to melt away her hardened exterior, and tears streamed down her face.

Blinking her eyes open, Alessa stared up at the wispy white clouds high above. "Oh, Kai. I wish you were here with me." She inhaled deeply, dropping her gaze to the cliff edge.

A light breeze caressed Alessa's cheek, and she wiped her tears away with a smirk. "Yeah, yeah. I understand what you're saying. You are here with me." Placing her hands on her hips, she smiled sadly. "But it's not the same," she said, her voice shaking.

Collapsing to her knees, she knelt, silently listening to the deep rumble of the waves as they bounced off the rock. Her shoulders slowly sagged, and she watched the waves ripple across the sea.

Alessa sighed aloud. "Quade and Sera were right. The waves may not be dramatically crashing against the cliffs, but this ... this is the most beautiful thing I have ever seen."

Two days later...

Damon lifted his hand to his head and groaned. Feeling the familiar tug of an IV, he blinked, trying to clear his blurry vision. "Where am I?"

"You're in the Official Fortress's infirmary," spoke an unfamiliar voice from across the room. The man was dressed in red and black medical scrubs while holding a tablet.

"Why am I in an infirmary? And did you just say the 'Official Fortress'?" Damon looked around the illuminated room. "We're not already in Greece, are we?"

The physician chuckled, pulling the tablet to his chest. "Yes, we are. You slept through the first day of festivities, which wasn't too much of a loss. It's always the most boring day of them all."

Damon's eyes widened. "How many days have I been unconscious?"

The physician side-eyed Damon as they displayed his three-dimensional chart in mid-air. "About two days, and I wouldn't say you were simply unconscious, more like dancing with death. You were very much on the edge of crossing over into Hades. Had your friend not told us what combination of alcohol and drugs you ingested, we may not have been able to counter their effects."

Damon pulled the IV from his skin and applied pressure using his light blue bedsheet. "My friend?"

"Yes. She came in several times to make sure you were still alive. She also admitted to being the initial cause of your being unconscious."

Damon laughed to himself, thinking back to Alessa punching the side of his neck. *Atta girl.*

"Without her intervention, you may have very well continued—"

"Yeah, I get it, Doc," Damon interrupted. Standing unsteadily, Damon eyed his leather jacket on the back of a nearby chair and his luggage in the seat. "Am I good to go?"

The physician's eyebrow arched. "What if I said no?"

Damon half-grinned while he jumped up off the bed. "I'd still leave."

The physician sighed, and he closed Damon's three-dimensional chart before returning his attention to the tablet in his hands. "That's what I thought. Just make sure you eat something soon. And I have to advise against any libations tonight. I finally got the drugs and alcohol out of your bloodstream; please don't end up back in my care so soon."

Grabbing his bag and slinging his jacket over his shoulder, Damon flashed a sarcastic grin. "Deal."

Entering the hallway, Damon collided with another man's solid chest.

"Ugh!" both men grunted in unison.

Looking up, Damon's face scrunched in recognition, and he dropped his jacket and bag. "Cassius?"

He had not seen his eldest brother since before he had been sent to the Colorado base. Cassius's light blond hair now fell to his shoulders, and his muted olive green irises bore an eerily familiar resemblance to their father's.

After a quick rub of his shoulder, Damon's brother grinned. "It's so good to see you."

They pulled each other in for a hug, and Cassius smacked Damon's back while in their embrace. "How are you doing now that you're no longer being controlled by that bitch?"

Damon scowled while pulling away. "You heard?"

Cassius rubbed the facial hair along his jawline. "Are you kidding me, brother? Everyone has. It's kind of hard to keep something that significant out of the mouths of Spartans."

Shrugging his shoulders, Damon exhaled loudly. "I guess so." Damon looked his brother up and down. "I didn't realize you'd be here."

"Who, me?" Cassius tucked his chin. "What would it look like if the next in line to become king of the East missed out on a celebration as big as this? I've been coming for years. It should be me asking what you're doing here." He stepped closer to

Damon, concern etched into his expression. "How'd you deal with the airplane ride?" Cassius asked in a hushed whisper.

Reaching down, Damon gripped the handle of his bag. "It was fine. I just finally decided to join in on the fun."

Cassius narrowed his eyes in disbelief. "Fun, huh? That doesn't sound like the Damon I know."

Damon flung his jacket over his shoulder. "Yeah, well, sometimes people change." He stepped to the side, trying to excuse himself. "If you'll excuse me. I need to get ready."

Cassius licked his bottom lip curiously, watching Damon walk away.

"Have you checked on Damon today?" Lexi asked as she and Alessa dressed for the second evening of celebrations.

Standing before the full-length mirror, Alessa let down her curled dark hair. "I did earlier. I'll go back after the night's festivities." She ran a brush through her loose waves.

Alessa's light cream-colored bodice plunged between her breasts, secured by the soft fabric strung up and over both of her shoulders. Thin golden ropes stretched beneath her breasts and across her abdomen, from one side of her to the other.

Clinging to her muscular frame, the ombré gown transitioned in a beautifully arranged pattern of light cream, black, and red. The raven black fabric wrapped around Alessa's waist before fading back to red and cream near the hem of her skirt.

Stepping her left sandaled foot forward, her pale thigh stuck out, revealing the high slit in the gown's skirt.

Alessa spun around, admiring the low-cut fabric that stopped just shy of her tailbone, exposing her back entirely.

"Almost ready?" Alessa yelled across the room.

Lexi opened the bathroom door, nervously smoothing down the sequins on the bodice of her emerald-green dress. "I think so."

Alessa's eyes widened, and her jaw dropped. "Um ... wow. Lexi, you look—"

Lexi threw her hands up in the air. "Ridiculous? Ugh. I knew it! I knew I shouldn't have—"

Rushing over to Lexi, Alessa grabbed her friend's hands. "No, I wasn't going to say that." Alessa tilted her head to the side and giggled. "I was going to say, incredible. Hades, you wearing that dress is making me question my sexuality."

Squeezing Lexi's hands, Alessa winked before grabbing her lipstick.

Lexi pressed a hand against her chest and blushed. "Really? You don't think it's too much?"

Alessa held the red lipstick in front of her lips as she looked back at the reflection of Lexi in the mirror that stood before her.

Lexi's sweetheart neckline was covered in what appeared to be vines stitched into the top layer, extending over her shoulders. Her bodice was see-through behind the vines that cascaded down the skirt, fading into the layers.

"I'd be shocked if you didn't turn a few heads." Alessa outlined her lips in red before coloring them in.

Lexi laughed nervously. "Um, no. I uh—I have to check something real quick. I'll be down in a few minutes."

Alessa smacked her lips together and placed her hand on the door handle. "You sure you don't want me to wait for you?"

"No, you can go on. I just had a thought, and if I don't act on it right now, I'll dwell on it all night. I promise I'll be right there. Go on."

Alessa stepped out into the hallway and, shutting the door behind her, she heard a man whistle.

Camden wrapped his arms around Alessa and buried his lips in the side of her neck. "You look incredible, my fiery one," he purred in his Russian tongue.

Pushing him away, Alessa beamed. "You are such a flirt. Everyone is going to look sexy tonight. This get-up is nothing."

Camden's eyebrows raised. "Oh, really?"

She looked the tall ex-Bodyguard up and down.

He wore a silver-and-white paisley vest over his long-sleeved white dress shirt and black slacks.

"You don't look too bad yourself." Alessa wrapped her arm around his. "Even if you are dressed too formally, in a few too many layers."

With a questioning glare, Camden cocked his head to the side. "You Spartans and your sex parties."

She grinned, knowingly. "Why don't we head to the celebration, and you can see for yourself?"

Camden glanced back at the closed bedroom door. "Isn't Lexi coming?"

Alessa pulled on his arm. "She said she's looking into something and then she'll join us."

Passing by the lit torches on the wall, Camden and Alessa made their way to the top of the large staircase. Releasing Alessa, Camden walked towards the railing as if in a daze. "Wow…" he trailed off.

The ceiling was painted in various shades of gold with a vast chandelier in the center, lined with traditional candles as well as electric ones.

There were close to four thousand Spartans in attendance, but only a few hundred lined the sides of the expansive room, drinking and laughing amongst themselves, whilst others danced to the music being played by the live orchestra.

The thousands of other Spartans were elsewhere, scattered amongst the grounds of the vast fortress, enjoying their night as the gods had intended.

Placing her hands on the railing beside Camden, Alessa sighed. "Breathtaking, isn't it? There are four things Spartans excel at: how to drink, fuck, throw a party, and fight."

A scantily dressed Spartan woman passed by Camden. Running a finger along his muscular forearm, she maintained eye contact while licking her lips.

Alessa's eyebrows rose as she giggled. "Point in case."

Clearing his throat, Camden turned away from the woman and blinked exaggeratedly. "I think I need a drink and a dance to get this night started off right."

Entertained by Camden's reaction, she smiled. "You got it."

Camden held out his hand, and Alessa placed hers atop his.

As he guided her down the stairs, Spartans were pleasuring one another in every corner of the room, and wine was being poured down the throats of others from a fountain with multiple spigots.

Scanning the expansive room, Camden cleared his throat as his neck flushed red. "You weren't kidding; this is quite the party."

Alessa chuckled while looking down at her feet as they stuck out from beneath her dress with every step.

"What? Back in Colorado, it didn't quite get like this."

"Oh, just wait," Alessa snickered. "The night is still young."

At the bottom of the stairs, Camden directed Alessa onto the dance floor. "Oh! I actually know this one."

Giggling, Alessa felt her tensions melt away with every step and sway. Camden wrapped his arm around her waist, spinning Alessa round.

Leaning into each other, they laughed light-heartedly as the song picked up pace and they raced to keep up with the other dancers.

Breathing heavily, Camden and Alessa ran from the dance floor, smiling as they each grabbed a drink.

A man whispered in Alessa's ear as she tilted her head back to take a swig of wine. "My wife's not here, interested in a dance?"

Nearly choking on her drink, Alessa turned to confront the man who dared to treat his wife with such disrespect. "Ah! Quade!" she squealed in excitement, wrapping her arms around his neck.

He pulled back, holding Alessa at arm's length. "Thought I'd snatch you up for a dance while I've been relieved from guard duty for a few minutes."

Alessa gave her drink to Camden before extending her hand towards her friend. "I'd be honored."

Camden looked as though he had been slapped in the face and huffed unhappily. "Sure, I'd love to stand awkwardly with two drinks in my hands."

After a few seconds of contemplation, Camden decided to go ahead and have fun without Alessa, and he downed both glasses of wine.

Setting the empty glasses on a table, he glanced across the way at three women who were eyeing him from head to toe.

Their eyes paused on Camden's groin, and after seeing his decent-sized bulge, the women grinned seductively.

CHAPTER THIRTY

As Quade and Alessa stepped onto the dance floor, the orchestra began to play the instrumental cover of "Just Pretend" by Bad Omens.

Standing in front of each other, they bounced their knees, impatiently awaiting the start of the dance.

Both stifled their laughter as Quade bowed ridiculously low while spinning his hand in an exaggerated circle. Holding their arms at a ninety-degree angle, opposite each other, they stepped forward, then repeated the move with the other arm.

Dropping their lifted hand, they clung to each other's waist, rotating in a circle to the beat of the music.

"It's been a while since we last danced," Quade remarked.

Alessa rolled her eyes while flashing a playful grin. "Yes, well, we've both been a little busy."

Breaking eye contact with the women across the room from him, who were becoming physically aroused, Camden set the empty glasses on the tabletop before stretching his neck to the side.

Glancing up at the orchestra, his breath faltered as his gaze landed upon Lexi descending the staircase.

Her modest, dark green gown looked out of place amongst the brightly colored fabric that barely covered most of the other Spartan women.

Camden watched Lexi as if in a trance as she moved amongst the guests.

Craning his neck, Camden moved further from the dance floor so he could watch her, making her way, unknowingly, towards him.

Finally meeting his eyes, Lexi's face lit up as she ran for him.

Wrapping her arms around his neck, she pulled him in close. "Oh, thank goodness I found you. This must be what it's like going to a high school reunion in the general population. I know everyone, but I don't like anyone."

Camden turned his face into her neck and inhaled her sweet scent.

Pulling away, Lexi stepped back and looked Camden up and down. "Let me get a good look at you."

Camden found himself at a loss for words as he stared at the beautiful Spartan.

"Well, I must say you clean up rather nicely. I didn't get to see you all dressed up at the last dance." She grinned.

Stepping forward, he placed both hands on her waist. "How tall are you?"

Caught off guard by his question, Lexi's eyes narrowed in confusion. "I'm five-foot-three. Why?"

His lips smirked lazily. "You are exactly one foot shorter than I am."

Her eyes darted off to the side rather than meet his intense stare. "Okay?"

"I'm just thinking about what that would mean, as far as acrobatics," Camden trailed, his voice husky.

Lexi's breathing hitched, and they slowly leaned into each other until her head was craned back as she looked up into his eyes. "Camden—"

"May I have this dance?" he asked, dragging Lexi onto the dance floor before she could respond.

Her mouth hung open in surprise as they joined the dancers mid-spin.

Lexi was amazed that Camden knew the choreographed steps, and as he took her in his arms, she leaned back into his firm chest. "How do you know what to do?"

"Alessa needed a distraction the week before we left, so I asked if she could teach me a dance or two in between your and my sparring sessions and my helping you research."

Lexi's cheeks flushed as jealousy coursed through her veins.

* * *

Following the other dancers trotting around the room in a giant circle, Quade grabbed Alessa's hand. "Is it just me, or have your feelings changed toward Damon?"

Not expecting Quade's accusation, her jaw dropped as her head whipped to stare at him.

"I'm known for being observant, but you do know you don't owe anyone an explanation." Quade gave Alessa's hand a gentle squeeze. "The heart wants what it wants."

Looking forward, unable to verbalize a coherent thought, she closed her mouth.

"I just want you to be happy and be taken care of. By whomever you choose." Quade glanced over at Camden.

Looking at Camden dancing with Lexi, Alessa sighed. "It's

not like that between us." Shaking her head back and forth, she stepped into Quade's arms. "It's hard to explain."

Quade gripped his friend's hand, bringing her closer. "Then don't. Just live your truth. It's your life, no one else's."

Alessa's cheeks blushed as she struggled to change the subject. "Speaking of lives, I cannot wait to meet your little girl. Have you decided on a name?"

Quade grinned as he thought about his pregnant wife and how he was about to become a father for the second time. "We haven't discussed names quite yet." He spun Alessa around before continuing. "I never imagined my life could be like this. A beautiful intelligent wife, soon to be two healthy children, gods willing..."

They stepped to the side, their feet moving in unison.

Alessa looked up into her best friend's eyes and sighed. "You're like the brother I never had. You've always been there for me, through thick and thin." Alessa swallowed, her skin growing warm with emotion. "I guess what I'm trying to say is, thank you."

Quade's smile faded as he pulled Alessa in for a warm embrace. "What do you mean *like* a brother?" He pulled away as they continued the dance. "For all intents and purposes, I *am* your brother."

Alessa relaxed into Quade's arms. "You know, you deserve all the happiness."

Quade smirked as he pulled her in for another spin. "As do you."

* * *

Damon approached the top of the staircase, looking intently for Alessa amongst the Spartan women, but only saw Cassius.

His dress attire was much less scandalous than his older brother's.

Sitting on a golden throne while both men and women draped themselves on and around him, Cassius was scantily clad in a decorated sheet. His glass was kept full of a dark red liquid.

Damon shook his head. Copious amounts of alcohol, no doubt.

The bottom of Damon's cream-colored long-sleeved shirt was rolled up, gripping his muscular forearms. His black leather strap wrapped around his back, just above his black slacks, and was designed to hold weapons across his chest. Listening to the orchestra, Damon spotted Alessa amongst the Spartans on the dance floor.

A flashback of them together at the dance back home at the Colorado base appeared before his eyes as he stepped down each stair.

Damon's feet hit the marbled floor of the lavishly decorated ballroom, and he craned his neck to the side. Moving through the crowd as if destiny were in control, he never lost sight of Alessa, watching her black, red, and cream-colored skirt float above the floor.

As the song transitioned into "Glow" by Livingston, Damon weaved in and out of the bodies crowding the sides of the room as he moved towards Alessa.

Spinning around, Quade's eyes met Damon's, and a non-verbal understanding passed between the men. With an imperceptible nod, Quade looked back to Alessa. After spinning her around, he stepped to the left, allowing Damon to sweep in and take his place on the dance floor.

Coming to an abrupt stop, Alessa smelled the familiar scent

of musk and cinnamon before looking up into Damon's deep sapphire blue eyes.

Her lips parted as Damon stood before her, as tall and handsome as ever.

Standing still, Alessa's breath escaped from between her lips.

Damon held his hand, and she hesitantly placed her hand atop his before he pulled her in close.

Placing her free hand upon Damon's shoulder, Alessa followed as he moved to the beat of the music.

Stepping to the side, their shoulders alternated pressing in and out, and then, mid-step, Damon pushed Alessa into a spin. Twirling her around while holding her hand above her head, she rotated a full three-hundred-sixty degrees. Alessa faced the tall Spartan once more, falling back easily into the procession of side steps while they leaned into each other.

Suddenly, every dancing Spartan stilled, and the leading partners kicked up their heels, Damon included.

Meanwhile, while bending her knees, Alessa lifted onto the balls of her feet and shifted her legs from right to left in a semi-circle.

After standing upright, she hinged backwards at the waist as Damon reached behind her while still holding her left hand.

Alessa fell backwards and leaned to the left as the fingertips on her free hand wrapped around Damon's muscular forearm.

Damon stared deep into Alessa's eyes as he pulled her close. Extending his arm, Damon let go of one of her hands, and as she stepped back, her torso rotated away from him.

Spinning to face Damon, Alessa fell against his defined chest. As she placed her left hand within his, he positioned his free hand on her lower back.

Stepping forward, Damon forced Alessa to walk backwards on the tips of her toes.

Their eyes never broke contact as he pressed her backwards, and their bodies moved in sync as they crossed the crowded dance floor until Alessa placed her palms against his chest, pushing him back.

Grabbing her by the wrists, Damon pulled Alessa back in, and she rushed forward as he turned to the side.

Encircling his neck with her left arm, she pushed up off the palm of his flattened hand with her free hand.

Holding Alessa firmly behind her back, Damon spun her twice in a circle, with her front leg extended horizontally and her back leg tucked.

The light fabric of her skirt flared up and out as they gazed longingly into each other's eyes.

As he set her down, her smile widened before he lifted her arm up and spun her around once more.

A few minutes later, as the song came to an end, Damon and Alessa breathed heavily as they stood mere inches apart.

His gaze dipped down to her lips while he licked his own.

Closing her eyes, Alessa wrapped her fingers around Damon's palm and pulled away. "I can't..."

Running off the dance floor, she burst through the double doors and onto the balcony.

Recognizing that she needed a minute to herself, Damon ran his fingers through his dark hair in frustration. He slowly walked over to the doors, awaiting the right time to join her.

Placing her shaking hand on her chest, Alessa inhaled the warm night air.

Whispering the third line of the Oracle's prophecy, she closed her eyes.

"Violence and rage shall threaten the world in the guise of a humanlike creature while a deception most keen must be severed unseen to secure the twin flames' future."

Her eyes opened wide, and she gasped. "The Frenzied. That's who the prophecy must be referring to, but who are the twin flames?"

Her mind darted back and forth between Damon and Camden. "It doesn't matter what my heart wants; I have to choose what the prophecy demands of me, or all of humanity could be damned."

With racing thoughts, Alessa paced back and forth across the large balcony. Her black, red, and cream skirt kicked up around her ankles with every step.

Blinking the tears from her eyes, she wiped them away with the back of her hand as they fell. "It's not fair!" Alessa shouted at the top of her lungs into the black waves. "It's not fair."

"Life isn't fair," a disembodied voice whispered from behind her.

She gasped. "Kai?" She sniffled as her head whipped back and forth, searching for the source of the disembodied voice. "Kai!"

Just below the furthest lit torch hanging on the outside wall, two people held each other in a tight embrace.

"Oh, shit. I—I'm sorry, I'll just—" she stammered, excusing herself, but as the person facing away from her, in the embrace, was flipped around, his back painfully struck the wall, and he grunted aloud.

The Spartan man's eyes were wide open, as was his mouth, hanging ajar in a silent scream.

As the person with their back to Alessa bit through the side of the Spartan man's neck, blood poured down the front of his shirt, and his entire body shook as blood gurgled from his mouth.

Alessa's eyes locked onto the man's familiar face, and she gasped in recognition. She instinctively sprinted forward while crying out, "Quade!"

CHAPTER THIRTY-ONE

At the sound of Alessa's scream, Damon's eyes activated silver.

Sprinting to the balcony, he snatched a smaller blade off the wall, beside the glass double doors.

The doors slammed open as Damon pivoted towards the gods-awful sounds and sprinted for Alessa, his blade held tight in the palm of his hand.

***

Without hesitation, Alessa stuck out her arm, wrapped it around the Frenzied's neck, and rammed her forearm beneath its jaw, closing off its airway.

Using all her strength, she pulled back on her right hand using the opposite arm.

After reluctantly releasing Quade, the creature clawed frantically at Alessa's arm. As she walked the Frenzied backwards, Quade collapsed in a growing pool of his own blood.

Her muscles strained as the creature's appendages flailed, desperately trying to rotate in Alessa's arms.

Its teeth gnashed together as Damon frantically sprinted toward them. "Alessa!"

Stepping between the fallen warrior and the creature, Damon lifted the knife and slammed it into its eye socket.

As he twisted the blade, the Frenzied froze for a moment before screeching. Screeching loudly, the creature ran at Damon.

Damon retracted the blade and yelled for Alessa to get out of the way. "Move!"

Releasing the Frenzied, Alessa ran around Damon to get to Quade.

He lay on his back, looking up at the night sky as deep red blood poured profusely from his wound.

Assessing his injuries, Alessa stammered, knowing how serious they were. "Oh—um..." She peered down at her skirt before bending over and ripping the fabric.

"Hold on. You just ... hold on. You hear me?" Alessa demanded while tearing the bottom of her skirt.

Falling to her knees, Alessa lifted Quade's shoulders up off the ground, and while holding him, she applied pressure to his neck.

Her irises glowed red as she peered deep into his brain. Focusing on Quade's microchip, Alessa forced it to release platelets and clotting factors. "This is not your time. Do you hear me?"

Even as she willed the microchip to produce as many anti-coagulants as possible, Alessa knew in her heart it would not be enough to reverse the damage.

Swallowing hard, she looked over at Damon, desperate for help, but he was still fighting the Frenzied.

Quade's eyes closed weakly, and he coughed up burgundy-colored blood.

Alessa's eyes flared brighter red as she struggled to keep her fear in check. "Oh gods, no. Please no. Your babies need you. Sera—Sera needs you. I need you. Don't leave us. Please don't do this."

Quade slowly opened his eyes, and his right hand reached up to touch the side of Alessa's face.

Holding tightly onto Quade, unable to hold back her tears any longer, Alessa broke down crying. "No, Quade, no."

Smiling sadly with tears in his eyes, Quade pressed his fingers against Alessa's cheek, and as the last remaining strength left his body, Quade's arm fell limp.

Blinking as his head turned to the side, Quade took a final breath before his chest stilled.

Kneeling on the ground, covered in her best friend's blood, Alessa shook her head back and forth in denial. "No—No. No, this cannot be happening."

Catching his breath, Damon turned around to find a Spartan man in Alessa's arms. "Fuck," he breathed while wiping off the bloodied blade onto his black pants.

Running to Alessa's side, Damon knelt beside her and reached for the man. Grabbing his shoulder, he lifted the male Spartan, and after recognizing his face, he inhaled sharply. "Quade!" He looked at Alessa. "How did this happen?" Damon scanned the balcony, panicked.

"I—I don't know. He was on guard duty before we danced. He must've just returned when—" she gulped.

Alessa lifted her friend's torso and rocked back and forth as she held him against her chest.

Damon glanced up at the top of the hill, and his eyes narrowed. *Do I see movement?*

Dashing over to the balcony, Damon peered over the edge and cursed. "Shit!" he muttered in Greek.

Hundreds of the Frenzied were running down the hillside and climbing up the deep grey stones on the sides of The Fortress. At least a dozen Frenzied littered the ground below after having fallen to their deaths.

"We've gotta go." Damon ran back to Alessa. "There's an army of the Frenzied coming. We have to warn the others."

She looked down at her friend. "What about Quade? We can't just leave him here."

Thanks to his microchip's adrenaline rush, Damon bent down and easily scooped Quade up in his arms. "Get inside! That's an order, Spartan!"

Wiping her nose as she jumped up, Alessa sprinted towards the doors. Yanking them open, she ran ahead of Damon and yelled into the large room. "The Frenzied are here!"

Every Spartan stared in shock at her blood and tear-streaked face, and her haphazardly torn skirt.

From his place on the dance floor with Lexi, Camden pivoted towards the sound of Alessa's voice.

Rushing inside after her, Damon looked for his brother. "Cassius!"

Cassius readjusted his robes and sat upright in his place on the throne with a look of bewilderment on his face.

Damon leaned back, holding Quade's limp body in his arms. "Activate the emergency protocol."

The room broke into chaos as partygoers ran frantically.

"Grab us weapons," Camden ordered Lexi. "Now!"

As the Spartans ran away from the exterior glass doors and windows, Camden pushed his way through the panicking crowd, towards Alessa.

Reaching back, Cassius uncovered a hole in the wall. Looking directly into it, a green light scanned his eye.

After confirmation of his identity, a red button appeared, and Cassius slammed his fist into it.

Alessa's eyes darted around the room, looking for anything to fight the Frenzied with. Noticing some of the Spartans darting over to the side of the doors where a collection of weapons lay against the wall, she followed suit.

Grabbing knives, Alessa stashed them in the tight bands wrapped around her thighs. *Good thing we Spartans are always dressed for battle, even during what was supposed to be a fucking celebration.*

After slipping one of the chest straps over her shoulders, Alessa secured several grenade-type weapons, a few more blades, and a deadly boomerang.

Alarms blared as Damon looked around the room for somewhere safe to hide Quade.

Realizing his brother was far too intoxicated to properly fight, Damon turned to him. "I need you to find shelter and take this man with you." He swallowed. "He is one of the fallen."

"What? No. I'm going to fight," Cassius slurred.

Damon glared at his older brother, not willing to back down. "You are the future of Sparta and are far too inebriated to fight. You need to put your pride aside and consider what would happen if you were to die tonight."

Cassius glanced nervously around the large room before accepting defeat. "All right. Give him to me."

Damon transitioned Quade's body to his brother's arms. "I'm sorry," he said to Quade, touching the red-soaked, sticky fabric, clinging to his friend's torso.

Finding a keypad on the wall, Damon entered a sixteen-digit passcode, and the lower half of the wall opened, exposing additional gear.

He snatched weapons of various sizes and secured them on his chest strap. After grabbing a powerful sniper rifle for himself, Damon secured a compound bow. He swung a large bag of specialty arrows over his shoulder.

Finally reaching Alessa, Camden grabbed her by the elbow and turned her to face him.

Alessa was void of emotion as she stared straight through him.

While looking down at the front of her blood-soaked dress, Camden grabbed Alessa's biceps and pulled her in close. "What happened? Are you injured?" Grasping the sides of her face, Camden shook her head gently.

Alessa glanced off to the side. "I'm fine. It's not my blood." She pulled away, continuing to grab weapons.

He shook his head in confusion. "Then whose blood is it?"

Placing her hand on a sword, Alessa stilled, and after a steadying breath, she responded. "It's Quade's."

His lips separated. "Was that who Damon was—"

Alessa interrupted Camden by handing him the sword. "We don't have time for this right now; any second, they're going to be coming in through the balcony. You and Lexi need to gather weapons and get into position."

The rest of the room was calming down as Spartans who were already geared up positioned themselves with weapons raised, facing the glass doors.

Camden sprinted for Lexi while Alessa hurried up the stairs to Damon, who was standing at the top.

With his chest held high, Damon held a compound bow out to Alessa. "Are you focused?" he asked, his eyes betraying concern.

With a curt nod of her head, Alessa inhaled deeply, and while grasping the bow, she took the ground quiver from Damon. "I am."

Damon handed her the bag of arrows. "We can mourn later, once we survive."

The whir of metal security doors descending from the tops of the exterior doorways vibrated through the marble floors and limestone walls.

Hearing the inhuman screeches coming from just outside the door, Alessa hurriedly plucked arrows from the bag and filled her ground quiver. "We're too late."

Damon aimed his rifle as Alessa nocked her arrow on the bow.

"They're here," he growled just before the first of the Frenzied crashed through the closed glass doors.

CHAPTER THIRTY-TWO

Shards of glass flew towards the first line of Spartans as they stood at the ready.

The Frenzied sprinted forward, and their inhuman screeching echoed throughout the room.

As their arms waved around haphazardly, Damon shouldered the butt of his rifle, and while looking through the scope, he shot one after the other, straight through the creature's foreheads.

Alessa joined Damon in the fight, releasing the first of many arrows. Each one struck a different Frenzied in the neck, the eye, the chest; before a tiny bomb exploded inside each arrow, tearing the creatures apart from the inside. But as each dead Frenzied hit the floor, another one pushed through the entrance.

Panicked shouting resonated throughout the building as the creatures gained access to The Fortress.

"You realize as soon as those doors slam shut, we'll be trapped in here with them," Alessa shouted over the commotion.

Damon smirked as he reloaded his gun. "We can handle them. Just as long as—"

Interrupting Damon, the thick metal doors jerked to a noisy stop.

"What the fuck?" he growled, his attention re-directing towards the frozen door blockades.

They glanced over to the side of the room where one of the Frenzied had typed in the secret code, halting the doors' closure.

Alessa's jaw dropped as she side-eyed Damon before gripping tightly onto her bow and her quiver filled with arrows.

His eyes widened, and his knuckles turned white as he sprinted away from Alessa. *How could they know? Only a handful of Spartans know that code.*

Positioning themselves to target the Frenzied as they fell in through the broken glass doors, they aimed at the incoming creatures on opposite sides of the staircase. Stretching their arms over the railing, Damon and Alessa shot one after another.

Alessa threw her grenade-type weapons in the thick of the Frenzied before chucking her boomerang, slicing through several of their skulls.

As the front line started to break down, Damon pursed his lips. *I need to find a way to get down there.*

Damon eyed Camden, who was fighting with his back to Lexi. *That's it!*

Damon extracted an experimental orb from his bag and focused on it, inserting the code into its core. "Camden!" Damon hollered, but the ex-Bodyguard couldn't hear him over the sounds of battle.

"Camden!" Damon bellowed, again, from high above.

Finally hearing his name, Camden peered up and shot

Damon a questioning glare. "I'm a little busy down here!" he yelled back.

"Put this in the hole in the wall!" Damon shouted, holding up the glowing orb and pointing behind Camden at the wall.

"What?" Camden shouted back in confusion.

Damon reared back, preparing to throw the orb. "Insert it ... into ... the wall!"

Camden yelled over his shoulder. "Lexi, cover me!"

After Damon released the orb, it sailed through the air, over the heart of the battle.

Stretching his hands up, Camden caught the hard, glowing orb and ran to the wall before shoving his arm in as far as it would go.

A gear-grinding noise began, and Camden snatched his arm out of the wall, backing up as he watched the glow intensify from the small hole.

Damon hollered and grinned excitedly as the code reactivated the doors.

The loud gears jolted back into place, and the thick metal door blockades began their descent once more.

Turning his attention back to the battle, Damon saw the Frenzied sprinting up the large staircase.

Looking across the room, he watched as Alessa used the last of her arrows to hold them back.

Panicking, he cursed in Spanish. "Motherfucker. I'll never get to her in time."

"Fuck you!" Alessa yelled, extracting two smaller, sharp blades that had been crisscrossed behind her back. Lunging forward, she sliced one of the shrieking creatures.

The Frenzied's mouths hung wide as if their jaws had been torn from their faces, and the whites of their eyes were now black.

Spinning around in circles, slicing them through two at a time, Alessa held back the urge to vomit as their putrid smell wafted into the air.

As their bodies piled up in front of her, the creatures continued climbing over the fallen, desperately trying to get to Alessa.

Damon stretched his hand up and over his back, locating the small grappling hook cannon that was tucked into the straps crossing his torso.

Raising the cannon, he aimed at the thick golden chain securing the large chandelier to the ceiling, and pressing the trigger, the grappling hook and the attached rope flew up into the air.

"Come on, come on," Damon urged while watching the Frenzied push Alessa further back into the railing.

As the metal hooks spun around and secured themselves to the chain, Damon sighed in relief. Pulling his arm protectors into place, he wrapped the end of the rope around his thick forearm before he jumped up onto the top of the railing.

Balancing precariously, he locked eyes with Alessa. While staring into her bright red irises, Damon pushed off the railing and jumped into the air.

Realizing what Damon was doing, Alessa pulled the shield from her back and pressed the trigger to expand its diameter.

After chucking her two blades one at a time into the skulls of two different Frenzied, Alessa held her expanding shield up as she dug the balls of her feet into the floor.

As the shield quadrupled in size, she strained against the weight of her attackers.

With a boisterous yell, Alessa pushed the shield forward, releasing it into the group of Frenzied, then she turned and sprinted for the railing.

Dangling by one arm, Damon swung across the room, over the battle taking place on the dance floor. As he began his ascent, he gripped the rope tightly with one hand, reaching out towards Alessa with the other.

At a full run, she jumped onto the railing and pushed off with one foot, launching herself into the open air.

Damon held his breath as he watched Alessa fall. *Come on, come on...*

As their bodies collided, they grunted in unison.

Wrapping his arm around Alessa, Damon pulled her in

close, and as they dangled from the rope attached to the chandelier, they clung to one another; their eyes locked in a smoldering stare.

Suddenly, a loud cracking noise came from above as they swung back across the room.

Tilting his head back, Damon cursed in Greek. "Fucking Hades."

The chandelier had snapped at the hanger loop and was barely hanging on.

"Move!" Damon shouted down at his fellow Spartans, who were in the path of the chandelier.

Letting go of the rope, Damon held Alessa against his chest with one arm as he pulled a small glowing orb from his chest strap and hurled it directly below them.

The chandelier lost its final hold and fell, quickly catching up to them. Every Spartan warrior on the dance floor lunged for the sides of the room as the chandelier fell.

The orb shattered against the tiled floor, and a plasma-like substance erupted, absorbing Damon and Alessa into its protective embrace.

Damon covered Alessa as the chandelier crashed down onto the top of the protective goo, and the metal bent around the exterior of its protective casing.

Camden grabbed Lexi and shoved her behind him, putting himself between the projectiles flying off the chandelier and the Spartan woman.

The metal door barricades were about a foot off the floor, but the Frenzied were still frantically crawling in, one after the other.

Their blood-curdling shrieks intensified as the heavy doors held them in place, crushing their skulls.

Cassius hollered from the top of the staircase, yielding a large sword, "Barricades are in place!"

Amidst the chaos, Damon and Alessa stared deep into each other's eyes.

Feeling the mixture of excitement and arousal, Damon's eyes drifted down to Alessa's full lips, and he couldn't help but lick his own.

"Damon! Damon!" Cassius bellowed as he fought his way to get to his brother.

Snapping back to reality, Damon looked up at Cassius; his eyebrows furrowed in confusion.

"Barricades are in place!" Cassius repeated while fighting off more of the Frenzied.

Looking at the hole in the wall, Damon grabbed Alessa's hand, and they ran. Stopping in front of the hole, he instructed, "Keep them off of me."

Spinning around, Alessa plucked a sword from a fallen Spartan and raised the weapon to block an attacking Frenzied.

As Damon entered another code, the little red light scanned his iris, confirming his identity.

After a good thirty seconds of Alessa fighting off the Frenzied, a whooshing sound was heard, immediately followed by a thunderous echo of screeches from outside the walls.

The Frenzied on the inside of the Fortress stilled all but their necks that craned towards the blood-curdling noise.

"What is that?" Alessa covered her ears, along with the rest of the Spartans.

Damon yelled over the inhuman shrieks. "Any Frenzied within a quarter mile of here is being burned alive."

Snapping out of their stupor, the creatures tilted their heads back and shrieked simultaneously before returning to the fight.

Uncovering her ears, Alessa picked up a nearby sword from a fallen Spartan, and as a Frenzied eyed her, it charged.

The creature's jaw hung in an unnatural angle as it lunged for Alessa.

Slicing its head clean off, she breathed heavily as the creature collapsed.

Damon grunted before one of the Frenzied tried to bite him from its place on the floor. "I really wish right about now they had microchips you could blow up."

Standing still, Alessa thought back to the conversation in which Quade had mentioned another way to possibly take the Frenzied down. "There is something I could try."

Sending out an invisible wave to gather information on the technology present in The Fortress, she recognized the familiar hum of electronics inside each and every one of the creatures' hearts. Alessa's eyes sprang open. "Cam! Lexi! I need you!"

Hearing her cry for help, Camden and Lexi swung their weapons as they hurried towards Alessa and Damon.

"What is it?" Camden asked breathily.

Alessa's eyes darted around the room. "I think I can stop them, but I need your help."

Lexi grunted as she deflected an attack. "Anything."

Alessa nodded her head in gratitude. "I need you to keep them off of me. I'll be helpless as I focus."

Damon sliced through the arm of an incoming attacker. "As you focus on what exactly?"

Alessa squeezed his bicep, reassuringly. "Just trust me."

Turning away from Alessa, her friends formed a protective circle as she closed her red eyes and exhaled.

Sending out another invisible wave, Alessa began to violently shake as she collected information on the locations of all of the Frenzied's pacemakers.

Opening her eyes, the Spartan warrior had glowing, speckled yellow fragments floating in her bright crimson irises, and blood began trickling down from her right nostril.

Ignoring the excruciating pain radiating throughout her, Alessa pictured the pacemakers inside of their chests exploding, and as she screamed in agony as every one of the Frenzied dropped dead.

After the creatures' bodies hit the tiled floor with a simultaneous booming thud, an immediate eerie silence ensued.

Alessa's eyes rolled into the back of her head, and as she fell unconscious, Damon spun around and lunged for her.

"Alessa!" he grunted as she collapsed into his arms.

Camden's jaw dropped as he scanned the room. "What the hell just happened?" The ex-Bodyguard glanced down at Alessa. "Is she okay? Did she do that?" he asked, tilting his head at the dead Frenzied littering the floor.

Damon held her unconscious body tightly against his chest. "I think so."

Lexi wiped the back of her hand across her forehead, smearing bright red blood. "We need to get her to the infirmary."

Camden glanced over at Lexi and winced. "She's not the only one." He placed his hands on either side of her face and pulled her in for closer inspection. "You need to get that cut looked at. It's pretty deep."

A slight blush popped up across Lexi's cheeks, and she ushered them up the stairs to the infirmary.

CHAPTER THIRTY-THREE

Alessa peered down at her elaborately beaded crimson gown. "What is this?" She fingered the decorative gems while scanning The Fortresses' pristine ballroom.

The tables weren't turned over anymore, the drinking glasses hadn't shattered, the weapons hung from the walls, untouched, and the floors weren't slippery with blood.

It was as if tonight's battle hadn't occurred.

Holding her white gloved hands up in front of her, she squinted in confusion. "What in Hades is going on?"

Standing across the large room was a familiar Spartan warrior, dressed in a suit and sporting a sad smile.

She held one hand up to her mouth in surprise. "Quade?"

Without a moment's hesitation, Alessa sprinted across the dance floor and leaped into her friend's arms.

"Quade! I'm sorry. I'm so sorry," she sobbed into his chest as he stroked the back of her hair, reassuringly.

Stepping back, she looked up at him. "What am I supposed to tell Seraphine? And Soren?"

Regaining consciousness, Alessa panicked as Quade's outline became hazy. "Quade, come back!"

While fading into the darkness, Quade muttered, "Don't blame yourself; it was my destiny to protect you."

Alessa sprang upright in bed while shouting her friend's name. "Quade!"

Shaking the fatigue from his shoulders, Camden stood up from the chair in the corner of the room. "I'm sorry, no." He walked to her bedside. Sitting down beside her, Camden grasped Alessa's hand. "He didn't make it. Remember?"

Staring straight ahead, Alessa snatched her hand back. "Yeah, I remember." Her eyes grew wide in a panic. "Is Lexi okay? Damon?"

Camden pretended not to be offended by her reaction and rubbed his hands up and down his thighs. "Uh, yeah. They're both good. Lexi got a cut on her forehead, but it's already been looked at. After receiving treatment, it's close to being healed already."

Alessa yawned while rubbing the sleep from her eyes. "How long have I been out?"

Camden rubbed his chin where a five o'clock shadow had appeared. "Almost an hour."

"What?" she demanded, throwing the bedsheets off her legs. "My people, they need help—"

"You did help them," Camden interrupted, holding her in place. "Don't you remember?"

Alessa struggled against his grip. "What could I possibly have—"

Camden moved his hand to her shoulders, looking her

straight in the eyes. "With your technopathic abilities, you fried every one of the Frenzied."

Remembering the agony that had filled her skull while the light burst from within her, Alessa winced. "Oh, yeah. Uh, I did."

Camden smirked while looking into her piercing blue eyes. "I guess practicing really has paid off. You did good, Spartan."

"Okay, but I really do need to get up and help my fellow medics. There isn't an endless supply of trained professionals here, and I'm sure those that have already been working are getting tired."

Camden sighed and stood up from the bed. "There's no talking you out of it, is there?"

Alessa stood up in front of the tall ex-Bodyguard and grinned. "Have you ever known me to back down?"

Over the next five hours, Alessa and the other medically trained Spartans worked nonstop to stabilize the wounded.

Those who were unable to be saved were held and sung to as they transitioned into the underworld.

Searching for Alessa, Damon peered into each room as he walked quickly past them, but upon hearing a familiar melody, he stilled.

Alessa was gently rocking a mortally wounded Spartan warrior back and forth while humming the song he had taught her years ago.

The injured Spartan's chest rose jaggedly, and blood was pooling beneath them, soaking into the towels.

Stepping into the room, Damon grabbed several fresh towels off a rack that had been pushed into the corner.

"Here, let me," he crouched down before Alessa and the wounded warrior.

With Alessa's help, he propped the Spartan up onto their side and replaced the towels that had been soaked through.

"Thank you," Alessa whispered.

She looked down at the gravely injured Spartan and attempted to comfort them. "You did well, Spartan. Be at peace now."

While Alessa ran her fingers through their hair, the gravely injured Spartan gasped for breath one final time before their body went limp in her lap.

"That's seventy-two," she sighed, gently moving the body onto the floor.

Not knowing how to bring up Alessa's dreamsharing with him, Damon swallowed hard before speaking. "I know this might not be the best time, but we really need to talk about—"

Alessa waved her hand dismissively. "Whatever it is can wait. I can't deal with anything else right now. If I allow myself to feel the weight of what's happened, I won't be any use to anyone."

Damon rubbed his hands on his legs and pursed his lips together. "Got it."

The doctor on-site rushed past the doorway, pushing a gurney with a patient on it. Holding their wound together with his bare hands, he shouted into the room. "We need all the help we can get!"

Alessa jumped up and darted towards the door before she yelled back at Damon, "Make sure the body is looked after."

Watching Alessa run from the room, Damon pursed his lips together in frustration.

A memory played inside Damon's mind, of his mother, his sister, and him sitting in front of a large body of water.

His mother was braiding his younger sister's hair while she was sitting on a log behind the girl. "You are still young, my boy, but someday you won't find love so distasteful."

Damon threw a rock, and it skipped across the surface of the lake. Watching the rings of water spread, he huffed. "I want nothing but to be a warrior."

A smile spread across his mother's face. "Your wants and needs will change throughout your lifetime."

Damon picked up a smaller rock and tossed it into the water, yet again. "I guess dreamsharing sounds pretty cool."

"Ah ... You have been listening to your elders' stories." She swallowed before looking out across the water at the colorful sunset. "There are many different types of love, but dreamsharing is very rare in that it can only be achieved by soulmates."

The word 'soulmates' repeated in Damon's mind as he picked up the fallen warrior and walked out of the room.

A few hours later, the Spartans were all departing, heading back to their homes.

Damon, no longer plagued by anxiety, sat with higher-ranking Spartans toward the front of the airplane, while Alessa sat near the back with Camden and Lexi.

Knowing Quade's body lay all alone in the rear of the plane made Alessa queasy.

With the announcement of the airplane's imminent landing, Alessa closed her eyes as her heart sank. *I'm going to have to see Seraphine brokenhearted. I wonder who broke the news to her since I was busy tending to the wounded.*

With the airplane's landing, Alessa jerked forward, and she gripped the arm handles on either side of her seat.

Noticing Alessa's distress, Camden laid his warm hand atop hers and lightly squeezed her fingertips.

Alessa's lips lifted at the corners, grateful for his grounding her when she needed it most.

As the plane stopped moving, the Spartans sat in silence, awaiting the go-ahead to begin unloading.

The pilot's voice boomed from the speakers, ordering them to their feet. "Please stand in reverence of the fallen."

Exhaling a shaky breath, Alessa joined the other Spartans who were already standing at the ready to honor those who had fallen.

Silently, they watched the seventeen body bags be pushed down the aisle towards the plane's exit.

As the last of the bags passed by the front rows, Damon stepped into the aisle, excusing the last bag's escort, and took their place.

Alessa choked back tears, realizing whose bag it was. *Quade.*

The remaining Spartans turned their attention to Alessa and bowed their heads in unison.

After a moment's hesitation, Alessa understood that she was being allowed to be the first one to disembark from the plane after her best friend's body.

Squeezing Camden's hand, she left her seat and followed the black bag outside. Alessa held her hand up to shield her eyes from the bright, late afternoon sun, and her gaze landed upon Seraphine.

She stood at the front of the crowd, red-eyed and with a swollen belly still occupied by her late husband's baby.

Seraphine eyed her husband's body bag as it was carefully

carried down the stairs. As were the rest of the bodies, Quade was set atop a moving table and moved toward the individual mourning families.

Little Soren held tightly onto his mom as she lifted his fingers to her lips. Tears streamed down her cheeks as she kissed the back of his hand.

Quade's escorts pushed his wheeled table, stopping in front of Seraphine before respectfully backing away.

Pulling the zipper down, Seraphine exposed her husband's pale face, and as her gaze landed upon the mortal wound on the side of his neck, she squeezed her eyes shut. Tilting her head back, Seraphine's eyes raised to the heavens, and her mouth opened, releasing a gut-wrenching cry.

Alessa felt her knees buckle, but was caught by two strong arms from behind.

"Don't let her see you like this," Damon whispered in Alessa's ear. "Her husband just died. You need to be strong for Sera."

Alessa nodded imperceptibly. *Damon's right; this isn't about me.*

Exhaling through pursed lips, Alessa found her footing before descending the stairs.

She approached Seraphine, stopping directly in front of her. Looking into her friend's tear-streaked face, Alessa's voice cracked with emotion."I—I'm so sorry. I failed Quade. I failed you—"

Seraphine lunged forward, wrapping her arms around Alessa's neck. "Shh. You did no such thing." She held Alessa at arm's length and smiled sadly.

Alessa cleared her throat, trying to keep her emotions in check. "Would you like some help preparing—"

Seraphine shook her head adamantly. "No. These are the last moments I will have with my husband. I wish to be alone with him." Seraphine peered over her shoulder at the Spartan warriors standing united behind her. "I'll have Chambers stand guard just outside the door for any heavy lifting." Seraphine absentmindedly rubbed her pregnant belly.

Staring at her friend's moving hand, Alessa swallowed the lump that had formed in the back of her throat. Looking one last time at Quade's face, Alessa's vision began to tunnel.

"Let's get moving," Seraphine instructed Chambers before she squeezed Alessa's hand. "I'll see you tomorrow at the ceremony."

Alessa pressed her lips together into a straight line. Watching her best friend walk away beside her dead husband, she could feel herself starting to hyperventilate.

"Run. We'll follow," Camden whispered into her ear from behind.

Alessa bit down on her lower lip, turned on her heel, and darted into the woods.

Sprinting around the trees, she jumped over the fallen logs as her pounding heart threatened to jump out of her chest.

Alessa's lungs burned with every inhale, and upon reaching the edge of the cliff, she came to a screeching halt. Staring out across the beautiful landscape, she balled her hands into fists.

Alessa felt herself close to losing control as tears poured down her face and her eyes flickered red.

Falling to her knees, Alessa's body shook as she crossed her arms across her chest.

Camden fell to his knees before Alessa. Wrapping his muscular arms around her, he buried his face in the crook of her neck.

Lexi came to an abrupt stop, her chest heaving from having run so hard. "I hope ... it's okay ... that I—"

Alessa reached an arm up for Lexi and pulled her down. Trembling, Alessa held her red-haired friend with one arm while Camden kept her grounded in his. "Yes, I need all the help I can get."

Lexi squeezed Alessa tight. "We're here for you."

***

With every fiber of his being, Damon resisted the urge to chase after Alessa. Knowing he needed to report on what happened in Greece, he stayed put—his hands clasped tight together behind his back.

His father strolled his way, concern etched into his aged face. "Damon, you're alright then." He glanced at his son from head to toe. "Good, that's good. We're looking forward to hearing from you, as the information we've gotten so far is sketchy at best."

Forcing himself to move, Damon stepped forward, marching beside his father to the intelligence center.

"We did finally get some video confirmation of what happened. For some reason, it isn't good quality and is poorly pieced together, but it's better than nothing."

Damon faltered for a moment. "Do you have footage of"—he cleared his throat—"Quade being attacked?"

Damon's father turned to look at his son. "We do. But if you'd like to—"

Damon shook his head adamantly back and forth. "No, no. I need to see what happened. Do we still not know how they got past our security or how they gained access to The Fortress?"

His father sighed and placed his hand on Damon's shoulder. "That's the thing. Nothing was out of place. There are rumors someone has infiltrated the Spartans and gained access to sensitive information, but we can't pinpoint the perpetrator."

"I see." Damon entered the smaller room inside the building where a handful of Spartan High-Borne Wellborns stood before a collection of monitors.

"Sir. Damon," the speaker acknowledged their presence before starting the video feed. "This is the footage captured from last night's attack. Prepare yourselves."

Standing next to his father, Damon inhaled a shaky breath, his fingernails digging into the palm of his hands.

Indistinguishable screams were heard in the background as the video played. All eight guards, bloodied and dead in various positions, were strewn about the room.

The image blurred before jumping to Damon's brothers' quarters, where it showed him slam his bedroom door shut behind him and stare at his reflection, no doubt willing his microchip to burn off the alcohol he had consumed so he could join the fight.

"Is there a camera in the descendant's suites?" Damon asked, surprised there was a camera in any of the bedchambers.

His father shook his head and flicked his wrist dismissively.

Suddenly, the center monitor displayed a dark picture of the balcony. "Quade..." Damon mumbled, stepping closer to the screen.

Watching Quade, alive and standing next to the railing, was strangely cathartic. He waved at another guard who had been positioned near the wall. He must've been giving them a break. *Wrong place, wrong time, man.*

Damon sighed, knowing the video was about to take a turn for the worse, and there was nothing he could do to stop it.

He could tell Quade had heard something by the tilt of his head and his change in attentiveness. The warrior leaned over the railing before jumping back to grab weapons from his chest strap.

Quade threw several of his blades down the side of The Fortress when a group of five Frenzied snuck up behind him.

Damon stepped forward in a desperate attempt to turn back the hands of time and save his friend.

Utterly helpless, he watched Quade be attacked and surrounded by several Frenzied. The Spartan warrior fought off four of the five, throwing them from the balcony, until suddenly Alessa's outline appeared on the screen.

As she ran to the opposite side of the balcony, the final Frenzied whipped around, prepared to lunge at her, when Quade grabbed the Frenzied in an unfortunate manner that allowed them to twist around in his arms.

Knowing what was about to happen, Damon's breath hitched, and his stomach twisted in knots.

Alessa whipped around, holding out her hands apologetically, until she realized someone was being attacked.

Her face fell as she cried out for Quade, and the scene transitioned to another view of the attack.

Removing a hand from his hip, Damon wiped the tears that clung to his eyelashes and exhaled slowly. *Quade sacrificed himself to save Alessa.*

As the footage of the Spartans' massacre continued playing before the group, Damon cleared his throat. "Any idea who's behind the attack?"

The entire room stared at him in silence.

"We are all in agreement that this was an attack, correct?" Damon huffed angrily. "I mean, not a hell of a lot of people are capable of seeing the Official Fortress in Greece, let alone knowing its exact location, how to get in, and when we'd all be there."

Damon's father placed a hand upon his shoulder. "We have already begun looking into who had security duty, knew all of the codes, everything necessary for this type of aggressive maneuver."

Damon pivoted on his heel. "Has Lucas or Cain been considered the primary aggressor?"

Damon's father cleared his throat. "I'm not sure how they would be capable of something like this. Cain is simply a senator now, and Lucas is still in hiding."

Reaching behind himself, Damon massaged the knots in the back of his neck. "Come on, now. We're smarter than that. From what I've been told by Sera, they suspect Ambrosia is the cause of the Frenzied, and not only did they know the code to stop our safety doors from closing, but at least one of the creatures was coherent enough to follow orders. We haven't seen that level of intelligence thus far from a Frenzied."

Damon turned to the man sitting at the computer and pointed a finger at him. "That reminds me, every single password should be changed."

"On it," one of the other High-Borne Wellborn Spartans agreed before exiting the room with three others.

Feeling his skin begin to crawl, Damon excused himself. "I need to seek solace. I'll be unavailable for the rest of the night."

He bowed out the exit door before running, alone, to the rock wall.

Slowing down, Damon tore his black and red fitted iron

chest plate and his black compression shirt from his torso and threw them into the grass and dirt. Snatching up the small pack full of chalk, Damon secured the strap around his waist before pulling himself up onto the rock with a loud grunt.

His eyes activated silver as he climbed higher, and as his adrenaline coursed through his veins, sweat dripped down his forehead and onto his chest.

Visions of Quade's smiling face flashed before Damon's eyes as he struggled to maintain focus. "You don't have a choice," he said through gritted teeth. "You have to do this. For Quade."

He peered up at the remaining fifty feet of the wall.

His muscles had begun to shake from exhaustion when the memory of Alessa jumping from the balcony into his arms manifested in his mind, and he got a much-needed boost of adrenaline.

Pulling himself up inch by inch, Damon caught a glimpse of the top edge of the wall.

With a wild grin, he stuck his fingertips into the chalk before reaching out sideways for the best way to the top.

Pushing off to the side, he grabbed the rock, nearly losing his grip before his other hand grasped a sharp edge jutting out from the wall.

"Whew," he laughed nervously, dangling from the top of the one-hundred-fifty-foot wall. Damon's muscles strained as he reached up and over the edge, grabbing hold of a root of a small tree.

Hoisting himself up and over, Damon rolled onto his back, looking up into the sky, which had transitioned from day to dusk.

Breathing hard, he lay with his legs straight and arms splayed for a good five minutes.

Finally pushing himself into a sitting position, Damon stared at the brightly colored sky; its vibrant reds and oranges blended into the dark pink and purple hues.

Tears quietly streamed down his face, and Damon's lips lifted ever so slightly into a pained smile. "We made it, brother. We finally made it."

CHAPTER THIRTY-FOUR

The following afternoon, after getting dressed for the fallen Spartans' farewell ceremonies, Alessa stared at her reflection in the full-length mirror. Her fingers slid down the front of her warrior's uniform as she mindlessly caressed the corset's boning.

Closing her eyes, she pictured Quade's smiling face, and with the gut-wrenching realization she'd never see him earthside again, tears fell down Alessa's face.

She thought about Quade's unborn daughter and her heart broke thinking about how she'd never know the warmth of his touch or experience his contagious smile. His baby would only experience her father through pictures and stories passed on by his loved ones.

Alessa jumped with the sound of knocking on the door frame.

Looking in through the open door, Lexi asked, "Are you ready?"

Alessa wiped her tears away and shook her head back and forth. "No, but this isn't about me. Sera and Soren need us to be there. And the rest of the fallen Spartans deserve our respect as well."

Camden strolled up behind Lexi, securing his cuff buttons. "Your elder has gone to join the others."

Alessa blinked away her remaining tears and exhaled through puckered lips. Gathering herself, she buried her raw emotions before brushing past Lexi and Camden.

As they emerged over the hill, Camden's breath was taken away by the sheer volume of people standing in the grassy fields. "Fuck me," he muttered in Russian.

Thousands of Spartans stood tall before the fallen warriors who lay on their elevated wooden planks, their bodies cleansed and wrapped.

Camden leaned down, above Lexi's head, and whispered, "I never realized how many Spartans were living at this one compound."

Lexi whispered back, "At any given time, there can be five to fifteen thousand living at each compound. I'd say we're close to eight thousand right now. Just so you know, when we get down there, I'll need to go with Alessa to the section of warriors to show our respects. You'll be expected to stand off to the side, over there." She pointed to a group of Spartans.

Camden's eyes narrowed as he stared at those standing away from the warriors. "Who are they?"

Lexi dropped her arm. "They're the Spartans whose primary isn't battle. The teachers, scientists, and everyone else who help make our communities run smoothly."

Nervous about leaving Alessa, Camden glanced over in her direction.

Lexi squeezed his hand. "She'll be surrounded by her people. Nothing's going to happen to her."

Alessa's heart rate increased as she stared at the fallen. *You can do this.*

"Alessa?" Lexi asked. Holding out her arm, she pointed towards the large group of warriors.

Alessa marched in front of Lexi, weaving in between the other Spartans as if in a daze. Reaching the front of the warriors, Alessa saw Seraphine holding her son's hand. She swallowed hard and urged herself to stay calm. *Don't lose it. You need to keep your shit together.*

Soren looked up at his mother with tears streaming down his cheeks, and Seraphine looked back down at him, whispering encouragement.

Alessa's vision began to swim as the music started to play, and she fought against the sudden urge to glitch. *Oh, not now. Please, no.*

Seraphine and Soren slowly approached the dark brown wooden slats. Reaching out a hand, Seraphine rested her palm upon her dead husband's chest before her shoulders rose and fell in a silent cry.

In Alessa's hallucination, Kai's smiling face alternated with Quade's, and she began to hyperventilate.

Alessa walked backwards through the crowd, bumping into chests and shoulders unapologetically. She wiped the sweat from her brow before turning away from the ceremony. "I can't..." she mumbled.

Struggling to hold back the all-consuming despair that was threatening to takeover, she sprinted towards the treeline.

Alessa ran through the tall trees, using all her energy to resist the urge to glitch as she dodged dangling tree branches and jumped over fallen logs.

She glanced up, and through the tree canopy, a faint purple light flashed across the sky.

She fell to her knees and squeezed her eyes shut while she rocked back and forth. "No, no, no, no," she cried, furiously rubbing her hands together.

A pair of muscular arms wrapped themselves around Alessa.

"Let it out," Damon encouraged.

Alessa shook her head back and forth, continuing to hyperventilate.

Damon took her head between his hands. "Let it out, or it will consume you."

With her heart threatening to beat out of her chest, Alessa panted as her irises flickered between blue and red. "I'm afraid … I will … hurt you."

Smashing a specialized Strongroom Bubble on the forest floor, Damon established a protective barrier, but rather than protect Alessa from outside forces, it protected the outside world from her.

Knowing that even though he couldn't hear her with the barrier in place, Alessa could still hear his muffled voice, Damon encouraged her. "Trust me; I'm protected. Just let go."

Unable to hold back any longer, Alessa imagined Quade, blood bubbling from his mouth and neck wound, before picturing Kai's pale face, lying dead in her arms, and wailed so loudly that even the gods took notice.

Hades gasped, his head jerking to the side. "What in the—"

"World was that?" Nyx interjected.

Kai's face scrunched up in alarm. "If I didn't know any better, it sounds like my sister."

Glaring at Kai, Hades' eyes shot daggers. "Nyx, your annoying pet is talking again. Shut her up."

Nyx chuckled while running her fingers through Kai's long blonde hair. "Why would I do that? She simply speaks the truth."

Hades huffed and his forehead scrunched. "How would we be able to hear a lowly human if she weren't summoned to our realm by either one of us? That isn't possible. There are too many voices earthside to pinpoint just one."

Staring at the god, Nyx arched an eyebrow. "Unless she is powerful enough to overshadow the rest."

<hr>

After screaming and crying for nearly twenty minutes, Alessa had collapsed from exhaustion.

Damon wrapped his arm around her waist and slowly helped her walk to the field where they used to lie next to Kai.

Setting Alessa down, he instructed Alessa to lie down. "Go on now, lie down."

Gripping his hand for balance, she sighed. "Damon, I—"

"Just do it."

She let go of Damon's hand and plopped down in the short patch of grass.

"Now, look up," he demanded, lying beside her.

Lifting her eyes up to the heavens, Alessa gazed at the bright stars. "Wow," she sighed. "I forgot how many of them there are."

Damon watched her every move, as if in a trance. "Haven't looked to the heavens for a while, have you?"

A sad smile crossed her lips. "Haven't had a reason to."

Damon rolled onto his back and chuckled. "Do you remember that one time Quade ate so many hot dogs at the eating competition that he ran to the side of the stage and threw up?"

Alessa snorted at the memory. "How could I forget? For over a year, he couldn't even look at a hot dog without feeling sick to his stomach."

Over the next few hours, Damon and Alessa exchanged stories of Quade and Kai until a comfortable silence blanketed between them.

As they lay beneath the stars, Damon inhaled the cool night air, considering how to word his question. "Alessa, how did you enter my dream? You know, the one with the"—he hesitated—"plane crash?"

"I don't really know," she slurred.

Looking off into the distance, Damon nodded his head slowly before continuing. "That wasn't just any dream. It was a memory of when I was on the plane that crashed with my family in it." He inhaled a shaky breath.

"My father gave me explicit instructions not to tell anyone of my being present on the plane during its crash. So, I lied and said I was elsewhere." He scoffed, looking down at the blades of grass he held between his fingers. "He believed the psychological trauma I endured could have hurt my possibly inheriting the title of king of the East."

Damon awaited her response but was met with silence.

"Alessa?" He sat up. "Alessa, did you hear—" Looking down, he realized she was asleep on her side, facing him.

Lying down, Damon placed his head on his arm and sighed. "I want you to know I never wanted anything other than the best for you. Me ... staying here ... isn't working for either one of us. I'm clearly holding onto something that isn't there anymore, and it's preventing you from moving on with your life. As much as it pains me to admit it, I think it's time I leave so you can finally be at peace."

With a sad smile, he whispered into the dark of night. "Good night, sydämen liekki."

Seraphine hissed at the bright light as she opened her eyes. "What in the world—"

Holding up a hand, she looked around the room, her eyebrows scrunching up as she recognized the building but couldn't place it. "Wait ... is this...?"

Seraphine glanced down at her elaborate, violet gown, and she gasped, pressing her hands against her flat stomach. "This can't be."

Below the deep violet halter top, her abdomen was covered in gemstones sewn onto transparent fabric. The gems continued down the flowing skirt before it kissed the tiled floor.

"Where's my—" she began before cutting herself off.

Lifting her gaze, Seraphine's eyes narrowed in disbelief. "Quade?"

Her husband spun around with a broad grin on his face.

"Quade!" Seraphine cried as they ran towards each other.

Falling into his open arms, Seraphine wept uncontrollably.

Clinging tightly to one another, they stood in place until she pulled away to look up into his eyes. "How can this be? You're-you're..." she swallowed.

Quade placed his fingers below her chin. "Yes, my love. I am. But Nyx has graciously given me the chance to say goodbye."

"But I don't want you to go," she begged. "You have so much to live for."

He smiled sadly, tucking a strand of Seraphine's dark bouncy hair behind her ear. "I know it, but we have no control over when our lives are meant to end."

Bringing her head to his chest, Quade wrapped his arms around his wife. "You know our plans don't always match those of the gods."

She placed a hand on her empty stomach. "Where's our baby?"

"This is but a dream and you are simply a projection of your self. Our daughter is safe in your belly, at home." Quade grinned. Taking her by the hand, he spun Seraphine in a tight circle. "We don't have much time, so let's make the most of it. Dance with me."

Seraphine sighed, her voice shaking with emotion. "Oh, Quade."

As he swept Seraphine around the dance floor, a phantom orchestra began to play.

Locking eyes, Quade laughed, spinning his wife around in a wide circle. "How is Soren handling everything?"

"He's holding in there. He doesn't quite understand the gravity of you never coming home, but I think, eventually, he'll be okay."

Quade's smile didn't quite reach his eyes. "And this newest addition of ours, have you thought of a name?"

Seraphine bit her lower lip. "I had narrowed them down to Stacia, Evi, or Lena."

Quade tilted his head in consideration. "I like Lena."

With tears shimmering in her eyes, Seraphine grinned. "Lena it is."

As they danced to the music provided by an orchestra

unseen for several minutes, Quade and Seraphine held tightly onto one another, afraid to let go.

Suddenly, Quade looked off to the side of the room and sighed. "I am sorry my love, but our time together is nearing its end."

Seraphine clung to him. "I don't want you to—"

Quade held his wife close. "Shhh, my love. Tell Soren I love him, and say hello to our baby girl." He swallowed back tears. "And let her know that her Patér wanted so badly to meet her and to be in her life."

Swallowing the lump in her throat, Seraphine nodded.

"And congratulate Damon on making it to the top."

Seraphine's eyes scrunched up in confusion.

"He'll know what it means. And my love, one last thing."

They stopped dancing, and she placed her hand on his cheek. "Anything."

"Please let Alessa know it was not her fault. It sucks how it all played out, but I don't regret saving her for one second. It was my destiny." He shrugged. "And thank her for keeping me company in the end. She never left my side, and I am so grateful for her friendship."

Seraphine started to cry as Quade peered off to the side of the room again. "It's time."

He placed his hands on both sides of her face and pulled her in for a gentle kiss. "Goodbye, my love," he said before turning around to.

"Quade!" Seraphine cried out.

Spinning back around, Quade's eyes burned with need, and they rushed towards one another from across the room.

As Quade and Seraphine collided, their arms wrapped around the other and their lips pressed together while hot tears fell down their faces.

With the lessening of Quade's touch, Seraphine opened her eyes. Where her husband once was, there was but a faint outline of his physical body.

Pulling back, Quade looked into Seraphine's deep brown eyes.

As he faded away into the ether, his voice resonated, "I will always love you. Live your life, full and true."

As a bright flash of light replaced the space in which her husband had just been standing, Seraphine collapsed to the floor, all alone, with a broken heart.

Springing upright, Alessa sat in the grassy field beside a sleeping Damon. "Seraphine," she said aloud, feeling a sudden urge to seek out her friend.

Jumping upright, she ran to New Sparta's necropolis.

Alessa whipped around the corner where she found her pregnant friend asleep on the ground next to the freshly disturbed earth. A tombstone lay at the top of the rectangle of loose dirt with Quade's name and the dates of his birth and death.

Walking slowly towards Seraphine, Alessa's chest tightened.

Seraphine's eyes opened with a gasp, and her neck craned back to look up at the tombstone. The disappointment in her eyes gave away that she had hoped it was all a bad dream.

"Sera?" Alessa asked breathily.

Seraphine searched desperately for her husband, but her face fell with the nauseating realization of his earthly departure. "He's really gone, isn't he?"

Alessa's head bobbed up and down disjointedly. "I'm so sorry. Yes, he is."

Pushing herself upright onto her knees, Seraphine bit down on her lower lip. "When I'm feeling better, remind me to tell you about the dream I just had."

Alessa pressed her hand to the side of Seraphine's cheek. "Okay."

Seraphine placed her hand atop Alessa's and tilted her head, closing her eyes as tears streamed down her cheeks once again.

Bending into one another, Alessa held her friend tight as they mourned Quade's loss together.

CHAPTER THIRTY-FIVE

After a long, emotionally exhausting night, Alessa was walking home when she heard Camden shout her name in the distance. "Alessa!"

Her head jerked upright at his surprisingly chastising tone, and her deflated walk turned into a motivated march.

Sensing the tension rolling off Camden, Lexi set her mug of hot tea on the table between their chairs and, with raised eyebrows, jumped up. "And that's my cue to exit."

As Lexi discreetly slinked off the side of the porch, Alessa approached the front of the cabin.

Hollering at Camden, Alessa scowled. "Why are you speaking to me like that?"

Camden stood tall, his hands pumping. "Where were you?"

Alessa's eyes narrowed, and she tilted her head. "Comforting my friend who is in mourning." She marched up the front steps, brushing past him.

Irate, Camden followed Alessa in through the cabin's front

door. "Lexi told me Damon followed you when you ran from Quade's service."

Alessa started taking off her warrior's uniform in the middle of the living room. "That's why you're upset?" She scoffed. "Yeah, I freaked out, and Damon calmed me down, but that's it."

Camden eyed Alessa warily. "You're sure?"

Annoyed with his judgmental tone, Alessa's eyebrows furrowed. "What's with you? You're not one to get jealous."

Camden sighed and looked away. "I guess with you, it's different."

Flattered, but knowing better, Alessa spun around to face him, smirking. Facing away from Camden, she asked, "So you're telling me you feel nothing for Lexi? That I've stolen your heart away, and you never want to be with another woman ever again?"

Taken aback by her statement, Camden stuttered. "I—Why —Why would you bring Lexi into this?"

Ignoring his question, she held the front of her corset tight against her breasts. "Can you just help me, please?"

Camden laughed while inching forward. "You are one hell of a confusing woman, you know that? One minute you're annoyed with me, then you're accusing me of lusting after another woman, and now you're wanting me to undress you?"

Alessa peered at Camden over her shoulder and smirked. "Tell me I'm wrong."

His mouth hung open in hesitation.

Alessa spun around, amused. "Right. Just get my corset strings started for me. I'll take it from there."

Camden pulled the strings, releasing their hold. Strolling to the bathroom, Alessa spread the strings apart. "I need to jump in the shower before heading up to the intelligence center.

Oreius called me earlier to say he wanted to discuss a new finding with me, in person."

Camden grabbed his shoes and sat on the couch. "I'm ready to go when you are."

Stepping into the bathroom, Alessa shut the door behind her. "You sure you want to tag along? It might end up being nothing of importance."

Camden unexpectedly slammed the bathroom door open. Standing in the doorframe, he took up most of the space with his tall, muscular torso.

After having already dropped her corset, Alessa snatched a towel from the wall and covered her mostly naked body while her jaw dropped.

"No matter if we're friends or lovers, I'm sticking by your side. 'Til the end." He looked her up and down. "And even if we are just friends, we can be beneficial to one another."

She scoffed incredulously while gripping her towel tighter. "You mean like, 'friends with benefits'?"

He winked before closing the door. "Exactly."

Camden and Alessa strolled into the intelligence center side by side. "Oreius, you wanted to see me?" Alessa asked.

Oreius smiled sadly. "Hey, how's Seraphine doing?"

With a nervous clearing of her throat, Alessa shrugged. "I mean, the love of her life and the father of her children just died, so I'd say pretty fucking bad."

Oreius anxiously smacked his lips together. "Yeah, um, that's understandable. I'm sorry for your loss as well. I know how close you were."

Alessa leaned into Oreius, her face void of emotion.

"Thanks, but you didn't call me down here for condolences. What was so important?"

"Right," Oreius agreed. "We've maintained twenty-four-seven surveillance on Cain since his involvement with Greenfield Farms, in hopes he would drop hints as to where Lucas is hiding."

"Get to the point," Camden urged.

"Senator Cain has been working his way up in the United States government, encouraging the stripping of women's reproductive rights and autonomy." Oreius laughed nervously. "Somehow, he's been able to whisper in the ears of the most powerful people, and they've actually been helping him achieve the passing of the most ludicrous of laws."

Alessa followed Oreius to the group of monitors above one of the desks. "Like what?"

"Well, for example, he's the individual who presented the initial idea to overturn Roe v. Wade," Oreius explained.

Camden stood near Alessa protectively. "Why would he care about women's ability to obtain an abortion?"

Bobbing excitedly, Oreius pointed at Camden. "Precisely. We've been trying to figure it out."

Alessa moved closer to the monitor on which Cain's grinning face was displayed. "Why would you be doing this? Some kind of sick power trip? Revenge against women as a whole?" She glared at his white teeth and growled, "What is it, you bastard?"

Camden glared at Cain's picture on the monitor. "How is he getting everyone else on board? I mean, if I remember correctly, to make an idea a law, it takes quite a few steps."

Oreius nodded. "That is correct. We've been taking samples of the food they're being served, per their M.O., and there haven't been any additives or any thought-altering substances added to the lawmakers' food. It's as if they genuinely believe in him."

Alessa swallowed the hot bile creeping up the back of her throat. "It's like he's creating his own cult. Cain would never do anything without it benefiting him or his uncle. There has to be a reason behind all of this."

She slapped the nearby table and nodded in determination. "That's it. I want a team put together as soon as possible to head down to Texas. I'm done playing nice, waiting for them to make the next move. It's time we demand answers."

CHAPTER THIRTY-SIX

Damon sat on the edge of a large boulder in front of the lake near his cabin. His guitar rested on his thighs, and he strummed while singing aloud.

His voice vibrated across the water, and the lyrics took on a deeper meaning as he sang about something going wrong with his love.

Damon got to the point he was damn near yelling the lyrics, and with the song's final sentence, he felt at peace with the finality of this chapter in his life.

Staring off into the distance at the sunlight reflecting off the water, he sighed, resolved to leave that very afternoon.

Walking in through his front door, he leaned his guitar against the front table before marching to his closet.

Leaning up against the wall, Quade stood unseen and unheard. "You don't have to do this, brother."

Pulling out a large duffel bag from the back of the closet, Damon exhaled loudly.

Quade's ethereal form followed Damon as he packed his

things. "You know she still loves you, man. Just give her a little more time to figure it all out."

Shoving clothing into his black bag, Damon shook his head back and forth. "I'm hanging on to the past. I want Alessa to have a future, and she can't move on with me hanging around like a living ghost." He paused and laughed to himself, glancing off to the side of the room where an invisible Quade was standing. "Look at me, slowly losing my mind; speaking to you as if you were hanging around just to watch my love life burn."

Quade sighed. "If your mind is settled, you and I both know there is nothing anyone can do to change it. Just make sure you see my daughter before you leave. She is so beautiful." He swallowed back his emotions. "Seraphine did such a wonderful job. She was so strong. I'm so proud of her."

There was a knock at Damon's door, and his head turned.

Chambers was standing in the doorway, rubbing his hands together in excitement. "Damon!"

"What is it? What's happened?" Damon cocked his head to the side, awaiting Chambers to explain himself.

"Seraphine delivered a healthy baby girl. She's asking to see you and Alessa. Any idea where she might be?"

A sad smile spread across Damon's face. "No, I don't know where to find Alessa, but that's great news about Seraphine." He pointed back inside his cabin. "I have to finish up something real quick, but I'll be there shortly."

"I'll let Seraphine know." Chambers ran back down the path near the lake.

Picking up his bag, he threw some toiletries in before zipping it up. Standing near the front door, Damon looked around his cabin for the last time while gripping the neck of his guitar.

As an onslaught of memories with Alessa hit, Damon squeezed his eyes shut, and he focused on slowing his breathing.

"Goodbye," he said aloud before closing his cabin door.

Damon arrived at the birthing center at the medical clinic and turned the corner. Setting his things down outside Seraphine's room, he squirted the sanitizer hanging from the wall onto his hands. "Sera? You ready for visitors?"

"Damon? Damon, is that you?" Seraphine asked, her voice full of emotion.

He stepped into the large room. "Yeah, it's me."

"Oh, Damon." Seraphine broke down crying while holding her newborn daughter in her arms.

Running over to the side of her bed, Damon climbed in beside Seraphine and wrapped his arms around her. "I'm so proud of you," Damon whispered in Seraphine's ear. "And you know Quade is, too."

She smiled sadly. Choking back tears, her voice was tight with sorrow. "I know."

Damon looked at the sweet sleeping babe. "What's her name?"

The baby wrapped her tiny hand around his finger.

Seraphine beamed. "Lena. Her name is Lena."

Damon nodded in approval. "Lena. Strong and beautiful, just like all women in New Sparta."

Seraphine handed her baby over to Damon, and he snuggled the newborn against his chest.

Noticing Damon's flushed cheeks, Seraphine grew suspicious. "What's going on?" She peered up at him and sighed loudly, recognizing the pain in his eyes. "Oh. You're leaving, aren't you?"

He wrapped an arm around Seraphine while holding Lena with the other. "I think my time here has come to an end."

"But what about Alessa?"

Hesitating, he looked up at the ceiling and slowly inhaled. "I will always love Alessa, but she deserves to move on, and she can't do that with me here."

Damon ran a finger down the newborn's chubby cheek. "Lena, I want you to know how loved you are, and I'm sorry I can't stay, but I'll always be with you"—He pointed at the baby's chest—"in here, just like your patēr."

Tears streamed down Seraphine's face as Damon handed the newborn back to her.

Damon stood up and rubbed his hands against his thighs before heading for the exit.

Seraphine smiled through her tears. "Take care of yourself, Spartan. I hope we meet again, someday."

Damon glanced back at Seraphine. "You better believe we will."

Reaching into his bag, Damon pulled out a letter and set it on the table near the room's entrance. "Could you give this to Alessa?"

Lena whimpered, and Seraphine rocked the baby in her arms. "Shh, little one." She directed her attention back to Damon. "Are you sure you don't want to give it to her yourself?"

Glancing down at the floor, he sighed. "I'm sure. Goodbye, Sera."

Seraphine watched Damon walk out the door. "Bye, Damon."

Hiking through the woods he'd called home for the better part of a decade, Damon felt as though he were leaving the other half of his heart—of his soul—behind.

CHAPTER THIRTY-SEVEN

In her dream, Alessa was once again sitting at the counter of the same diner from her nightmare on the airplane.

She looked around the empty building for the Frenzied that were present the last time. "Why this nightmare again?"

Suddenly, the TVs hanging down from the ceiling behind the counter turned on, and loud static appeared on every screen.

A woman's face appeared in an ad for the artificial sweetener Ambrosia in a popular soft drink.

The image kept flickering between a healthy-appearing woman holding the soda pop and a Frenzied, carrying what appeared to be a beating heart. The creature's lips were cracked and bleeding, its eyes were dark and sunken in, chunks of its flesh were missing, exposing a cream-colored skull, and its hair was a rat's nest atop its head.

Alessa watched the images, engrossed. "What are you trying to tell me?"

Cain and Lucas appeared in the corner of the screen, both

smiling maniacally. Their lips separated before simultaneously yelling, "Jump!"

As the image zoomed in on the grotesque Frenzied, the creature jumped forward as if it were going to leap out of the screen.

Screaming in terror, Alessa covered her face and fell back out of the stool.

Waking up from her nap, she breathed rapidly. "Shit..." she cursed, bolting off the couch. "I have to talk to Sera."

Alessa sprinted the entire way to the medical ward, and upon reaching the building, she bent over and rested her hands atop her knees while gasping for breath. "Hey," she huffed to the guard on duty. "Is Sera here?"

His eyes scrunched in confusion. "Where else would she be?"

Alessa tilted her head, awaiting his explanation.

"Oh, has no one told you? She gave birth a short time ago."

"What?" Alessa looked past the guard. "Well, can I see her?"

"Of course; go right in," the guard encouraged.

"Thanks!" she called back over her shoulder as she walked in through the double glass doors.

"Damon just left," he said.

Alessa turned her head in surprise. "He did?"

The guard held up his weapon across his chest. "Any idea where he's headed?"

She stilled, her face serious. "What do you mean?"

The Spartan guard turned around, his back to the building.

"He had a duffel bag and his guitar. I assumed that meant he was—"

"No, I don't know where he was going," Alessa interjected as she began to walk away. "I really need to see Sera."

Sprinting down the hall, Alessa followed the sound of newborn cries and found her friend easily.

Stepping into the room, Alessa covered her mouth in awe. "Sera, oh Sera."

Stepping into the room, she sprayed her hands with the wall-mounted sanitizer and rubbed them together.

"Alessa!" Seraphine exclaimed. "Come meet your niece."

Distracted from her initial reasoning for finding Seraphine, Alessa's heart melted as she looked at the infant's face and saw Quade's features. Running her finger down the baby's forehead and nose, Alessa gasped. "Oh, Sera, she looks—"

"Just like him? I know." Seraphine swallowed.

Noticing Alessa's ashen skin tone, Seraphine's eyes widened. "Are you okay? What's going on?"

"Oh"—Alessa shook her head to clear her mind—"I came to tell you about another dream I had."

"Spit it out, Spartan," Seraphine snapped.

Alessa licked her lips nervously, standing beside the bed. "Cain and Lucas were on the same television screen as one of the Frenzied. She was holding a heart in her hands, and when they told her to jump, she jumped."

Seraphine's eyes narrowed in confusion. "She jumped?"

Alessa paced back and forth. "Yes. I think Nyx and Kai are telling us that the Frenzied are being controlled by Lucas and Cain. And it has something to do with their hearts. Like, maybe it's the pacemaker-type apparatus implanted on the outside of their hearts? The things I targeted when I took them down—I don't know." She shook her head in confusion.

"That's not a bad idea. You got all of this from a dream?"

Alessa nodded excitedly, nearly bouncing up and down. "Yes, just now." Alessa hesitated. "Sera, that's not the first dream I've had about the Frenzied. The first one was on the plane, when we were heading to Greece."

Seraphine stared at Alessa, her lips pursed together in silence.

"Looking back, I think my sister was trying to warn me that the Frenzied were coming. I'm so sorry I didn't figure it out in time."

Seraphine smiled sadly and reached out to touch Alessa's hand. "I do not blame you for what happened to my husband, not now or ever. But, if you feel strongly that these dreams hold truth, then I recommend you try to decipher their meaning before others are hurt, or worse."

Seraphine wiped her tears that were threatening to spill over. "Okay, then, we should start testing your theory right away."

Alessa placed a hand on Seraphine's arm. "You will do no such thing. We can give this information to your colleagues, and they can take over until you've rested. Now, can I hold my niece?"

Seraphine tilted her head, shooting Alessa an annoyed glance. "Yes. Here you are." She handed the baby over.

Alessa scooped the newborn up into her arms. "You need to rest for a few days, at the very least. Quade would never forgive me if I let you out of bed too early."

With a sigh, Seraphine yielded. "I'll give you that."

Alessa lapped the room with the content baby snuggled against her chest.

Seraphine inhaled slowly. "There's something I have to tell you."

Smiling at the newborn, Alessa responded. "Yes?"

Seraphine anxiously played with the tips of her fingers. "Quade came to me in my dreams the night we laid him to rest ... to say his final goodbyes."

Alessa's breathing hitched, and tears sprang to her eyes.

"He wanted me to let you know that he does not blame you for his death. It was his destiny."

Alessa blinked the tears from her eyes and sniffled.

"And he was glad it was you by his side in his final moments," Seraphine's voice cracked with emotion.

Alessa peered down at the tiny baby in her arms, and while smiling sadly, she wiped away the tears. "Thank you for telling me. I assume he talked to you as well?"

Seraphine rubbed her hands together. "He did."

Alessa cleared her throat, understanding that what he had said was clearly intimate and was not going to be shared. "Understood. The guard said that Damon had already seen the baby..."

"Lena," Seraphine finished for her.

"Lena," Alessa sighed with a smile. "So, he did get to see her before I did," she remarked playfully.

Seraphine's face dropped.

Alessa laughed nervously. "What's that look for?"

"He's leaving."

Alessa froze. "Like, on a mission?"

Seraphine shook her head. "No. For good."

"That's impossible," Alessa laughed incredulously. "He wouldn't just leave. Not without saying—"

Seraphine looked past Alessa, at the table. "He left you a letter."

Quade's ethereal form stood in the corner of the room,

unseen and unheard. "He's not gone just yet. You still have time to stop him."

After handing Lena back to her mom, Alessa hurried to the table, where a white envelope sat with her name on the front.

She tore open the envelope and pulled out the piece of paper. Her lips moved silently as she read the words written by Damon.

ALESSA,

THIS HAS GOT TO BE THE HARDEST LETTER I'VE EVER WRITTEN, NOT THAT I'VE WRITTEN A LOT OF LETTERS IN MY LIFETIME, BUT STILL.

IT HAS TAKEN ME A HELL OF A LONG TIME TO COME TO THE REALIZATION THAT I'M NO GOOD FOR YOU. I KNOW YOU'VE SAID IT IN THE PAST, BUT I WAS HOLDING OUT HOPE THAT YOU'D STILL COME BACK TO ME, SOMEHOW. SOMEWAY.

BUT HOW COULD YOU AFTER ALL THE PAIN I CAUSED? I GET IT NOW.

Alessa's lips parted, and she dropped the letter.

"What are you waiting for?" Seraphine urged.

An invisible Quade grinned from ear to ear. "Go get him."

Sprinting out the door, Alessa ran down the hallway and out the front of the medical ward. Heading for Damon's cabin, Alessa was panting as she replayed the rest of the letter in her mind.

AS MUCH AS I WANT TO BE THE MAN FOR YOU, IT DOESN'T LOOK LIKE THAT'S GOING TO HAPPEN IN THIS LIFE. I KNOW IT'S MY FAULT EVERYTHING WENT TO SHIT. MY MISJUDGMENT OF ONE PERSON'S CHARACTER CHANGED THE TRAJECTORY OF BOTH OF OUR LIVES.

I AM SO SORRY. FOR HURTING YOU, FOR BEING THE INDIRECT CAUSE OF YOUR SISTER BEING KILLED; FOR NOT LISTENING TO YOU SOONER.

Alessa burst in through Damon's front door. "Damon!" she yelled, frantically searching his cabin. "Damon, where are you?"

Running her fingers through her hair in a panic, Alessa realized he was already gone. Her heart leapt as she ran back through the front door, out into the woods. *Where would he leave New Sparta from?*

Remembering where he had parked his car just outside the forcefield, Alessa ran as fast as she could.

Her voice echoed through the trees as she jumped over fallen logs and broken limbs. "Damon! Don't do this to me," she begged, running as fast as her legs could carry her.

MAYBE THIS ISN'T THE LIFE WHERE WE END UP TOGETHER, BUT YOU BETTER BELIEVE I'LL SEARCH FOR YOU IN THE NEXT.

I'VE ONLY EVER WANTED THE BEST FOR YOU, AND IF THAT ISN'T ME, SO BE IT.
I SET YOU FREE, ALESSA.
GOODBYE.

Breaking through the treeline, Alessa froze as she saw a shimmering figure stepping through the forcefield across the meadow.

Alessa regained her wits and screamed at the top of her lungs. "Damon!"

Hearing his name, Damon looked back over his shoulder through the shimmering forcefield.

His breath swirled before him amidst the cold mountain air, just outside of New Sparta.

Realizing someone was running towards him, he pulled his guitar strap up over his head.

Alessa sprinted across the meadow, scattered with yellow wildflowers, while pleading with Damon to stop.

Recognizing the voice, Damon's forehead scrunched up in confusion as he looked past the falling snow, back into the warmth of New Sparta. "Alessa?"

Damon stepped back through the shimmering forcefield, and as soon as he set his instrument down and dropped his heavy bag, Alessa flew into his open arms.

Wrapping her arms around his neck, Alessa gasped for air.

"What's wrong? Baby, are you okay?" Damon asked, his voice dripping with concern.

Pulling back, she looked up into his eyes, and shaking her head back and forth, she begged, "Don't go. Please don't go."

Damon sighed and placed his hands on either side of her face, while staring into her tear-filled eyes.

"I love you, Damon. I love you, heart and soul. Please don't go. Don't leave me." Alessa stood up on the tips of her toes while pulling him down.

As their lips touched, electrified heat spread throughout them both, from head to toe.

Damon's breathing sped up to match Alessa's as they stared deep into each other's eyes.

Moving his hands down her backside, Damon scooped her up, and she jumped effortlessly into his arms.

She wrapped her legs around his waist and squeezed tight as they kissed deeply.

His lips caressed the side of Alessa's neck as he lay her down onto her back, under the heat of the late afternoon sun.

Unwrapping her legs from around Damon's midsection, she splayed her legs on either side of him.

He grasped the thin fabric of Alessa's dress and tore it down the middle. As her breasts fell free, he placed his hands behind her lower back and pulled her to his mouth.

Damon bent down and sucked Alessa's erect pink nipple between his lips, and her moans grew breathier. His mouth left her skin, and he knelt in the tall grass. Bending down into Alessa, his tongue licked up her shin.

Reaching her center, Damon jumped upright and shrugged out of his black leather jacket before peeling off his fitted black T-shirt. While slapping his shirt onto the ground, he traced Alessa's womanly curves as she lay nearly bare.

Damon pulled off his shoes and socks, and a sexy smile spread across his face as he and Alessa locked eyes; hers glitched red, and his activated silver.

Unbuckling his belt, Damon unzipped and dropped his jeans, allowing the outline of his erect cock to be seen straining against his black briefs.

He lay beside Alessa, his fingers trailing down her beautifully scarred midsection as he breathed into her ear. "This is going to be rough and fast. I've wanted you for far too long to control myself any longer."

Alessa gasped as his fingers slipped beneath her panties.

"But you better believe tonight I fully intend on pleasuring you all..." Damon's fingers pressed into her wet slit, and she gasped. "Night..."he continued as Alessa moaned with the increasing rocking motion of her hips. "Long," he said breathily before licking and biting the side of her neck.

Alessa arched her back as the pleasure combined with the pain nearly pushed her over the edge. She moaned loudly as his fingers spread around her wetness, flicking her clit in the process.

"Please," she begged breathily.

Turning her head, Damon bent down above her lips. "Use your words. Tell me what you want," he taunted.

Alessa's red irises glowed as she opened her eyes. "Fuck me."

With an aching growl, Damon kissed her hard. Bringing his hand up to his lips, he licked Alessa's sweet juices from his fingers while staring deep into her eyes.

Alessa pulled Damon in for a passionate kiss, and as she moaned into his open mouth, she set his body aflame.

Breaking away from her, his lips pressed against Alessa's puffy scar, stopping just above the top of her panties.

"Sorry for this," he apologized before ripping the lacy fabric and tossing it off to the side. Damon wriggled out of his briefs before throwing them atop their growing clothes pile.

He crawled back to Alessa and dug his fingertips into the back of her thighs, spreading her legs. Seeing her drip with anticipation, Damon growled, "Fuck, baby," before he dove into her center. His tongue thrust deep inside, and Alessa cried out in ecstasy.

"Oh gods, Damon!" She gripped fistfuls of his hair as his tongue increased in speed

As stars crowded her vision and she was about to cum, he pulled back.

Her mouth was wide open as Damon wiped his mouth, grinning devilishly.

Alessa's forehead scrunched up in need, and she groaned in frustration.

Grasping her wrists, Damon raised her hands above her head and, while resting them in the wildflowers, he wriggled his hips just below hers.

Feeling the tip of his cock rubbing against the outside of her center, Alessa's eyes rolled into the back of her head, and she moaned loudly.

The sounds Alessa was making sent Damon over the edge, and he thrust his hips.

His hard cock twitched with the familiarity of Alessa's ridges. As he rubbed against her slick walls, Alessa's body bounced up and down.

Damon ran his hand up her body, massaging her breast

before bending down to her nipple, once again sucking the sensitive skin. With every thrust, Alessa's face reddened and her lips separated in incomprehensible moans.

Driving further into her, Damon's free hand reached for Alessa's hands still stretched above her head. With their hands grasped tightly, the veins in the backs of his hands and forearms bulged as his jaw clenched.

"I've needed you for so fucking long," he professed, his voice deep and guttural with need.

"Damon," Alessa panted. "I'm going to—I'm going to—" Alessa repeated breathily.

Gripping tightly onto Alessa's intertwined fingers, Damon thrust harder and deeper. "Cum for me," he growled.

"Uh—Damon!" she exclaimed as her body spasmed around him.

Damon spilled into her, his cock twitching as her contractions milked him. "Oh fuck, Alessa."

Damon pressed in as deep as he could, and Alessa wrapped her legs around his waist.

Her lips separated into a lazy smile as sounds of pleasure escaped from between them.

Catching his breath, Damon leaned in and kissed up the side of Alessa's neck.

He withdrew himself and pressed his lips against Alessa's. As the pressure released inside her, she inhaled.

Barely lifting himself, he hovered just above her lips. "I love you, sydämen liekki. In this life and the next."

Blinking the tears from her eyes, Alessa smiled. "Forever."

Wiping the tears from her cheeks, Damon kissed her one final time before standing up. Damon peered down at her naked body and sighed. "Hmm ... sorry about that."

She glanced off to the side at her destroyed clothing and giggled. "Uh, yeah. You kind of ripped my clothes to shreds."

"Hold on a second," he called out, running back for his bag while tugging on his T-shirt.

Damon dug through the bag's contents and handed Alessa a dark blue T-shirt and black briefs. He shrugged with a smirk. "It's better than nothing."

"Um..." She took the clothing from Damon, smiling wryly. "I don't think we're going to be able to hide what happened if I wear your clothing."

Damon shrugged on his leather jacket. "I have no intentions of hiding anything from anyone." Damon took his shirt out of her hands and helped her wiggle into it. Staring deep into Alessa's eyes, he exhaled. "You mean everything to me, and I will make damn sure everyone knows it. I'm never letting you go again."

Alessa's heart stilled, and she licked her lips while staring at his. *Gods, that's sexy.*

Damon leaned in and placed his fingertips beneath her chin, tilting her face up to his. "Do you understand, sydämen liekki?"

Her eyes unglitched back to their natural bright blue hue. "I do."

Reaching down, Damon helped Alessa into the briefs. "This'll keep me from dripping all the way down your legs. At least until we get home." He winked, standing her upright.

"We're going back to your cabin?"

Gripping her hand tighter, Damon pulled her into him. "I am nowhere done with you tonight. I want your body aching and sore by sunrise."

Alessa's breath escaped her as Damon bent her backwards in a passionate kiss.

Standing her upright, he let go of Alessa and grabbed his guitar. Damon slung the strap over his neck and snatched up his black heavy bag.

After picking up her torn clothing, Alessa walked side-by-side with Damon. "So, about never letting me go"—she cleared her throat—"I may need to leave soon."

Damon's head jerked to the side, and he stared at Alessa.

Her cheeks flushed. "I asked to have a task force sent to investigate the forced pregnancies. We need to try to figure out why they're so prevalent in Texas, and why Cain started the law to make abortions illegal. It's got to be connected somehow."

"Sounds great. When are we leaving?" Damon asked matter-of-factly.

Passing the large trees, Alessa caressed the rough bark of each one. "We?" she asked with a chuckle in the back of her throat.

Damon shrugged as they continued further into the forest. "I meant what I said. I'm never letting you out of my sight again. As long as I live, you'll be by my side. I will protect you with my dying breath."

Alessa's lips parted in surprise, and her cheeks blushed as she continued marching forward.

"Okay, then," she laughed under her breath. "Well, it will probably be in the next few days. At least I'm hoping it will be." She cleared her throat nervously. "Speaking of leaving, where were you going?"

Damon walked ahead of Alessa. "I was thinking one of the compounds overseas, so as not to risk seeing you for a while. I wanted to give you adequate time to..." he trailed off.

Staring at his muscular back, her voice softened. "To what?"

"Find happiness," Damon said, his voice strained.

"But how could you just leave? Without saying goodbye? I thought I meant more to you than—"

Damon dropped his bag and rushed to Alessa. Placing his hands on either side of her face, he brought his lips close to hers. "You are everything to me. But I wasn't leaving because I wanted to—it wasn't about me. I did what I thought was best for you."

She placed her hands atop his, feeling his strength. "But how could you just leave me after—"

Shaking his head back and forth, Damon's eyebrows furrowed. "You weren't alone. You had Sera, Lexi"—he swallowed—"Camden. I saw the way you two were with one another, how he never left your side. I thought that maybe you were trying to move on but couldn't fully because I was in the way."

Stretching her neck up to Damon, Alessa pressed her lips against his, and when she pulled back, she sported a half-grin. "Cam and I have never been more than good friends. He's been there for me through everything." She cleared her throat. "He was there when you couldn't be. Even when I hated you, I loved you. It's always been you, and it will forever be you."

Damon's focused gaze burned with passion, and he grabbed the back of Alessa's neck, pulling her in for a deep kiss.

As their tongues danced, Alessa moaned into his mouth.

His eyes sprang open, and his irises activated silver. Dropping his guitar carelessly onto the ground, he growled, "Fuck my stuff. It's slowing us down," before swooping Alessa up into his arms.

CHAPTER THIRTY-EIGHT

Alessa clung to Damon, giggling, as he jogged the rest of the way to his cabin.

Damon kicked in his front door while holding Alessa in his arms. Kissing her deeply, he set her down slowly, as if in slow motion.

He backed away from Alessa as his wristband lit up. "Shit, I forgot I told them I was leaving. Give me two minutes so I can cancel the cleanup crew, or else we will have some unwanted guests tonight."

Alessa laughed as he playfully bit the side of her neck.

Stepping back onto his small front porch, Damon closed the front door behind him and spoke into his wristband.

Alessa set her clothes on top of the entry table before walking slowly around the cabin, inspecting his new furniture.

Looking at his new bed, she was no longer plagued with visions of Brielle. *Damon loves me. He has always loved me.*

Kicking off her flats on the way to the bathroom, Alessa stripped Damon's briefs and his shirt from her body and turned the shower's handle.

Stepping over the curb, Alessa stood beneath the warm running water, allowing it to run down her face.

After canceling the cleanup crew, Damon came back in through the front door, and he tilted his head while listening to his running shower. Undressing on his way to the bathroom, he stepped in through the open door and saw the outline of Alessa's naked body behind his shower's opaque glass frame.

He slid into the shower behind her. *Fuck me, she's perfect.*

Grabbing her hips, Damon pulled her backside against his erection, and a small whimper escaped Alessa's lips as she wrapped an arm behind him.

He spun her around, splashing the water before she pulled his lips to hers.

While balancing on the tips of her toes, the water streamed down her hair and the back of her torso.

After caressing Alessa's lips with his own, Damon stepped back, and reaching for the shampoo, he squirted a small amount of liquid into the palm of his hand before running his fingers through her dark hair.

The weight of the water pulled down on her wavy hair, straightening her thick strands down past her shoulder blades.

Working the suds through her thick hair, Damon's body visibly reacted to Alessa's every moan.

He grabbed his navy blue loofah from its hook, poured body wash onto the coarse sponge, and rubbed it back and forth just below Alessa's jawline. He worked his way down her chest, gently circling her nipples, urging them to points.

The radius of his circles increased as he massaged further down onto her abdomen.

Her puffy scar was clearly visible, but it didn't bother him like it used to.

This was a part of who she was now, and if they were to

move on together, he'd have to forgive himself for not being there when she needed to be saved. *But never again will that happen. I will die before I let harm befall Alessa.*

While cleaning her backside, Damon gently bit into the top of her shoulder.

She shuddered as his lips caressed the light red marks left behind.

Bending down, he cleaned both of her legs, breathing deep as he made his way up the inside of her thighs.

Turning around to face him, Alessa tilted her head back towards the ceiling while backing away from Damon, into the water.

The soap rinsed down her pale skin, into the drain, and as she turned around to ensure the front of her was rinsed off, Damon let out a guttural growl.

She half-grinned. "It's your turn, now."

She squeezed shampoo into her hands before pointing at the shower floor.

Kneeling down, Damon placed his palms against her lower back, pulling her into him.

Alessa's back blocked the warm water from hitting Damon in the face as he kissed up the scar on her stomach.

She ran her fingers through his hair, then grabbed the loofah and applied body wash. Starting at his neck, Alessa moved in circles just as he had moments earlier on her.

As she moved down his body, Damon stood up so she could easily reach further down.

Turning him so that his back was against the water, Alessa finished cleaning his legs.

They stared into each other's eyes as she knelt in front of his erection. Throwing the loofah off to the side, she wrapped her fingers around his tip and stroked his length that had been slickened by soap.

He hissed as pleasure shook him to the core. "Mmm," he hummed, his eyes rolling back into his head.

As the water rinsed the soap from his body, Alessa looked up at Damon with a mischievous grin and slid her lips over his cock.

Pressing his palms against the sides of the shower, his head fell back in ecstasy, and as she ran her tongue up and down his shaft, Damon peered down.

Watching Alessa's head bob back and forth, he growled, "Oh gods!"

After a minute, she had him breathing deep while he was pumping into her mouth.

Pulling Alessa upright, Damon lunged forward, and wrapping his fingers around both sides of her neck, he pressed her back up against the shower tile.

Feeling her body bend to his will, Damon lifted her hand up above her head, pinning her against the cold tile.

As their fingers entwined, Alessa's eyes flared bright red, and the lights in the bathroom flickered.

Pulling back, Damon's eyebrow arched. "Oh. Have I struck a nerve?"

Alessa grabbed a fistful of his hair with her free hand and pulled him eagerly back into her as her other arm remained outstretched.

"God dammit, woman. You drive me crazy," he panted in between kisses.

Turning off the shower, Damon stepped over the curb, dripping wet, and lifted Alessa out after him.

Rotating her wet body to face the mirror, Damon palmed

Alessa's breasts. "I want you to watch," he whispered into her ear before licking and sucking on two of his fingers.

"Damon..." she panted as he played on either side of her slick entrance.

As he rubbed back and forth on her clit, her knees buckled.

Damon held her up by the front of her neck, and Alessa's hands darted to his, gripping his fingers in ecstasy.

Her breathing quickened as his fingers ran back and forth against her. "Uh! Yes. Yes," she moaned.

As she was about to peak, Damon thrust his fingers into her.

With a gasp, Alessa wriggled. Rocking back and forth, she encouraged him to press in further and go faster.

Watching her face redden, Damon licked his lower lip. "Open your eyes, baby."

She opened her eyes, and staring back at her in the mirror was the red-eyed version of herself she had learned to hate.

Turning her head to the side, Damon pulled her attention back to the mirror with his free hand. "I want you to see how beautiful you are. Do not take your eyes off your reflection."

Feeling the warmth spread throughout her body, Alessa began to pant. "Damon, I'm going to cum."

"Go ahead and let go. I want you good and exhausted once I'm finally done with you tonight," he said in a guttural voice.

"Uh!" Alessa moaned as her entire body shook in Damon's one-armed embrace.

With her legs quivering on his hand, Damon's fingers felt every contraction within Alessa, and his cock ached with the need to release. "Good girl," Damon cooed into her ear.

They locked eyes in the mirror, and he lightly bit the side of Alessa's neck before he brought his fingers up to his mouth.

Whipping around to face Damon as he was licking her juices from his fingers, Alessa jumped up into his arms.

His hands scooped up underneath her ass, and she wrapped her arms around his neck, kissing him urgently and deeply.

Carrying her from the bathroom, Damon turned the corner before pressing Alessa's back up against the wall, next to his bed.

Holding her, he lowered her while simultaneously thrusting his hips.

Alessa's breath escaped as she felt the tip of his cock press up against her center.

Having just orgasmed, she was tight, but Alessa was wet enough that all it took was a few pumps, and Damon had eased himself in.

His erect cock plunged deep inside, and as he hit her sweet spot, she tightened around his girth.

They both moaned into one another's open mouths as pleasure wracked their bodies.

Lifting her off the wall, Damon withdrew himself and carried Alessa to the bed. After tossing her onto the mattress, he dove on top, but was surprised by Alessa rolling him onto his back.

"What do you think you're—" he started, but was silenced as Alessa sat atop Damon, sliding all of him in, slow and deep.

Feeling her tighten around him once again, Damon cursed. "Fuck me."

Grinding her hips, Alessa smiled wickedly. "I'm trying."

Digging his fingertips into her hips, he thrust further into Alessa, forcing her back to arch as she cried out in pleasure.

Damon's skin lit aflame as he watched Alessa's head thrust back toward the ceiling.

After brushing her hair out of her face, she watched his eyes roll back, and he released a guttural moan as she bent down to lick and bite up the side of his neck.

Flipping her onto her back, Damon lifted Alessa's hips to his and thrust deep.

Their rhythmic panting matched one another as his speed increased.

She dug her fingertips into his muscular forearms while begging, "Damon, please."

He leaned in to her. "What, baby. What do you want me to do?"

"Cum with me," she gasped. Grabbing him behind the neck, Alessa forced Damon's lips down to hers.

She bit and sucked on his lower lip, sending Damon over the edge.

Letting go of her hips, Damon's body weight pressed against Alessa, and their bodies sank further into the bed.

She moaned loudly as a flame ignited inside her lower abdomen.

"Say it, sydämen liekki," Damon urged breathily.

"I love you!" Alessa exclaimed upon climax.

Following closely thereafter, Damon moaned into Alessa's mouth as he pulsed, filling her with his warmth.

They kissed slowly and deeply before he pulled back, smiling. "I love you too."

CHAPTER THIRTY-NINE

The next day, Alessa awoke exhausted and sore, but in the best way.

After she wrapped the bedsheet around herself, she followed the grunts and groans that were coming from the back of Damon's property.

Swinging the back door open, her eyebrows arched, and her heart rate skyrocketed as Damon stood shirtless, throwing stars and blades at a target.

The knives sat in a bucket on the ground beside him, and with every stretch of his arms, the sweat dripping down from Damon's muscles shone in the sunlight.

Biting her lower lip, she watched him stretch as he leaned down for another blade.

Damon focused on the target, and while exhaling through pursed lips, he tossed a water bottle up in the air. Damon thrust the knife forward, and it sliced through the center of the water bottle before pinning it to the board.

Alessa tilted her head. "Impressive."

Damon ran to her, smiling. "Finally. You're awake." He pulled her in for a kiss.

Alessa chuckled. "Ah, yes. I am awake, but I see how easily it was for you to leave the bed."

His eyes grew dark as he looked down at her with longing. Placing one hand against the cabin's exterior wall behind Alessa's head, Damon raised an eyebrow. "I knew you needed to get some rest, and if I was going to remain lying next to you, I was not going to keep my hands off of you."

Leaning into Alessa, Damon's lips hovered just above her own, and his hot breath brushed against her skin.

Alessa trembled with need as she tilted her head back for a kiss.

"Damon! Hello?" Lexi called out from the front of the cabin.

Gripping the sheets tightly around her, Alessa's eyes widened. "What is Lexi doing here?"

Damon's back straightened. "I have no idea."

Lexi walked up the stairs, onto Damon's porch, and peeked in through his open front door. "You home?"

Damon sprinted from the side of his house, running up behind Lexi on the stairs. "Lexi!" he exclaimed a little too loudly. "What are you doing here?"

Her eyes narrowed suspiciously as she looked Damon up and down. "Why do you look so nervous?"

Damon chuckled. "I'm not. You just caught me doing some exercises out back. What's going on?"

"We've been trying to get a hold of you all morning on your com." Lexi glanced down at his naked wrist. "But I see why we weren't able to."

Damon rubbed the skin on his wrist where his band should be. "Yeah, um..."

"I don't really care why you don't have your com on. I'm just here to let you know there's a group being sent to Texas this evening to further investigate Senator Cain. The main objective is to discover the reasoning behind the increase in forced pregnancies and the consequent death of women. You and a group of your choosing are expected to lead the investigation."

Leaning to the left, Lexi looked past Damon. Seeing Alessa's dress in a bunched-up pile on his entryway table, Lexi's eyebrows raised in surprise.

"I—I'll let you get back to your day," she said, backing down the stairs. "Just make sure you and your selected officials are good to go by tonight."

Walking in through the entrance, Damon shut the door.

"Is she gone?" Alessa asked after having shrugged into one of Damon's T-shirts.

"Yeah." Damon nodded as he plucked his black bag off the floor. Plopping it down on the edge of his bed, he started unpacking the previous day's contents to pack things suitable for their mission. "Looks like we're going on a field trip, just like you said we would."

Alessa leaned up against the wall blocking the door from the rest of the home's interior. "Why'd she leave so fast? And why is your front door wide open when you were in the back?"

Damon shrugged as he took clothes out of his large bag and placed them on his bed to pack into a smaller bag. "I don't know. One second, she was fine, then she looked past me and freaked out. And my door was open because I had forgotten the water bottles on my front table, so I ran in to grab them. Must not have gotten the door latched on my way back out."

Alessa peered to the side, and her eyes grew wide as she saw her balled-up dress on the side table. "Oh shit."

Damon's head darted up at Alessa. "What?"

"Um..." She rubbed her biceps. "I think she may have seen my dress."

Damon stiffened. "And? Are you ashamed to be with me?" he asked defensively.

Alessa charged forward. "No, absolutely not. That's not at all what I'm worried about. If she tells Camden before I get a chance to, it could be—"

"Bad. It could be bad," Damon huffed.

"Exactly. Cam's been there for me, and he knows how badly I was hurt—"

Damon placed his hands on Alessa's upper arms. "And I've apologized time and time again. I swear to never—"

Alessa sighed and set her hands atop his. "I know, and I have forgiven you. But Cam may not be as easy to persuade. He was there for me through it all." Alessa slipped her shoes on. "He deserves an explanation. From me."

Damon stood silently in the entryway, unsure of what to say or how to react.

Removing her hand from the door handle, Alessa ran back to Damon, flinging herself into his arms. Pressing her lips against his, she poured all the love she felt for him into the kiss.

Pulling back, Damon exhaled, and his shoulders fell as his tense frame relaxed. "I trust you."

Alessa smiled while looking into Damon's deep ocean blue eyes. "I'm yours, and you're mine. Forever."

In his brightly colored room, Hades sat on his throne made of black onyx and grumbled, "Fuck."

He grabbed a severed hand off the white marble side table and tossed the limb high into the air for Cerberus to catch.

Nyx strolled in stealthily, eyeing the giant glass globe in which Hades had been keeping an eye on the Spartans. "I assume you saw Alessa's declaration?" She smiled smugly.

Taken by surprise, Hades jumped, and with a flick of his wrist, the image of Alessa and Damon holding one another in a loving embrace faded into a foggy haze. His eyes darted off to the side of the room as he crossed one leg over the other nonchalantly. "So what? The lowly human is only one step further—"

Nyx grinned knowingly. "You mean two? Two steps further." She sashayed across the room, her dark, sparkling gown dragging along the floor. "You really have no concern?" she taunted.

His face growing red, Hades lashed out. "She still has to survive what's to come in order for the prophecy to be upheld."

"They both do," Nyx corrected.

Hades' head sprang upright, his forehead scrunched in confusion. "Come again?"

"Oh." Nyx laughed mockingly. "I forgot how young a god you are. You know how you can tell as soon as a soul is departing earth for the underworld? The second a soul is created, I get this tingly feeling"—she pointed to her chest—"right here."

The false sky above them, within the room, darkened as his playful demeanor vanished. Brief flashes of light shone through the swirling, deep grey clouds as artificial lightning bolts mirrored Hades' deep-seated feelings of panic.

The god's face dropped, and his cheeks reddened, realizing what it meant for his winning the competition. "Yes, well, let's see how she deals with the next obstacle."

CHAPTER FORTY

Lexi's mind was a jumbled mess as she ran all the way back to the intelligence center. "Am I sure I saw what I think I saw? Yeah, no—that was definitely Alessa's dress. Which, honestly, makes sense because Damon suddenly changed his mind about leaving last night. That would make sense—her having changed it for him."

Approaching the building, she slowed her pace.

With Lexi's skirt no longer flowing behind her, she nearly tripped as the soft fabric entangled itself around her ankles. *Do I say anything to Camden? Will he freak out? And if he does lose his shit, will it be because he loves Alessa or because he's concerned about his best friend? Ugh. I hate that this bothers me so much.*

"Hey, Lexi." Camden noticed the crease deep between her eyes. "You okay?"

Biting down hard on her lower lip, Lexi nervously giggled. "Yeah. Why wouldn't I be?"

Camden side-eyed her before turning his attention back to the monitor. "Okay, then."

Chambers walked around the corner. "Oh, good, you're back. What did Damon say when you told him?"

"Um, yeah, he'll be ready to go." Lexi plopped down in the chair next to Camden.

"Has anyone gotten a hold of Alessa yet?" Chambers addressed the room.

Camden exhaled and stood up. "She's been pretty messed up since Quade's passing. I'll look for her back at her cabin."

Lexi blushed, and she mumbled under her breath. "She already knows."

Camden spun around. "What was that? How could she possibly know?"

Lexi's eyes nervously darted back and forth between Chambers and Camden. "Oh, uh..." *Shit.* "Um ... I think I saw her ... stuff ... at Damon's this morning," Lexi confessed.

Camden paled, and he felt as though he had been punched in the gut. "Come again?"

Lexi stammered. "I—I think Alessa—"

Camden held up his hand. "Stop. Just stop."

"Cam, I'm so—" Lexi leapt out of her chair, reaching for Camden.

Camden silently marched out of the building as the remaining Spartans stood unmoving around the room, their mouths hanging ajar.

Chambers laughed to himself and shook his head back and forth. "Hasn't anyone ever heard of the enemies-to-lovers trope? It's like that, but Damon accidentally killed her sister."

Lexi stared at Chambers, and her jaw dropped in shock.

He shrugged before nonchalantly taking a bite out of an apple. "What? It's true."

* * *

After taking a quick shower at her elder's cabin, Alessa got dressed and rushed out the door to find Camden.

As she stepped out onto the front porch, Camden was already running toward the cabin, his hands balled up into fists.

The fabric of Alessa's dress floated behind her as she hurried down the front steps. "Cam, just listen—"

"You went back to him? Really, Alessa?" he demanded, rushing forward.

She met him halfway to the road. "Of course, I did—"

Camden grabbed Alessa by the upper arms and shook her. "How could you? After all he did—"

Taken aback by his aggressive reaction, Alessa defended herself. "You're the one who discovered it was worms. You're the one who helped me find it in my heart to forgive him; what are you—"

Camden stepped back, and while stumbling in a circle, he ran his fingers through his blond hair. "For the gods' sake, Alessa. He fucked Brielle!"

Her breath escaped, and she stumbled backwards, shock written across her face.

Camden struck his chest desperately. "I mean, what else could you have wanted? What else could I have done to make you want me?"

Suddenly realizing his lashing out was not one of anger but one of misunderstanding, Alessa approached Camden and tilted her head in sympathy. "I can't thank you enough for being there when I had no one else in the world. But, Cam, I want you to dig deep and answer one question for me..." She placed her hand over his heart.

Camden stepped forward, taking Alessa's hand within his own. "Anything."

Peering into his hazel eyes, she tilted her head to the side. "Do you truly love me and only me?"

Camden's jaw dropped, but before he had the chance to respond, Alessa interjected. "I'm talking about the kind of love that makes your insides light aflame. The all-consuming love that makes everything else in the world not matter. Am I the *one* person you cannot imagine living without?"

Camden hesitated."I—I—"

Alessa's eyebrows rose, and she shrugged. "See? If I were your soulmate, you wouldn't have questioned it, and that's okay. Cam, you are one of my best friends. I would lay my life on the line for you, but what we have is not the same as romantic love."

She wrapped her arms around his neck, pulling him down for a hug. "I don't want you to miss out on finding true love because of me. I'm not worth it."

Pulling back, Alessa kissed his cheek gently. "Thanks for being my rock when I needed one. I promise to always be the same for you."

Camden blinked away hot, angry tears. "Was that all I was to you? A courtesy fuck?"

Feeling as though she had been struck in the gut, Alessa's arms dropped from his neck. "No, I would never use you like that. We both needed one another that night. Cam, I swear—"

Camden sneered. "Well, I'm glad you got what you needed from me before going back to Damon."

Alessa turned around, enraged, and flipped Camden off on her way back to her cabin. "Fuck you, Cam! You're going to feel like a real asshole when you come to the realization that I'm right."

Hands pumping, Camden yelled after her, "Yeah, well, you're a fucking idiot for going back to him!"

Slamming the door, Alessa slid her back down the wood and sat with her head in her hands. *That was not how I saw that going.*

CHAPTER FORTY-ONE

Camden marched up the grassy hill to Lexi, who was sitting beneath a tall tree. The bright, hot sun bore down on him, increasing his irritable mood, and he yelled at Lexi. "Alessa fucking went back to him!"

She rolled her eyes without so much as looking up from her book. "I assumed as much."

Breathing heavily, he paced back and forth in front of her outstretched feet through the light green grass. "And she had the gall to tell me I don't love her, as if she knows—"

"Well, do you?" Lexi interjected.

Camden stilled, defiantly placing his hands on his hips. "Do I what?"

Her fingertips gripped the book's edges, and she looked up at the tall man through her eyelashes. "Do you love Alessa?"

Camden shook his head dismissively before he resumed pacing back and forth with an annoyed scoff. "What kind of question is that?"

Lexi stared intently at Camden as he walked back and

forth. "Okay, then, let me ask you this: what does love mean to you?"

He tilted his head and shrugged. "Alessa rescued me from certain death, we stuck by each other's sides when we didn't have to, I comforted her after her sister's death; after Quade's death—"

Lexi slammed her book shut. "I didn't ask what you did for one another. I asked if you loved her and what love means to you."

His jaw clenched, and he stood stiff-backed. "You don't do those things for just anyone—"

She snickered and jumped to her feet. "No, you don't. But there are different types of love: familial, platonic, playful"—she paused, her head tilted back, looking up into Camden's eyes—"passionate."

Swallowing back his feelings of uncertainty, Camden faltered. "Uh—"

"Exactly." Lexi shook her head while half-shrugging in defeat. Picking up her com, she slapped the band onto her wrist.

Camden's jaw dropped as he stared at her in confusion. "Why do I feel like you're mad at me?"

"Because I am!" Lexi snapped. "All I ever hear about is Alessa and how her actions aren't the right ones and how you think she should do better, but guess what, Cam? Alessa is living her life the best she knows how to. I think you need to stop being so obsessed with someone who is in love with someone else. Open your eyes," she grumbled.

Camden frowned, and his shoulders dropped as he struggled with confusion. "To what?"

"Ugh!" Lexi stormed away, yelling back over her shoulder, "Just figure your shit out and leave me out of it."

Plopping down in the tall grass beneath the tree, Camden murmured to himself as he watched Lexi stomp away. "What the hell was that all about?"

CHAPTER FORTY-TWO

Behind a large desk, two well-dressed news anchors sat next to each other.

The woman with bouncy blonde hair spoke first. "In other news, the violent mobs have lessened in frequency, and their numbers seem to be dwindling."

The red-headed news anchor nodded excitedly. "Yes, this is great news for the affected communities."

The blonde's eyebrows drew together. "But there's no real explanation for their sudden disappearance, so there remain more questions than answers."

The redhead agreed. "Precisely. Law enforcement has found hundreds of Frenzied's decaying bodies. After their autopsies, the medical examiners confirmed they died due to a combination of emaciation and enlarged hearts, also known as cardiomegaly."

The blonde peered over at her colleague. "Did they say what the cause of death is?"

The redhead answered, "So far, the assumption is that the

violent individuals are not eating much, if at all, after their transition. And the reasoning behind their heart being enlarged is still unknown."

The first news anchor nervously tucked her blonde hair behind her ear. "No one has gotten to examine a live specimen yet, which makes them near impossible to study."

Clearing her throat, the redhead chuckled nervously. "How about we talk about some more positive news? The local football team is in the state finals. Go Rangers!"

The blonde beamed into the camera. "And President Barnes has an important announcement, so let's head on down to the White House to hear what he has to say."

Positioned behind bulletproof glass and a podium, the president cleared his throat as those surrounding him kept their distance. The older man stood tall in his pressed navy-blue suit and red tie as he stared at the reporters before him.

"Thank you for clearing your busy schedules to be with me today," the president began. "I'd like to start by saying that those who are working beside us to diligently rid this country of the vermin that have been allowed to go unchecked for far too long will be greatly compensated and awarded for their dedication. If you are interested in becoming one of the collectors, please visit your local police station to apply."

He glanced to the side of the room and took a deep breath. Returning his attention to the reporters and the cameras, he flashed his pearly white teeth. "I have asked you all here today to make several announcements regarding the future of the United States. I have signed into law some spectacular, long-overdue changes.

"First off, abortion is no longer legal in any state in the United States, as of one week from today. Second, it is now illegal for any person to file a false police report. If an individual is found to have made a report based on flimsy evidence, they will face a minimum prison term of one year.

"Lastly, to ensure our citizens' health is being taken seriously, our government has been granted access to every American citizen's health records. This allows those who require more assistance to easily receive aid by being moved to facilities equipped with the resources to provide the additional support."

The president beamed, and the reporters clapped loudly as he glanced off to the side of the room once more. His gaze met Lucas Greenfield's, who was unseen by the crowd and cameras, and Lucas nodded agreeably.

Sneaking up beside Lucas, Cain buttoned his cuffs while tilting his head toward the president. "How'd you do it?" he asked quietly. "I understand being manipulative, but this goes beyond that."

Lucas grinned maliciously as he continued to admire his puppet, the president. "Money talks, and I've got plenty of it."

Cain leaned into his uncle. "How does it feel to get everything you ever dreamed of?"

Lucas grabbed his nephew's tie and adjusted the fabric, pulling it tight against his neck. He sneered before casting his gaze across the crowd, and plucking a white handkerchief from his front pocket, Lucas flicked the fabric. "You see all those people, grasping onto everything this old coot says, no matter how insane the idea may be? Every single one of them wants power, and they blindly believe he will be the one to give it to them."

Cain glared at the crowd through his half-mask. "They're sheep..."

Lucas snickered while tucking his handkerchief into his nephew's breast pocket. "Being led to slaughter." He patted Cain's chest with the palm of his hand. "It's about time for you to make your speech." Lucas grinned enthusiastically. "Make me proud."

CHAPTER FORTY-THREE

Opening the front door to their Texas rental home, Damon exhaled. "Welcome to our home for the foreseeable future."

Alessa peered into the tall entryway. "Wow. It's huge!"

Her head tilted back as she admired the bright colors. The mural painted the on long wall depicted a vine that had grown uncontrollably up the stairs to the second story.

Damon laughed to himself. "That's what she said."

Whipping around, Alessa stared at him, her mouth ajar. "Damon!"

He shut the door behind him with a grin. "I couldn't help myself."

Sunlight streamed in through the clear skylight. "Stunning," Alessa mumbled while looking up.

Damon dropped his bag before flinging his leather jacket onto the back of the couch. Hurrying over to Alessa, he scooped her up.

She squealed as Damon carried her toward the stairs.

"We have at least an hour alone," Damon said in a husky voice.

Alessa flashed a cheeky grin and peered up at Damon through her eyelashes. "Is that why you were so urgent about us leaving when we did?"

Damon grinned wickedly as he ran up the stairs with a laughing Alessa in his arms.

Camden grumbled to himself while pacing back and forth in front of the small lake. "The fuck does Lexi mean by 'what does love mean to me'? Of course, love involves things people do for each other. It'd be absurd to think otherwise."

Looking at the sunlight reflecting off the water's surface, Camden growled. Holding his hand up to block the bright light, he cursed in Russian.

Thinking back to all the times Lexi had been there for him, Camden played the memories in a montage within his mind. He shook his head back and forth, clearing himself of the images. "Why was she so angry about me talking about Alessa? She couldn't be jealous, could she?"

Staring at the sunlight reflecting off the lake, Camden had a sudden epiphany. He stumbled backwards as he replayed Lexi and his interactions over the last few months in his mind. He relived their laughter, their playfulness, their jokes, their sparring sessions...

His jaw dropped as he stumbled away from the lake. "Shit. Lexi's right. I don't love Alessa."

Camden swore under his breath, sprinting for the armory. "Dammit. Lexi better not have left for Texas yet."

Turning the corner, Camden saw Lexi reaching for weapons hanging on the wall. Placing his hands on his hips, he bent over, breathing hard. "Oh, good. You're ... still ... here."

Lexi glanced at him out of the corner of her eye while up on her tiptoes, reaching for weapons to pack from the wall. "What's the matter with you? Why are you out of breath?"

With his hands still on his hips, Camden approached Lexi. "I need to talk to you."

She grunted while grabbing a sharp blade off a shelf. "Can't you see that I'm kind of busy?"

He snatched the blade from her hand and tossed it into her bag sitting on the floor. Throwing Lexi over his shoulder, Camden declared, "This can't wait."

"Whoa! Cam," she shrieked, striking his back. "What are you doing?"

Setting her down in front of a nearby tree, Camden shook out his arms before running his fingers nervously through his hair. "Okay..."

Lexi eyed Camden suspiciously as he walked away from her. "Seriously, what's going on with you?"

Whipping around to face Lexi, Camden stilled. "Do you love me?"

Lexi laughed nervously. "What? Cam, we don't have time for this. I'm about to leave."

He rushed toward her, stopping just shy of his lips touching hers. "I need to know. Because"—Camden licked his lips while looking down at Lexi's—"I may have just come to the realization that I love you."

Her eyebrow arched in disbelief. "How can that be when just a few short hours ago you were sure you were in love with Alessa? Sounds to me like you don't know what you want."

She walked to the side of Camden, but he stuck his arm out, wrapping it around her midsection, holding her in place.

Rotating Lexi toward him, he bent down and, while

holding her neck and lower back, he pressed his lips against hers.

As Lexi's body reacted to his touch, her back arched, urging his kiss to deepen.

Pulling away, Camden peered down, and as she blinked slowly, her ragged breathing normalized.

As she grinned up at him, his heart fluttered. He bent down and pressed his forehead against hers. "So, this is what love feels like."

Lexi touched the side of his face as a soft smile formed at the corner of her lips. "Took you long enough." She tilted her head back and pulled him in for another long kiss.

The heat from their bodies intensified as did their need.

"I want to taste you," Camden whispered huskily into Lexi's ear.

Her eyes sprang open with need. "But I've got a mission," she said hesitantly.

"Like hell you do." Camden marched toward the open door to the room full of weapons. Eyeing Chambers, Camden hollered in his direction. "Hey, Chambers, you good if Lexi sits this one out?"

Chambers' eyes narrowed in concern. "Yeah, we've got more than enough of us heading down tonight. She's good, though?"

"Oh, she's about to be real good." Camden smirked before winking.

Understanding his message, Chambers laughed as he waved Camden out. "Okay, then."

Camden marched back to where he had left the red-headed Spartan and scooped her up into his arms. "You've been excused. Now, where can we get some privacy?"

CHAPTER FORTY-FOUR

Later that evening, Alessa and the other Spartan women were in the rental home's bathroom getting dressed for their first night out. "Where's Lexi? I thought she was joining us," asked Alessa.

One of the other Spartan women shrugged before smacking her magenta-painted lips together. "Must've changed her mind."

After applying bright red lipstick, Alessa exited the bathroom to find Damon dressed in black from his button up shirt down to his black slacks and shoes. He was in the middle of the living room, standing on a wooden coffee table, addressing the houseful of Spartans.

"So, to reiterate, Spartan women, you are to pretend to be inebriated at your chosen location and then exit the establishment alone to entice the nefarious patrons to follow you outside. Each group has been assigned to different ragers, frat parties, bars, and dance clubs within a twenty-five-mile radius. Again, you are to pretend to get drunk or be drugged.

Under no circumstances are you to actually drink enough alcohol to be incoherent.

"Spartan men, your job is to keep your eyes on every one of our women to make sure they stay safe. You've each got your assignments and partners. It's time to head out."

Jumping down from the table, Damon eyed Alessa, and seeing her bright-pink top and black leather skirt, he growled. Grabbing her around her waist, Damon kissed up the side of her neck.

Alessa playfully pushed him away and adjusted her top. "Okay, okay. This outfit is not for you." Grabbing a half-moon purse, she slung it over her shoulder.

After filtering out through the front door, the Spartans split up into their designated cars that were idling out front.

Sitting down beside Alessa in the back of the car, Damon laid his warm hand on her upper thigh. Inching up her skirt, his fingers played with the edges of her panties.

"Damon..." Alessa warned as her cheeks reddened in response to his touch.

"I can't help myself," Damon professed. Bending into her, he pressed his lips against Alessa's neck before whispering into her ear, "I spent far too long unable to touch you. Good luck getting me to stop now."

Hearing the need in his voice, Alessa's lips separated, and her breathing became ragged.

"Oh, but there is this one thing." Damon pulled back and dug into an inner pocket of his leather jacket.

Watching him search, Alessa tilted her head. "What are you doing?"

He pulled out his mother's ring. "I believe this belongs to you."

Alessa beamed. Taking the alexandrite and diamond ring, she slid it onto her finger.

He reached back down into his jacket pocket and withdrew a second piece of jewelry. "And one more thing."

As Damon held up another ring, Alessa's eyes widened in surprise.

The black band wrapped around the ring's entirety, connecting beneath a magenta and blue-green princess-cut alexandrite.

"I know this isn't the most romantic of locations, but our lives don't exactly leave much time for planned romance. But I promise to take you on one hell of a honeymoon if you agree to marry me. So, what do you say, sydämen liekki? Will you be mine forever?"

Alessa nodded excitedly, her smile widening. "I will. I— I do."

After sliding the ring onto her finger, above his mother's band, Damon grabbed the side of her face and kissed her smiling lips.

As their kiss deepened, the driver hissed. "Whoa, there. I have not been paid enough for you to be doing that in my back seat."

Alessa pulled away and sank back into the seat, laughing, as Damon flashed a wicked grin.

Following Alessa into the noisy nightclub, Damon never took his eyes off the scantily clad Spartan.

Her shimmery, hot-pink backless halter top and short black leather skirt clung to all the right places.

Watching Alessa's hips sashay back and forth, Damon found it challenging to maintain his distance.

Pumping his hands, Damon went further down the bar so Alessa would appear as though she was alone.

It didn't take long for men to start hitting on her, and not just one at a time; they came in droves.

Damon was starting to attract attention from others in the club and was having to look around the giggling women to keep an eye on Alessa. *It's incredible how an engagement ring doesn't deter men from going after her in the least bit. If anything, it encourages them.*

Damon's vision zoomed in on a tiny pill being dropped into Alessa's cup by a tall man with slicked-back hair.

Holding his anger in check, Damon's jaw twitched, and his body stiffened as he fought back the urge to run over and drop-kick the man.

Peeking at Damon out of the corner of her eye, Alessa nodded once to let him know she saw the pill. Distracting the men by dropping her purse, Alessa turned around and withdrew a small vial from a tiny pouch hidden inside her skirt.

Pouring the powder into her drink, Alessa counteracted the drug the man had dosed her with.

A couple of inebriated women tugged on Damon's arm, and to maintain his cover, he allowed himself to be dragged to the dance floor.

<hr>

"I—I'm not feeling well," Alessa slurred, pretending to trip over her high heels as the group of men led her to the side of the dance floor.

As the pink liquid splashed over the edge of her cup, two

additional Spartan women showed up. "Hey, Britt, you doing okay?" one asked, using Alessa's fake name.

Alessa's head bobbed up and down as she sagged against the wall. "Yeah, no, I'm just feeling a little—"

The tall man who had dosed her stepped in. "She's probably just dehydrated. We were about to get her some water." He flashed an insincere smile. "You want anything as well?"

The two Spartan women played dumb and smiled back. "Yeah, that'd be great."

As the leader of the group of men went to the bar, three men stayed back.

After helping Alessa to a nearby bench, the Spartan women took the drinks from the tall man upon his return. "Thanks," they said in unison before discreetly pouring their powder into each.

They all drank half their drinks to appear as though they had ingested enough of the drug to produce disorientation.

The caramel blonde Spartan woman brushed Alessa's hair out of her face. "She's not getting any better. I think we'd better grab her a cab and head home."

The red-headed man spoke up as he stepped in close to the Spartan. "Oh, we can help with that."

As the four devious men surrounded the Spartan women, the black-haired man scooped Alessa up into his arms and headed for the side exit.

The dance floor filled with white smoke as the fog machine activated and green lasers reflected off the dense vapor, blocking Damon's view.

The two Spartan women began shaking their heads as if to clear their minds, and a couple of the men reached behind them, giving each other a high five. "Whoa. The room just started spinning," one of the women complained as they stepped out into the alleyway.

Damon's jaw flexed as he excused himself from the dance floor, discreetly following the group. Glancing to the side of the smoke-filled room, he caught the attention of the other Spartan men and instructed them to follow him with an urgent jerk of his head.

As the men pushed the remaining women out of the building, the heavy door slammed shut.

Alessa hung limp in the dark-haired man's arms, pretending to be unconscious while her fellow Spartans played along.

"I feel funny," the first woman slurred as she purposefully broke the heel off one of her shoes while staggering forward.

The men frantically looked up and down the alley for witnesses before they dragged the two Spartan women into a nook between two smaller staircases.

"These bitches actually thought good men still exist in the world," the blond spat while hastily unbuttoning his pants.

"No, please, don't," the second woman cried out while pretending to weakly fight back.

After setting Alessa down, the tall man spun around and, while cackling at his friend's remark, he unzipped his slacks. After pulling his pants and briefs to his knees, his eyes lifted, and his breathing hitched.

Alessa was awake and alert, standing before him with an unhinged grin.

Peering down at his erection, she laughed maniacally before glaring at him. "Is that all you've got?" she taunted.

No more than ten seconds later, Damon burst through the exit door, looking toward the sounds of loud grunting and curse words coming from halfway down the alley.

Jogging to the dark alcove, the other male Spartans joined Damon just in time to watch the show.

Flying backwards through the air, the tall man grunted as his back hit the brick wall behind him. He slid down to the wet ground with his pants and briefs still wrapped around his ankles.

While wiping her hands, Alessa rolled her eyes in disgust as she walked out after the man who had been kicked across the alley.

The red-headed man was gasping for breath while still on his knees, after having been punched in his Adam's apple.

One of the other Spartan women had her legs wrapped around the blond man's throat in a choke hold, and the second Spartan mercilessly snapped the neck of the man she had been fighting.

With a huff, she shrugged nonchalantly. "He wasn't playing nice."

Damon flashed a sideways grin. "It's all fun and games until someone gets hurt."

The woman scoffed and arched an eyebrow while stepping over the dead body. "You're one to talk. We all know what you're capable of."

Damon puffed his chest. "Thanks for the compliment, Chelsea." He turned his attention toward Alessa. "Did you get anything?"

She shook her head back and forth. "No. They were just pieces of trash looking to get lucky without having to be decent human beings."

Damon wrapped his arm protectively around Alessa's

shoulders. "Guess they should've vetted their prey better. The women in this world are lucky to have you to take out the trash."

"Ready to get back in there?" the Spartan men asked of the women.

Damon looked over at the men. "No, we are going home. This won't be solved in one night, and there's no reason to push the women. This is emotionally and physically taxing for them. Let's just hope when we check in with the others later that they got more information than we did."

Alessa sighed and took Damon's hand within her own as it dangled off her shoulder. "I could go for a good night's sleep. Or at this hour, a good morning's sleep. I haven't been sleeping very well as of late."

The Spartans walked to the front of the building, Damon and Alessa closer than the rest. "I wonder why that is," Damon whispered with a smirk.

CHAPTER FORTY-FIVE

A couple of weeks later, Damon softly kissed Alessa as she slept.

"Mmm..." Alessa moaned before slowly blinking her eyes open. "What was that for?"

Damon sat down on the edge of their bed. "A wake-up call."

Rubbing the sleep from her eyes, Alessa rolled onto her stomach, burying her face in the pillow. "Oh? Do we have somewhere we need to be?"

Jumping up, Damon playfully smacked Alessa's backside. "We do."

She squealed and flipped over onto her back with an indignant grin.

Sporting a confident smile, he winked before continuing his explanation. "We've got some connections at the local morgue, and with your background in medicine, I think it would benefit us to go see some of the victims."

After a quick yelp and giggle, Alessa sat upright, her eyes wide and alert. "You mean I'll have full access to examine some of the women who have passed away following the forced impregnations?"

Damon stared at Alessa in concern and pursed his lips. "Your excitement kinda freaks me out." He held up his thumb and first finger. "Just a little bit."

She threw the bedcovers off and jumped up to get dressed. "It has nothing to do with being excited. My being able to physically lay eyes on the victims could help us figure out why the deaths are occurring."

After slipping into a bra, Alessa tugged on a shirt. "It won't change the fact that they shouldn't be happening in the first place. Fuck Cain and all the people who voted for this," she cursed under her breath.

Damon watched her wiggle into a pair of jeans and grinned before he slipped into his leather jacket. "Yeah, well, you should have at least an hour."

Alessa hurried to their bathroom to brush her hair and teeth. "Great! That's more than enough time," she mumbled with the toothbrush sticking out the corner of her mouth.

After ringing the bell, a tall woman clacked her heels toward the Spartans awaiting entrance into the single-story building.

While being escorted into the morgue, Damon shook the medical examiner's hand. "Dr. Peters."

The woman winced as she placed her cold hand within his. "There's no need to use my assigned name, Spartan. Every security camera has looped footage playing." She withdrew her hand and redirected her attention. "And you must be the infamous Alessa."

Alessa chuckled as she tucked her hands nervously into the

back pockets of her blue jeans. "I'm not sure what you've heard."

The medical examiner crossed her arms. "Your microchip faltered, causing your activation to glitch. You can influence technology, and you killed damn-near every Frenzied that attacked the Official Fortress without lifting a finger."

Alessa blushed and half-shrugged. "I mean, a finger or two was lifted."

"Anyway, you're here to examine the bodies, correct?" the medical examiner asked as she walked away.

Damon and Alessa hurried down the dim, cold hallway after the medical examiner.

Pushing through metal double doors, the three Spartans approached two rectangular metal tables, each with a dead body adorned with a white sheet.

Looking down at the first of the women, the medical examiner lifted her tablet to read the description of the deceased woman. "This woman's family identified her as Jeanne Fryer. She was twenty years old and was attending university. After being denied the morning-after pill, she became pregnant. Immediately after finding out about the pregnancy, she attempted to obtain an abortion but was apprehended while crossing state lines. A short while later, she died while in police custody."

Alessa's forehead creased in concern while she was examining the woman's waxy skin. "How could this have happened?"

The medical examiner looked up from her tablet and stared directly into Alessa's eyes. "She was grossly neglected. This poor woman died in the care of those who had sworn to protect her."

Alessa's nose wrinkled in disgust as Damon pumped his hands in frustration.

"What the fuck?" he cursed.

The medical examiner's face fell. "If that surprises you, wait until you see the effects of the fetus on the woman's—Jeanne's—body." She pulled back the white sheet, exposing the woman's naked torso, down to her hips.

The woman's stomach had horrific, dark stretch marks engraved into the thinned skin on her enlarged abdomen.

Alessa turned to the medical examiner. "You haven't yet—"

"No. I was waiting for you. Besides, I've done enough of these by now to know what the autopsy will likely show."

The medical examiner gloved before picking up a small blade from the metal table. "Ready?"

Alessa stepped closer to the table, and Damon's face turned a shade of green.

"How about you keep a lookout? By the door," Alessa suggested.

Swallowing hard, Damon agreed with a nod of his head, nearly bolting toward the exit doors.

The medical examiner scoffed before dragging the blade across the woman's upper chest and down the midsection, making a Y-cut towards her pelvis.

Alessa swallowed as the blade went up and over the distended belly, slicing through the claw-like stretch marks. "What happened before her death?"

The medical examiner exhaled as she cut deeper. "The reports are sketchy at best. No one was monitoring her while she was incarcerated. Which is terribly negligent, especially due to her pregnancy, but the other women who were in the shared cell said she had been complaining of back and stomach pains for weeks. Which makes sense, what with her rapidly expanding belly. The report said that in the final moments before her death, she screamed in agony, complaining of a shooting pain in her abdomen and shoulders. Just before losing consciousness, Jeanne said she felt dizzy."

Alessa bowed her head in respect. "I'm so sorry humanity failed you," she apologized before glancing up at the medical examiner. "Are we thinking uterine rupture?"

Impressed, the medical examiner half-grinned at Alessa. "It has been the case in every autopsy I have performed thus far, so I assume this would be no different."

Pulling apart the tight skin, fat, and muscle stretched across Jeanne's abdomen, they watched a grossly deformed, full-term baby emerge.

The examiner's nose wrinkled. "Wait. This can't be," the examiner said, extracting the mangled fetus from the woman's abdominal cavity.

Alessa placed her fingers against her lips in shock. "How could she not have known about ... this? How far along was she again?"

The Spartan medical examiner scowled. "The report said it had only been six weeks since the attack."

Alessa stumbled backwards while shaking her head back and forth. "There's no way. That is a full-term baby. But it also isn't a baby at all." She stared at its deformities, extending from head to toe, and a shudder of fear went through her.

"This is unlike anything I have ever seen. The rest of the deaths I've encountered have followed the same timeline: rape, forced impregnation, and an increased rate of growth of the fetus, resulting in rupture of the uterus. However, this is by far the largest one I have extracted. This is the size of a 38-week fetus, but its appearance is—"

"One that would not allow its survival," Alessa interjected.

The medical examiner set the small body on the shorter silver table beside the deceased woman.

"Precisely. Just from a quick glance, I don't see a mouth or nose, its heart is on the outside of the body, the skull only covers the left side of its brain, and its appendages are ... well." The medical examiner pointed at the fetus. "Useless, for lack of a better term."

"I can see for myself what they are." Alessa turned her back on the medical examiner. Taking slow, deep breaths, she attempted to calm her rapidly beating heart. "Whatever is happening to these women is intentional. We're being experimented on."

The medical examiner pursed her lips together. "Unfortunately, I have to agree."

Alessa excused herself as she swallowed the bile creeping up the back of her throat. "Um, excuse me, but I have to go confer with my—" She put a hand over her mouth, holding back the urge to vomit.

Continuing her examination, the medical examiner waved her hand in dismissal. "I hope this has helped you."

Bursting through the double doors, Alessa was focused on deep breathing as she sprinted past Damon.

"What happened?" Damon yelled, scrambling to catch up to her.

She burst through the exit door and bent over the railing.

Damon rubbed Alessa's upper back as she vomited into the patches of yellow grass and dirt.

She stood erect while wiping her lips with the back of her hand. "They're experimenting on women." She inhaled deeply. "The victims are being forced to carry these creatures, and we have to find out why."

CHAPTER FORTY-SIX

One month later...

Chewing the mint-flavored gum, Alessa smacked her lips together. "Think tonight's gonna be the night?"

"I sure hope so," Damon sighed while stretching his neck to the side. "The time away has been nice and all, but I'm ready to get home and sleep in my own bed."

"I can't wait to get home and sleep in your bed as well." Alessa flashed a wicked grin at Damon.

The cab stopped in front of a red brick building on the corner of the street. "We're here," the driver announced.

Damon and Alessa walked up to the building and in through the front door.

She yelled at Damon over the music. "Are Dani and Dru on their way?"

"They'll be here." Damon tilted his head towards the counter, and Alessa smiled, following close behind.

Holding up his first two fingers at the bartender, Damon shouted, "Two shots of tequila, please."

Alessa cocked her head and grinned mischievously. "I thought we weren't supposed to get drunk while working."

Damon flashed his handsomely crooked smile. "It's just one drink."

The bartender handed Damon two full shot glasses.

After holding one out to Alessa, he wrapped his arm around hers, and they exclaimed, "One, two, three," in unison.

After downing the liquid, Damon let out a loud exhale. "I gotta hit the restroom. Don't do anything stupid," he yelled, pushing through the crowd.

Alessa backed up against the countertop and pressed her fingers to her lips. *Oh man, that made me nauseous.*

She was focused on deep breathing when a man approached her from the crowd. "Are you okay?" he asked with a southern twang. "You don't look so good."

Holding up a hand, she forced a smile. "Yeah, I'm thinking that tequila had a bit of a kick to it."

"It's kinda hot in here, you wanna head outside for some fresh air?" He held up his hands innocently before tilting the brim of his Western hat downward. "My mama raised me to be a gentleman; you don't have to worry about me tryin' no nonsense. I damn well know anyone in this bar could walk out there at any second."

Alessa's stomach rolled, and she rushed to the side exit.

Falling through the doors into the fresh air, Alessa inhaled deeply as she placed her hands on her hips. "Oh, you were right. I feel much better," she breathed.

Feeling the man's hot breath on the back of her neck, Alessa tensed.

His voice suddenly deepened and grew more authoritarian,

the southern accent gone. In its place was a light Russian accent. "You are a pretty little thing, aren't you?"

Taking Alessa by surprise, he held her in place and licked up the side of her neck.

Realizing he was a Bodyguard, Alessa played along, pretending to be helpless.

Trying to weakly break free from his grasp, she squealed. "What do you think you're doing?"

"Only what I was told to, darlin," the man said in a forced southern twang.

She pretended to panic as the Bodyguard pushed Alessa further down the alleyway, away from the side door. "Please don't do this."

Grasping her arms tightly behind her back, the man grinned as he slammed her chest up against the building. "Don't worry. This won't take long, and then you and I can both be on our way."

While pressed against the brick wall, Alessa feigned tears. "Am I going to end up like all those other women?"

The man stilled for a moment. "How do you know—"

Alessa sniffled. "It's been all over the news. The victims are dying. Please don't kill me. I don't want to die."

His grip tightened around her wrists as he unbuttoned his pants. "Well, hopefully our little soldier won't kill you."

Dropping the facade, Alessa's irises glitched crimson in color.

"Soldier?" she asked, her voice strong and unwavering as his pants hit the ground.

Wrenching her wrists from his grasp, Alessa broke free and whipped around to face the Bodyguard.

Narrowing her eyes, she stared up at him, searching his

brain for his microchip. Gaining control of his chip, Alessa pointed at the wet ground. "Down," she demanded.

As the man's knees hit a small puddle, water splashed, and Alessa exhaled in satisfaction.

The Bodyguard knelt before her, his body unnaturally stiff.

"I need answers," she began. "First, why did it take so long for your kind to target a Spartan? We've been hunting you for over a month."

The man glared menacingly. Unable to resist her hold on him, he reluctantly answered. "We can sense those that have microchips, like us, but I can't see yours. Why is that?"

With a shrug, Alessa looked off to the side. "What can I say, I'm special."

Drool fell from the Bodyguard's lower lip. "You're ... the one."

Her face scrunched up in confusion. "What the hell is that supposed to mean? Look, I don't have time for your riddles." She squatted down to his level. "Why are you attacking women?"

The Bodyguard stared into her eyes, emotionless. "To impregnate them with super-sperm."

Alessa tilted her head. "I thought Bodyguards couldn't make children."

"We couldn't ... before. Mr. Greenfield gave us the ability to procreate."

Hearing the man mention Lucas, Alessa's eyes narrowed. "Why would he do that? Why is that beneficial to him?"

The Bodyguard's body began to tremor, and he hesitated before answering. "Mr. Greenfield wants to create super soldiers."

Alessa's eyes flared, and she whipped out a small knife. Pressing it against the Bodyguard's throat, she asked through clenched teeth, "By raping women? Couldn't they have been created in test tubes or something?"

His Adam's apple bobbed up and down, slicing his flesh on the sharp blade. "They tried that."

Alessa tightened her mental grip on the man's microchip, causing him to wince painfully. "And?"

His eyes opened wide. "They never developed with working organs. It was determined they had to be grown within a human host."

Blood dripped from Alessa's right nostril as she struggled to remain connected to the Bodyguard. "Tell me more."

The man's entire body trembled as he tried to defiantly press his lips together.

Alessa's eyes flared as she yelled, "Tell me!"

In one breath, the man explained, "Mr. Greenfield's scientists experimented on women we kidnapped. Once it was confirmed they were in their ovulation stage, they would be injected with super-sperm as well as given a boost of supplements to encourage pregnancy. They were kept sedated."

"What happened to those women? Clearly, that didn't work, or else you wouldn't be doing this."

Before beginning his explanation, he scowled in defiance. "They died. Every single one. The scientists finally determined the soldiers would not survive in a body that was not living as it should be, so the experiment was paused until it was determined Elite Bodyguards could be carriers for the future super soldiers."

"Why are women still dying?" she demanded.

The Bodyguard separated his lips in a crazed smile. "The women are weak. Their organs can't keep up with the rapid growth of the infants, which is why—"

"Alessa!" Damon yelled from the doors to the bar before running toward them.

The Bodyguard's eyebrows raised as blood seeped out from beneath his teeth. "You are the one."

Her face dropped with the weight of his words. "Why do you keep saying that? What the fuck is that supposed to mean?"

The Elite Bodyguard's spine straightened as Alessa felt her hold over him falter. "You'll find out soon enough," he spat before his irises flashed golden.

With a loud crack, his neck suddenly snapped to the side at an unnatural angle, and his lifeless body collapsed to the ground with a sickening thud.

"Fuck! Alesssa!" Damon hit the ground before her.

Skidding along the wet concrete on his knees, he held her face. "Sydämen liekki, are you okay? You weren't supposed to do anything stupid."

Nodding her head up and down vigorously, she licked her lips. "I'm fine." She looked into Damon's eyes, full of concern, and exhaled loudly. "I actually learned quite a lot."

Damon's eyebrows furrowed. "Like?"

Alessa unglitched and fell forward into his strong arms, panting heavily. "You need to end the mission and have everyone report back to the rental. I'll explain everything once we're back there. I need the ride home to just ... decompress."

Recognizing the haunted look on her face, Damon agreed. "Alright. I'll make the call."

Alessa sat silently on the bed as Damon rushed around the room packing their things.

After a brief knock on their bedroom doorframe, a Spartan man stepped into the room. "What's with calling us all back? Did you get the information you needed?"

Damon glanced over at Alessa, who was still sitting on the bed, staring at the wall. Clearing his throat, he folded a shirt before tossing it into his bag. "Um, yeah. We did."

"Well, what is it? What's the scoop? Everyone's talking theories, but nobody's been told any—"

"Lucas is attempting to create an army of super soldiers by impregnating people with genetically altered super-sperm carried by Elite Bodyguards," Alessa interrupted.

"Oh, fuck," the Spartan man at the door cursed before running out of the room to tell the others.

Damon rushed toward Alessa and wrapped his arms around her.

After taking a steadying breath, Alessa continued. "They've been avoiding us since the moment we got here. The Bodyguard said they could sense us; our microchips, to be more exact."

Damon jumped up and threw things haphazardly into their bags. "How could they do that?"

Alessa shrugged and stammered. "I—I don't know. They started by experimenting on unconscious women whom they had kidnapped, but when that proved unsuccessful, they moved on to impregnating women while they were alert, allowing them to be awake during the"—she gulped—"creature's growth."

Damon stilled and stared at Alessa, casting a questioning glance.

"You should've seen it, Damon. The creature the medical examiner pulled out of that poor woman ... it was no human baby."

Damon finished packing and zipped his bag before pulling the handle up on Alessa's. "We've got to put a stop to these motherfuckers. For once and for all." Damon whipped around to look at Alessa. "It's that son of a bitch nephew of his, Cain, who is running the show, isn't it? He's the senator who introduced the abortion law, right?"

Alessa stood up and nervously rubbed her hands on her jeans. "That's why we need to get back so quickly. I need to talk to Sera. Maybe we can come up with a plan to put into place to prevent people in the general population from getting pregnant for the time being, just until all of this is sorted out."

They ran out to the cab scheduled to drop them off outside of town.

Pulling up to an empty field, large enough for every one of the Spartans to transport home with just one press of the transportation device, Alessa babbled to herself. "I hope Cam isn't still angry with me."

Overhearing her, Damon asked. "Why would Camden be angry with you?"

"Oh." Alessa laughed dismissively. "He thought that he and I were going to end up together or something. But I told him—"

"Why would he have thought that? You two were inseparable, yeah, but weren't you like brother and sister?" Damon interjected.

Alessa scoffed and mumbled under her breath, "You don't fuck your brother."

Realizing she had said the words aloud, Alessa's jaw dropped.

Damon's face immediately turned a deep shade of red, and the veins in his neck bulged as his jaw flexed. The car was still moving as he grabbed the door handle.

Snatching up his bag, Damon flew out of the car and marched towards the other Spartans.

"Damon? Damon!" Alessa ran after him.

As the cab drove away, Damon ignored her while yelling at his fellow Spartans. "Ready?"

Pushing the trigger, Damon erected the invisible barrier between themselves and the general population.

"Damon, I—" Alessa begged as she reached toward him.

Pressing the transport button on his wristband, Damon and every other Spartan in the field disappeared.

CHAPTER FORTY-SEVEN

Appearing at the edge of New Sparta, Damon tossed his heavy black bag and made a mad dash for the statues, where Camden stood amidst a group of Spartans.

"Shit," Alessa cursed before chasing him.

Seraphine was the first to notice Damon, and her eyes widened as she stepped out of the way. "Nope."

Chambers, Orion, and Camden all turned their heads to see what Seraphine was referring to when Damon's fist slammed down, hard and fast, into the side of Camden's face.

"Damon!" Alessa screamed at the same time as the crack of the ex-Bodyguard's cheekbone was heard.

Camden hit the ground with a grunt as everyone stood frozen in shock.

"The fuck was that about?" Chambers yelled as he jumped in between Damon and Camden.

"What the hell was that for?" Seraphine demanded as she fell before Camden.

Holding him beneath his jaw, Seraphine checked

Camden's eyes, instructing him to follow her finger. "Is your vision blurry, or do you have any floaters?"

Camden glared up at Damon as the Spartan paced back and forth.

Pointing down at the fallen ex-Bodyguard, Damon growled. "He slept with Alessa."

Camden pressed his fingertips into the side of his broken cheekbone. "Oh," he chuckled. "Let it go, guys. His hit is justified."

Alessa rushed up behind Damon, and her hands covered her mouth as she stared at Camden lying on the ground. "Shit, Cam, I'm so sorry."

Camden wiped the blood off his cheekbone while trying to shake the ringing from his ears. He jumped up and stepped forward, standing face-to-face with Damon. "That was a good hit; I'll give you that, Spartan." He tilted his head while sporting a diabolical smirk. "But if you ever try that again, I'll knock you the fuck out."

"Men are so stupid," Alessa groaned with a shake of her head. Shooting daggers at Damon, she pointed at him. "We will talk later, but right now I don't have time to deal with both of your egos. There are more urgent issues I need to address."

She directed her attention to Seraphine. "I need to speak with you. Now." Alessa grasped her friend's hand, helping her up off her knees, and pulled her to the side.

She glanced around before she spoke in hushed tones. "I found out why Cain introduced the abortion ban."

Seraphine leaned into Alessa. "Spit it out."

"It's worse than we could've imagined." Alessa swallowed before nervously licking her lips. Glancing at her group of friends, Alessa's eyes landed upon Camden. Blinking hard, she tore herself from his gaze. "They're forcing women to become pregnant and carry their army of engineered super soldiers."

Seraphine's lower jaw dropped. "What?"

Trying to calm her nausea, Alessa exhaled through pursed lips, and after putting her hands on her hips, she rocked back and forth. "Yeah, it's fucking terrible. These poor women are being ripped apart from the inside because they are not strong enough to grow a baby that quickly, if you can even call them babies. I think they're still experimenting with the fetus-making formulas. The fetuses are coming out with deformities that are incompatible with life ... thus far. Have you learned anything from the Frenzied specimens, especially the ones you've had since the attack in Greece?"

Seraphine swallowed and nodded excitedly. "Oh, yes. The first group you brought back from California died. They had no drive to eat, drink, or even rest. We tried to strap them down and give them nutrients through both an IV and a nasogastric tube, but they remained aggressive until they dropped dead of a heart attack. But the Frenzied brought back from Greece are different."

Alessa's forehead scrunched up as she crossed her arms. "How so?"

"Have you heard the reports that some are dying, but most of the Frenzied have disappeared into thin air?"

"Yes, we did hear some of the reports," Damon joined the conversation, stepping up protectively behind Alessa.

"The newer Frenzied have pacemakers implanted, or at least a similar medical machine to keep the heart pumping. I believe someone is collecting them and implanting the devices near their hearts, which is how you took them down during the battle. You targeted their electrical impulses generated by the machines, stopping their hearts from beating," Seraphine explained.

Camden rubbed the back of his neck. "Nice," he smiled at Alessa.

She couldn't help but give a hint of a smile in return. *Maybe he doesn't hate me anymore.*

"Actually..." Seraphine turned away from Alessa, deep in thought.

Alessa reached out and touched Seraphine's shoulder. "Actually, what?"

Seraphine shook her head, placing her hand atop Alessa's reassuringly. "Nothing. It can't possibly be related."

Just as Alessa was about to ask Seraphine to clarify, a very pregnant Spartan emerged from the transportation dock, yelling for help.

Seraphine held her hand over her eyes to shield them from the sun. "Amelia?" she mumbled, recognizing the Spartan.

Two Spartan warriors scooped the woman up under each of her arms, and she hobbled forward.

Stumbling towards Seraphine, the Spartan's swollen abdomen stretched on one side before pulsating on the other.

Camden jumped back in alarm. "What the fuck is that about?"

Falling forward, Amelia's arms wrapped around Alessa and Seraphine's shoulders. "Help me," she cried, panicking. "Please help me. Get it out of me!"

Seraphine pointed at the medical ward and screamed for help. "Get me a stretcher, now!"

With a scream, Amelia's water broke violently, splashing all over the ground.

Alessa grabbed the woman's hand and allowed her to painfully squeeze her fingers. "Come on, we've got you," she said, encouraging Amelia to start moving forward with a hand on her lower back.

"They're all dead; no one ever makes it," Amelia grunted.

"Who's dead?" Seraphine asked as they marched closer to the medical ward.

"All of the gen pop women being held..." Amelia gritted her teeth together, and spit flew out from between her lips. She inhaled and exhaled quickly. "Rory, Stacia..."

Realization dawned upon Seraphine's face. "You all were kidnapped? When?"

The skin on Amelia's stomach stretched so far it became translucent, and she shrieked as tears streamed down her face. "Get it out of me! Don't let it kill me, please."

Seraphine held the woman tightly. "We're moving as quickly as we can. How about we focus on getting you taken care of, and then you can answer our questions."

Struggling to tug Damon's rings from her finger during all the chaos, Alessa grunted as they finally pulled free. Holding them out for him to take, she placed the rings in his hand. "Keep them safe for me."

Damon's eyes darted back and forth between Alessa and Amelia. "Is there anything I can do?"

The stretcher reached them, and Alessa, Seraphine, and Damon helped Amelia up onto the top.

"Not unless you know how to deliver a baby," she hollered over her shoulder as she ran alongside the stretcher.

Slamming into the two swinging doors to the labor and delivery surgery suite, Seraphine barked out orders. "I need a c-section kit set up, and I need Amelia put to sleep as fast as possible so I—"

"I don't fucking care if I'm asleep! Get it out of me before I die!" Amelia cried as blood seeped from between her lips.

"Shit. Sera, she's bleeding internally. We've gotta get moving," Alessa gasped.

Amelia's vitals floated in mid-air above her, displaying her increasing heart rate and dropping blood pressure.

An electric scalpel appeared within Seraphine's grasp. "I'm going in."

What appeared to be claws scratching from inside Amelia's abdomen stretched her already thinned skin.

Suddenly, she let out a bloodcurdling scream, and her vitals bottomed out.

"Amelia, no!" Alessa pleaded, grabbing her shoulders and shaking them.

Exhaling loudly in defeat, Seraphine watched the floating line move left to right in a single line on Amelia's vital signs display. With determination, Seraphine pressed the blade against Amelia's swollen abdomen.

As soon as there was a big enough gap for the creature to fit through, it used its long claws extending from its slender fingers to crawl out. Gasping for air, its chest hardly moved, as if its lungs weren't developed.

As quickly as the vitals for the creature-child rose into the air above it, it flatlined and collapsed in a bloody mess atop Amelia's open belly.

Alessa's mouth hung ajar, and her hands began to shake. *The creature looks almost like ... a human child. They're getting closer to accomplishing their goal: creating an actual super soldier. Shit...*

Staring at the dead Spartan with the creature lying unmoving on her stomach, Alessa felt vomit burn up the back of her throat, and she ran from the room.

Running down the hallway, Alessa rubbed her hands together, still feeling the sensation of Amelia's firm grip around her fingers. Intense heat crept up the back of her neck as Alessa flew into the bathroom, and she pushed open the stall door, projectile vomiting.

Feeling another wave of nausea, she emptied the remainder of her stomach's contents into the toilet.

Nyx's disembodied voice echoed in Alessa's mind. "Why would they be interested in Spartan women? Why would Rory, Stacia, and Amelia all have been experimented on? Think, Alessa. You're almost there."

Looking absentmindedly into the toilet as it refilled with water, Alessa gasped. "Oh, shit." The color drained from her face as the realization dawned on Alessa. "They need Spartans' physical strength to grow the babies."

Wiping the side of her lips with toilet paper, she barged out of the stall.

A Spartan standing at the bathroom counter spun around in surprise. Feeling the need to explain herself, Alessa forced a false laugh. "Uh, sorry about that. I must've gotten that stomach bug that's been going around."

The Spartan scrunched up their nose in confusion. Shaking their head back and forth, they chuckled. "What stomach bug?"

Alessa pursed her lips and smiled awkwardly while washing her hands.

Eyeing Alessa's stomach, the woman dried her hands off. "You sure you, alone, don't have a *bug*?"

Scrunching her eyes up, Alessa chuckled to herself as the woman left the restroom. What did she mean by—

Alessa's head jerked up, and she stared at her pale reflection. Memories flashed in her subconscious, and her eyes darted to the side as she did the mental math.

In her memory, Seraphine injected her with the birth control in the upper arm, then stood before her. "You're good for the next six years," Seraphine said sternly.

Alessa's eyes dropped to her lower abdomen, and she laid her hand on it.

Seraphine's disembodied voice echoed in Alessa's mind. "Repeat after me, six years."

Alessa held up her fingers as she counted aloud. "One, Two, Three, Four, Five, Six..." her voice trailed as she realized she was late getting her birth control replaced by nearly ten months.

"Shit ... shit ... shit..." she cursed as she ran down the hallway with her hand protectively on her lower abdomen. Barging into the ultrasound room, she locked the door behind her and grabbed the external ultrasound wand.

As the computer asked for Alessa's retina scan, she grumbled under her breath. "Come the fuck on."

It took her all of five seconds to decide to falsify her identification, and she grabbed a generic trainee ID badge from out of a hidden drawer that only medical staff knew existed.

After flashing the badge in front of the scanner, the software logged her on, and Alessa lay back on the table.

Holding the wand above her abdomen, she waved it up and down, and back and forth until, floating on the screen to the side of her, was the perfect silhouette of a nine-week-old fetus. I'm pregnant?

Gasping, Alessa watched the jelly bean jump up and down

on the screen. How could I let this happen? I mean, I know how babies are made, and we have been doing plenty of it, but how could my needing my birth control replaced completely slip my mind?

A montage of Alessa's traumatic past year dawned upon her, and she tilted her head. Okay, I can't be that hard on myself. It has been one hell of a terrible year.

A sudden wave of protectiveness washed over Alessa as she considered the implications of what might happen if the Consilium or the elders found out she was pregnant. *Would they experiment on the baby?*

With one last look at the screen, she smiled to herself. You look like a dancing ember. Wiping a tear from the corner of her eye, Alessa shut down the program and pulled her shirt down. *What will Damon say? Will he be happy? We're not even married yet. Is that allowed with his high status?*

Without looking up, Alessa ran out into the hallway. Ugh ... I never followed that topic in school. I never thought it would ever pertain to me.

"Oh!" She smacked into Camden while rushing towards the building's exit.

"Hey! Oh, Alessa—" Noticing her erratic behavior, Camden stepped towards her with his arm outstretched. "Did she make it?"

Alessa's breathing faltered as her heart nerves threatened to take hold. "No, she didn't. Neither did the, um..." Shaking her head back and forth, Alessa ran her hand through her dark hair.

A look of concern crossed Camden's face as he placed his hand upon her shoulder. "Hey, are you okay?"

Alessa wiped her nose and nervously licked her lips. "No, yeah, I—I'm not sure."

Camden wrapped his other arm around her shoulders and

pulled her into his muscular chest. "I know I said some shitty things to you before you left, but you need to know I wasn't in the right frame of mind. I'll always be here for you, my fiery one."

Wiping the tears from her eyes, Alessa smiled. "Thanks, Cam. Is that what you've been calling me in your native language? Fiery one?"

Camden smiled and peered down at the top of her head.

She hugged him back. "I like it."

Camden sighed. "Besides, I think you and I ended up with the people we were meant to be with."

Alessa pulled back, looking up at Camden with raised eyebrows. "We did?"

Holding her out at arm's length, Camden laughed. "Didn't you wonder why Lexi never made it to Texas?"

As realization dawned, her jaw dropped in pleasant surprise. "Ah ... that makes a lot of sense. Well, I'm happy for you."

"Thanks for that, but what do you need to get off your chest? You look worried."

Hearing screams coming from outside the building, they ran for the exit. Looking up, they both saw a purple flicker in the sky as the grid protecting New Sparta powered down.

Standing beside Alessa, a nurse gasped. "The forcefield is down!"

Alessa's jaw dropped as she looked straight ahead at Damon. Realizing what was about to happen, she screamed, "Damon!"

Seeing the terrified look on Alessa's face, he yelled, sprinting towards her. "Alessa!"

White smoke floated up from the ground as explosions erupted all around them.

Camden was thrown into the air and knocked unconscious as his head smacked the side of the medical building.

Damon fought against the sleep-inducing smoke, and a Bodyguard appeared in front of him, yielding a sword.

Bending backwards, Damon not only dodged the blade as it swung across his body, but he also pressed his wristband against his temple, applying a gas mask to himself.

Whipping his wrist around in circles, the Spartan warrior charged the area around his fist before punching the Bodyguard, knocking him out with an electric shock.

Feeling the sting of a dart striking his thigh, Damon's vision blurred as he collapsed to his knees.

Alessa lay unconscious on the ground, and a Bodyguard appeared before her. Brushing the hair out of her face, the man spoke into his comm device to confirm her identity. "The primary target's been found and tagged."

He secured a collar around her neck, and with the press of a button, it glowed, signaling that it was powered on.

Damon plucked the small needle from his leg and tossed it to the side. Struggling to crawl, he reached out for Alessa, screaming her name. "Alessa!"

The Bodyguard picked her up from the ground and flashed a cocky grin at the flailing Spartan.

Gathering his remaining strength, Damon pushed himself upright with a thunderous scream. Sprinting forward, he lunged for Alessa just in time for them to disappear.

Landing hard on the ground, Damon balled his hands into fists. His veins bulged angrily as he screamed in agony while slamming them into the ground. "No!"

He dug his fingers into the blades of grass where Alessa had been a few seconds prior and watched in despair as the white smoke dissipated.

"What ... the ... hell?" Camden groaned as he came to, holding the side of his head.

Damon glared at him out of the corner of his eye as his chest heaved up and down. He plucked the dart from his leg and, after ripping off his electronic mask, he growled. "They took Alessa."

"What? They took—Shit ... Lexi." Camden's eyes bulged as he sprang upright. Teetering back and forth, he ran into the medical ward. "Lexi? Lexi!"

Damon smacked both sides of his face and shook his head before blinking exaggeratedly. With a loud exhale, Damon jumped up and followed close behind Camden. "Was she helping with the delivery?"

Camden blinked, trying to force the black dots from his vision. "No, she was here doing research into one of her theories." Camden glanced back at Damon. "Did I see you pull something out of your leg?"

Damon dismissed his comment with a wave of his hand. "It was a tranquilizer. Little did they realize I have some of the strongest Spartan blood, being a descendant of a king. It'll take a much higher dose to take me down."

Camden whipped around the corner and, upon entering the room, discovered dead Spartans scattered across the floor.

Peering in through the doorway before setting foot into the bloody scene, Camden's voice boomed as he hollered. "Lexi?"

Damon shook his head in relief as he looked around the room at all the dead male Spartans. "She's not here."

Camden looked lost as he stared at the bloodied bodies littering the floor. "Yeah, you're right. But where is she then? Where did they take them? And is ours the only compound targeted, or were others involved?"

Damon shook his head, and they left the room together. "I don't know, but we're getting them back."

Camden grinned wickedly as he pumped his fist in the air. "Fuck yeah, man. I'm all in. They have no idea what we're capable of."

Damon marched with purpose towards the exit doors, his eyes shining with ruthless determination. "They've mistaken me for the hero in this story, but I am no hero. I will gladly burn the world to the ground to save the woman I love."

Damon walked outside and threw his fist into the air. "With this act, they've declared war on the Spartan nation!" he bellowed into the gathering crowd.

His fellow Spartans held up their fists and hollered warrior cries as Damon mumbled under his breath, "Hold on, Alessa. We're coming for you."

CHAPTER FORTY-EIGHT

Brielle whipped around the corner to the large room, her heels clacking excitedly against the reflective tiled floor. "Did you get her?"

Cain turned his head as he lay Alessa down on the white bed. "We were successful in obtaining the primary target." He chuckled to himself, glancing around the large room at all the hundreds of Spartans, lying atop the white hospital beds. "It was very successful indeed."

Brielle crept up behind Cain, her disgusted gaze not leaving Alessa. With a scowl, she eyed the Spartan from head to toe as she stood beside her body. "What does Damon see in you?"

Brielle leaned in close to Alessa and watched as her eyes whipped back and forth behind her eyelids. "And they're all unconscious?"

"Yep." Cain turned away to type something into his keyboard. "We need to catalog every single participant, clean them up, and get their vital signs before we draw their labs."

Lifting her hand, Brielle smacked Alessa hard across the cheek.

Cain lifted an eyebrow behind his half-mask. "You feel better, now?"

Exhaling shakily, Brielle flashed a half-grin. "Yes, I do," she said before touching the collar around Alessa's neck. "What is this?"

Lucas walked into the room, announcing his presence with his boisterous voice. "It's a powerful defuser for their microchip. It scrambles the signal and disables their chip, meaning they'll have no choice but to be docile and cooperative."

Grinning wickedly, Brielle giggled. "Mmm. How fun."

Lucas arched an eyebrow at his nephew. "You've got this under control, I presume?"

Cain glanced down at Alessa and back at his uncle. "Yes, sir. You've trained me my whole life for this moment. I won't let you down."

"Good." Lucas gave a curt nod. "If you should need me, I'll be in the control room."

As Lucas walked away, Cain spoke to Brielle while typing. "This isn't about having fun. It's to ensure the future of a healthier human race."

Brielle held up her hands defensively. "Got it." She turned on her heel and looked through the clear glass rooms that extended as far as the eye could see.

Inside each of the ten-by-ten-foot cells were several Frenzied. Their eyes bulged as the flesh rotted away from their bones, and the glass had been smeared with blood; their fingernails left behind, stuck to the glass, within the streaks of red.

The Frenzied's teeth gnashed together as Brielle stood

before one of them, teasing it by pressing a hand against the cold glass. "Impregnating Spartans with super soldiers may not be a fun time for you, but you can't tell me you aren't getting a kick out of these little science experiments."

Cain sneered while logging Alessa's name and subject number. "They're not exactly the highlight of my day, but they'll be useful when the time comes."

He glanced off to the side of the room. "Hey, Tony. Have you given the Frenzied their lessons for the day?"

Holding up a tablet, Tony typed something into the command box and pressed a button with a satisfied grin. "They're receiving them now."

Every single Frenzied stopped moving, and their backs stiffened while they looked straight ahead.

Cain purred, "Good. That's good." He pressed enter on his keyboard before calling over the lead physician to Alessa's bedside. "Hey, Charles. This is the primary subject, Number 001. She is to be handled with the greatest of care. I want you to get her cleaned up before you check her levels. She got a bit banged up during the extraction."

The physician nodded stiffly. "Yes, sir. I'll get my people on it right away."

Cain stared intently at Alessa, imagining all the ways he could peel her perfect pale skin away from her bones. Blinking, he brought himself out of his fantasy and back to reality. "And don't worry if her numbers are off. We have time to get her into prime condition. She's going to be one of the last implanted." Cain leaned down, breathing hot air against her pink lips. "We want the embryos to be perfect when it's her time."

He stood upright, shrugged, and smirked wickedly. "Who knows? If she handles it well, maybe she can grow several of our little ones. They only take a few months to reach full-term."

Glaring down at Alessa, Brielle crossed her arms and pouted. "You promised me that when you're done with her, I get to play with what's left."

Cain peered over at Brielle. "Once she's deemed unusable, she's all yours. You have my word."

A maniacal smile spread across Brielle's face, and she squealed. "Wonderful."

"But until then, Alessa's off limits. You cannot touch her. Do you understand?"

Brielle clasped her hands behind her back and scoffed. "Yes, sir."

Cain pursed his lips tightly together. "I'm not kidding. She cannot have high levels of cortisol and epinephrine; it can harm her chances of successfully carrying the soldier."

Brielle glared down at Alessa.

The Spartan's dark hair lay behind her in a tangled mess, her cheek had a light-purple mark where Brielle had slapped her, and her chest slowly rising and falling was the only indication she was still with the living.

Digging her nails into the palms of her hands, Brielle held back the urge to lash out at Alessa once more. Instead, she whispered into the Spartan's ear, "Looks like I'll get my chance at taking your life after all."

The clack of Brielle's heels echoed loudly across the white tile as she strolled away, casually meandering between the hundreds of Spartan women lying unconscious in their white hospital beds, each with a glowing collar secured around their necks.

Inside the control room, Lucas stood behind a bulletproof glass wall, grinning maliciously at all the bodies he'd collected. "Looks like it's the beginning of the end."

CONTENT WARNING LIST

- Attempted SA - drugging
- Death - child - graphic
- Discussions about abortion
- Kidnapping
- Mental illness
- Child birth
- Abelism
- Gore

READY FOR MORE?

Keep a look out for Scorched, the fourth and final book in The Glitched Series.

ABOUT THE AUTHOR

Eisley Rose is the author of *Glitched, Shattered,* and *Forged.* She is also a registered nurse, a stay-at-home mom, and an entrepreneur who lives in the greater Kansas City area. She loves reading, writing, painting, attending concerts, playing tennis, watching movies, and playing board games with her family. Her love for science formed the backbone of this story, but she also adores anything creative and openly embraces the unique.

"If you choose to be one thing in this world, choose to be unequivocally, unapologetically, you."

— Eisley Rose

facebook.com/eisleyrosebooks

instagram.com/eisleyrosebooks

goodreads.com/eisleyrosebooks

youtube.com/@eisleyrosebooks

amazon.com/Eisley-Rose/e/B0CSMD89HQ

tiktok.com/@eisleyrosebooks

threads.com/@eisleyrosebooks

bsky.app/profile/eisleyrosebooks.bsky.social

REVIEWS APPRECIATED

Thank you so much for giving my book series a chance. I am forever grateful.

Please feel free to leave a review online.